Kowabana

'True' Japanese scary stories from around the internet
Vol. 1

Tara A. Devlin

Kowabana: 'True' Japanese scary stories from around the internet Vol. 1
First Edition: October 2017

taraadevlin.com

DEDICATION

To the country that helped me become the person I am today. And to you, the readers, for choosing to share in this journey with me.

CONTENTS

INTRODUCTION

When I entered university, I decided to study Japanese as my major. There was no special reason; I liked languages and I liked anime, so Japanese seemed like a good choice. The extent of my Japanese knowledge going in was “Watashi wa Tara desu” and “Kore wa pen desu.” Over the next three years it didn’t get much better. I did the bare minimum to pass and graduated being able to say “Watashi wa Tara desu” slightly more fluently than three years earlier.

As graduation loomed however, I was stuck with a difficult choice. Just what on Earth was I going to do with the rest of my life? I could continue my Japanese studies at university with the goal of becoming a translator or I could go to Japan itself and do something there. I ended up choosing the latter. Becoming a translator seemed way out of my grasp at the time.

I applied for the JET program around the same time I graduated. I was fresh off my 21st birthday and one of my classmates suggested it to me before we finished up for the year. The interview went okay but a few months later I received the letter informing me I wasn't picked.

I was heartbroken.

I cried quite a bit that day and didn't know what to do. By this point about six months had passed since graduation and I was struggling to find any type of work elsewhere. When I was done crying I went online, looked up some English conversation schools and started applying. I went to an interview with a particularly large chain and about two weeks later was told they'd like me to go to Japan to work for them.

I was finally going to Japan.

My mother spent two months saving every single penny she had so we could afford the ticket to send me there. To this day I'm still grateful to her for giving me the chance to experience the best years of my life. There's no way I can ever repay her. Thank you, Mum.

When I arrived in Japan, I very quickly figured out I couldn't understand a single thing. Three years of Japanese was basically useless. I took the four-hour trip from Osaka out to the countryside by myself and couldn't understand any of the train announcements or people around me. Fear was settling in. What was I going to do? I studied Japanese for all that time but now that I was actually here I couldn't understand anything. Some of my new colleagues met me at the station and took me to my new apartment and helped me get settled in. The very first thing I did that day was buy a second hand PS2 and *Resident Evil: Outbreak File*

2 so I could feel more at home.

So how does all this relate to Japanese horror, the subject of this book? Like many my age, I got my first real taste of Japanese horror with movies such as *Ringu* and *Ju-on*. My roommate moved out my first month in Japan and I spent the next two years living by myself. I lived very close to the video store, which is still a big business in Japan, and there I found an entire wall of Japanese horror waiting for me to consume. And consume it I did. Over a period of several months I rented every single horror movie the video store had and watched them alone in my sixth floor Japanese apartment. They were of course without subtitles. At first I couldn't really tell much of what was going on, but simply by living in the country and studying more than I ever did in university I slowly began to pick the language up. I could understand announcements. I could understand store assistants. I could understand conversations. Soon I could understand movies and when I did I tore through them even faster. Some of my favourite memories ever are those months where I watched nothing but Japanese horror movies, both big and small.

Around the same time I made friends with a girl who loved horror; a rarity for a Japanese lady. It turned out the city I lived in was quite old with a rich history and was infamous for its ghost spots. We used to drive around late at night looking for them and telling each other stories. One of my favourite memories to this day was the first time she told me a story entirely in Japanese and I understood every word of it. We were sitting outside a family restaurant, it was around midnight during summer so still quite hot and she was like, "Do you want me to tell you a story in Japanese?" Of course I said yes, and it was a fairly common tale, the one about how two friends go home after an evening out and one sits down on the couch. Her friend suddenly remembers something and asks the other lady to come outside to help her. When they leave she pulls out her phone and starts dialling the police. When the lady asks her what she's doing, she tells her that she saw a man hiding underneath the couch and he had a knife. It was the first time I heard an urban legend entirely in Japanese and I understood every single word. I was stoked.

The horror industry is huge in Japan. It's a part of their culture. While questions like "Have you ever seen a ghost?" might seem odd to a Western person it's not really that strange for a Japanese person to say they or a family member can see them, like you or I might see bread sitting on a counter-top. Children diligently visit their family graves and attend to altars in the family home. Obon is one of the largest holidays during which time the spirits of one's ancestors return home for a few days and the family showers them with gifts and tends to their graves. Go to any convenience store and you'll find the magazine rack full of books on the best ghost spots and terrifying 'true' tales of angry spirits and vengeful hauntings. Summer TV is full of ghost specials where Japanese celebrities sit around and watch badly edited home movies where they scream and cry at how terrifying they are and shield their faces in horror at even more badly photoshopped ghost photos. Summer especially is the season for horror. The chills are supposed to help cool you down in the awful Japanese heat.

Japan’s strong anonymous internet culture also brought about another fascinating phenomenon; that of the 2chan creepypasta. 2chan is an anonymous forum where people can post about any subject under the sun. The occult board is particularly active and many famous urban legends have originated as posts from this board. Perhaps you’ve heard of Hasshaku-sama, the extremely tall woman who likes to haunt young men, or Kisaragi Station, the station that doesn’t exist on any map. Due to the anonymous nature of the boards many people use them to post their ‘true’ stories of strange happenings and ghostly encounters without fear of anyone finding out who they are and calling them on their nonsense.

And that’s what this book is about. This book is a collection of translations from the 2chan forums. These stories are all posted anonymously; they have no known author. They’re posted by regular people in a casual environment so the stories are often very rough, to put it politely. They occasionally make no sense, they often have very little payoff, they can be full of slang and grammatical errors and just plain bad writing. I do my best to fix these things when I’m translating and make it understandable in English but sometimes there’s only so much you can do. Regardless, I really enjoy these stories and I love translating them. Sometimes you find a real gem and that makes it all worthwhile. Other times you find stories that have good ideas but poor execution. Other times you just have to wonder why someone took the time to post that at all. But at the end of the day, as a fan of horror and as a fan of Japan, these stories are a fascinating insight into the culture of modern Japanese horror. Japanese horror may be past its heyday of truly terrifying movies like *Ringu* and *Ju-on*, but it still lives on on the internet.

The book is split up into several sections. The countryside is a very common theme in Japanese horror so you'll find quite a lot of stories that take place there. There are also your regular hauntings, strange tales that take place in buildings (abandoned or otherwise), stories that take place while travelling and quite a few set around the Obon holiday. Obon is a common setting because it's seen as less strange to have a ghostly visit during this time. There are Japanese games such as Kokkuri-san (the Japanese version of a Ouija board) and hide and seek, creepy dolls and cursed items, horrors related to technology and some unexplainable disappearances. The last section features some of my favourites, a genre of Japanese stories called "Imi ga wakaru to kowai hanashi," literally, "Stories that are scary once you understand them." These are like a riddle with an explanation given at the end in-case you didn't catch it while reading.

I hope you enjoy these stories, the good and the bad, and you can always find more at kowabana.net where I post translations almost every single day!

COUNTRYSIDE

On a dark country road

* * *

This is a story my grandfather told me. I'll do my best to remember and write it down.

His name was Shinji, so I call him Shinjii. One day, Shinjii told me a strange story. This was the only time he ever told me such a story before he died several years ago.

When Shinjii was around six or seven years old, he had a brother who was two years older that died from sickness. His brother was terribly sick and didn't have much time left, so my great-grandfather, Shinjii's father, said that he should spend his remaining time at home, and they cared for him there. Shinjii played with his older brother in his room until he was unable to. Then, as his brother was getting close to passing, his father asked him to stop.

Then one night, his brother died. It was summer, and of course, they had no air conditioning. Not wanting to damage the body, his father decided to take him to the nearest place to do the funeral rites.

Shinjii's house was way out in the countryside, a place where there weren't even any roads a car could pass through. So their father decided to piggyback him there, and because there was no light on the road, Shinjii held a torch and they went together.

While shining the torch in front of them, Shinjii walked alongside his father, who was carrying his brother's dead body. It was a quiet country road during the middle of the night, so they didn't see any people. All they could hear were the sounds of bugs crying and their own feet on the gravel. The pair walked in silence. My grandfather said his father's face looked extremely tired.

After they walked for a while they saw the figure of a person in front of them. It seemed like the person was walking in the same direction as them, but was moving slowly. They didn't think too much about it and thought they would catch up to the figure in time, but as Shinjii casually cast his torch over the person's back, his breath caught in his throat.

He'd seen that outfit somewhere before.

He quickly remembered where.

It was the same outfit that his brother was wearing on their father's back right now.

His father noticed at the same time and whispered to him sharply, "Shinji, don't shine that!" He quickly lowered the torch and shone it on their own feet.

Because the figure was walking slower than them, they slowly began to close the distance. Shinjii started to get scared and wanted to stop walking, but he noticed that whenever he did, the figure in front of them stopped walking too. His father had probably realised the same thing.

Slowly they got closer to the figure. The person was just as tall as his brother. Before long he saw the figure's feet. He was barefoot. Even though the road wasn't paved, there were no marks or injuries on his feet.

They got even closer.

He could see shorts. He knew those pants. They were green and had cuffs. He also saw the shirt. It was a blue and white striped shirt. It was his brother's favourite.

He saw the back of his head…

At that moment his father grabbed his shoulder and said, "Don't look! Shinji! Don't look!"

Shinjii was slightly curious about 'it' but cast his eyes down. His father was muttering something. He couldn't hear very well, but it sounded like a prayer.

They finally closed the distance, and Shinjii and his father walked side by side with 'it.' His father was praying next to him. Shinjii kept repeating to himself not to look, but as soon as they stood side by side he realised that 'it' was looking at him. He said that the power behind his gaze was amazingly strong.

Finally, the two of them passed 'it.' But, Shinjii said, that was when it really got scary.

When they passed it, that is to say, 'it' was now behind them, that's when it happened. They couldn't hear footsteps, but it was definitely behind them. It was there, right behind them. He could feel it looking right at them.

My great-grandfather said, "Don't look back, Shinji. Whatever you do, don't look back." Shinjii couldn't even look at his father beside him, let alone look back. The reason for that was what his father was carrying on his back.

The two of them kept on walking down that country road with something following behind them. He just looked straight ahead and prayed they'd reach a place full of people soon. He didn't know when the figure behind them might call out his name or suddenly jump on him, so with his heart racing he kept on walking.

But in the end, the figure didn't call out his name or rush to attack him. The two of them arrived safely at their destination, delivered his brother's body to the morgue, and returned home.

Shinjii said there was nothing on the road on their way home. When I asked if 'it' was really his brother, he acted like he didn't know. He only said this:

"Ever since then, I can't get rid of the feeling that something's following me."

Shinjii said when that happens, he makes sure not to look back.

The old guy I saw at the park

* * *

This story happened about 30 years ago.

At the time I was a junior high school student. I lived in a small countryside village in Hokkaido where bears often roamed.

It was just before the summer holidays and I decided to spend the night studying for my end of term tests. I was starting to feel drowsy, however, so I grabbed the dog to go for a walk and headed for the park next to a nearby shrine.

In the darkness of the park, an old man walking his tiny dog showed up. He was someone I often saw while walking my own.

That night I once again nodded to him in greeting, and with a smile, he returned the favour.

The next day I went to take the dog for another walk after waking up when I saw police cars and people everywhere. They were in front of the old man's house.

"What happened?"

Apparently, the old man who lived there had gone missing two days earlier, and the police were searching for him. He was found dead in one of the nearby mountains. He'd hung himself.

Generally, you would go to the police station in order to confirm things, but this was the countryside where everyone knew each other, so the police drove his body to his wife first in order to have her confirm his identity.

After a few minutes, a white car slowly pulled up before their house. I can't describe it well, but I could just see the two legs of his dead body poking out from underneath a green vinyl sheet from the back door.

Later I found out that the old man was already dead the day he went missing… so who had I greeted!?

Even when I think about it now it terrifies me…

The thing I saw at the bottom of the river

* * *

My parents' house was out in the middle of nowhere. There were few places for kids to play when summer holidays rolled around. We just collected insects, read manga at friends' houses, or went to play in the mountains or rivers…

So, there was this river I often went swimming in. The current there was slow, but it was still dangerous. Swimming was forbidden, but we ignored it and went swimming there anyway.

Then one day something happened.

With nothing else to do, we went to play in the river. My friend A and I went fishing that day while B and C went swimming in the upper stream. Close to where B and C were swimming was a concrete barrier (like a dam). There was a deep, huge hole underneath it, so it was often used as a diving spot.

A and I fished for a while, but when we looked over at B and C, they were trying to climb the dam.

"Ah, they're gonna dive in, huh?" I said to A as we watched them. B and C noticed and waved at us, so we waved back.

B and C reached the top of the dam and dived in together. There were two large splashes, and A and I cheered them on. But when they came back up their actions were strange. They rushed onto the bank and were screaming about something.

Both of them were crying their eyes out.

"What's wrong?" we asked them, but they kept screaming.

"The hole, in the hole!"

There was nothing we could do, so A and I jumped into the river, put on some goggles and looked into the hole.

It was dark, so we couldn't see very well, but we saw something that looked like a clump of seaweed. When we looked closer and realised what it was, I felt like I was going to pass out.

It was a person.

A person with their back to us was swaying in the water like they had grown out of the hole. What looked like seaweed was their hair. We quickly got out of the river and ran to tell some adults.

According to what I heard later, the person had jumped off the dam and gotten their foot stuck under a rock in the hole, causing them to drown. It wasn't anyone we knew.

Since then, jumping off the dam has been completed prohibited, and swimming in the river is even more off limits. The four of us never swam in a river again.

Magagami-sama

* * *

There's this mountain in the village where my grandma lives, and in that mountain, there's this amazingly beautiful, emerald green pond. It's so green it's almost blue, it feels like a transparent pastel colour. Whatever you want to call it, it's really beautiful. However, the children of the village are told never to go near it.

Whenever I asked why, the answer was always the same. "Children don't need to know. Just don't go there."

But kids will be kids, so of course, I wanted to know more. I asked my grandma and adults from the village about the special features of the pond. If it was really that beautiful, I wanted to see it for myself.

The other kids in the village felt the same and whenever I went to visit we'd start talking about going to see it. However, because the adults were warning so strongly against it, well rumours started amongst the kids that, "If you go to that pond, you'll never come back."

"I heard that it's bottomless, so if you fall in it you'll die," people would say, so we never actually put our words into action.

But when I entered junior high school and returned to the village, the kids I used to play with when I was a child (as follows: Taro, Jiro, Hanako. Taro and Hanako were twins. Jiro was their cousin) were like, "If you really can't return from there, then how come everyone knows what the pond looks like?"

"If there really was a bottomless pond these days they would fill it in." They started to say things that were more realistic, and I agreed.

"Is there really even a pond? It's not just some story they made up?"

So, in the end, we decided. "Let's go check it out!"

The four of us met up early in the morning and made for the mountain. The mountain itself was only small, so even if we got lost we figured we'd be able to find our way out by nightfall. We didn't take the situation very seriously. Taro, Hanako and I were now junior high school students, and Jiro was a second grader who did judo. He said if worst came to worst and a bear or some wild dog attacked, he would do some overhead throw and defeat them, haha. It made us feel better even though we knew it was impossible.

While we were talking about these things and tired after walking around for close to three hours, we found a strange place where the trees grew really densely. I can't explain it very well, but in just that spot the trees were really numerous, like they'd been forcibly planted there. There weren't even any animal trails.

"It's absolutely here, look how suspicious it is," Hanako said from the front of the line. She was a tomboy, and although we three boys were trembling, she went straight through a gap in the trees ahead of us.

There was nothing we could do, so we followed her. Then, just as we thought, there was the pond. *Centre of the Earth*? Whatever that movie is called, it was just like a scene out of that. In reality, it was clearer than I ever imagined, it was so beautiful. But thanks to the trees it was kinda gloomy, and a small cabin beside the pond spoilt the view.

At first, everyone was really excited, and we collected water from the pond in bottles that Hanako had prepared. But that little cabin continued to make us feel uneasy. Rather than calling it a little cabin, it was long, like a small hut had been lengthened out. Just looking at it, it was dirty and creepy. Like a mountain witch or something lived there.

Then Jiro was like, "If there's a mountain witch in there I'm just gonna overhead throw her~" and went inside. We went to follow him, but then out of nowhere Taro spit out, "No way, I'm not going. I'll stay here."

Hanako was sick of him acting like a weakling, but Taro stubbornly refused to concede.

"If you wanna go, then just you and Jiro-chan can go. Ume-chan (myself) and I will just wait here. Yeah?"

For some reason, I was the only one held back. I was scared, but I still wanted to go inside the cabin. But Taro was a scaredy-cat too frightened to put his plans into actions, and it would have been awful if something bad happened to him, so I decided to stay. I waved the two off as they entered the cabin and sat by the green of the pond to talk with Taro.

"Why don't you wanna go in there, are you scared?"

"I don't like it. It's scary."

"Well then, why is it okay for Hanako and Jiro-chan to go in?"

Taro replied, "Hana-chan is always mean to me, I hate her. Jiro-chan always acts tough, but it's all just words so I hate him too. So whatever. If they die I don't care. Hana-chan is always acting so big and mighty, and she treats me like dirt. Jiro-chan always hits me. I hate both of them. They should die, I just wish they'd die. That's why I came here, to have Magagami-sama kill them for me."

Amongst his string of abuse, there was a word I'd never heard before, so I repeated it.

"Magagami-sama? What's that?"

"None of the village kids know about her. Hanako and Jiro don't know either because they're idiots. But I know. Magagami-sama lives here. Old lady Kichizu told me about her because I'm smart."

"Yeah, but what is Magagami-sama!?"

"Ume-chan, you're kind to me so I'll help you out. But I can't do anything for Hanako and Jiro. They're idiots, they act tough, they're stupid, they should die. Magagami-sama will kill them for me."

It started to sound less like a string of abuse and more like a curse. At some point, he stopped calling them by their nicknames as well.

Taro kept going, spit flying from his mouth, and before long he let out a strange laugh.

"Hyoa hyoa hyoa hyoa hyoa hyoa. Hyoa hyoa hyoa hyoa hyoa hyoa hyoa hyoahine hyoa hyoa hyoahine hyoa hyoa hyoahine hyoa hyoa hyoahine hyoa hyoa hyoa."

It was disturbing. He sat there holding his knees, and then his neck turned to look at me as he laughed. He'd gone crazy.

Then I realised that Hanako and Jiro had been gone for a long time. I wanted to get away from Taro as well, so I headed towards the cabin.

"Stay here! Don't go looking for those two!" Taro called out. "It's already too late~" He smiled.

His face made me sick to my stomach, but I ignored him and went inside. It was pitch black and there was a strange smell. It smelt like something burning, or something rotting. The further I went in, the sicker I became. Then I heard a strange laugh from the room at the end of the cabin.

"Hyoa hyoa hyoa hyoa hyoa hyoa hyoa hyoa."

Reluctantly I went in, and Hanako and Jiro were sitting on the floor.

"Hyoa hyoa hyoa hyoa hyoa hyoa hyoa hyoa hyoa hyoa."

"Hyoa hyoa hyoa hyoa hyoahinuhinuhinu hyoa hyoa hyoa hyoa hyoa hyoa."

They were laughing the same way as Taro. It freaked me the hell out. I had to go call someone at once. I turned around. Then, right in front of me…

…a pair of white eyes were floating in the air. They were white, like white membrane covering the pupil of someone who'd gone blind.

I let out a terrible scream and drew back towards the wall. As I did, something felt sticky. I touched it again and the entire wall was sticky. Gross gross gross gross! I wanted to get out immediately, but I couldn't move because of the white eyes. If I moved they'd chase me, so I was terrified.

The white eyes continued to stare at me. 'Am I going to be cursed and die?' I thought. I didn't want to look at them anymore so I turned my face to the right. When I did,

"I told ya it was too late~"

Taro's face was hanging half inside the window. Taro's eyes were exactly the same as the white eyes floating before me.

"Hyoa hyoa hyoa hyoa hyoa hyoa hyoa hyoa hyoa hyoa hyoa hyoa hyoa hyoa hyoa hyoa hyoa hyoa hyoa hyoa hyoa hyoa hihihihihihi hyahahahahahahaha hyahahahahahahaha hyoa hyoa hyoa."

Taro laughed. Hanako and Jiro also laughed. The white eyes kept floating before me. I couldn't stand it anymore.

Half-crazed, I ran from the cabin and down the mountain. From behind I could constantly hear "hyoa hyoa hyoa hyoa." With tears and a runny nose flying everywhere, I fled.

When I reached the bottom of the mountain it was still midday. I thought it would have been night long ago. After descending the mountain and entering the village, the first person I saw was Taro and Hanako's grandfather.

"Ume! What's wrong, you… you! Youuuu!!!!"

Their usually kind grandfather came running at me with incredible speed, flecks of spittle running from his mouth.

"You went there?! You went there?!"

With a perilous look on his face, he shook me and I told him everything…

We went up the mountain and saw the pond and cabin. I told him Taro's story. The white eyes and sticky wall. The three of them going crazy. They were still up there.

I bit my tongue several times as I spoke. "You need to save the three of them. What were those white eyes? Have I been cursed too? What is that up there?" I yelled.

Their grandfather hugged me and said, "It's alright, it's alright. You're okay, Ume, you're okay. You were saved, you're okay."

I was okay? What about Taro? Taro was his grandchild, not me, why wasn't he worried about him? I started to panic, but then I realised I didn't want to get the sticky stuff on their grandfather so I pulled away from him. Then I saw what was on my own body.

It looked a lot like mayonnaise, but it was spotted with black and red. It felt like the texture of mayonnaise too. Plus, it stank. The smell pierced my nostrils.

In any case, my memories of the incident end around there. Next thing I knew I was lying on the floor of my grandma's house surrounded by adults. My parents were crying their eyes out. They sat nearby but didn't try to talk to me. Everyone else did the same.

Taro's parents were there too, but they were just silently crying while looking at me. Then I realised I couldn't move. I wasn't bound or anything, but for some reason my body wouldn't listen to me. I couldn't speak either, all I could do was open my eyes. 'What's this?' I thought, starting to panic, when Taro's grandmother came over to speak to me.

"Umebon, take a look at my right eye, would ya?"

Taro's grandmother lost her right eye in an accident long ago, so she had an artificial eye. I already knew that, so what good would looking at it do? But I did as she said and looked.

"What? It's the same as usual. The focus is a little strange, but it's your eye."

Suddenly I could speak. The adults all let out a cheer. "I'm so glad." "He's been saved." They all cried and hugged each other.

My parents hugged me as they cried, and even Taro's parents cried. "We're so glad, Ume-chan. So glad."

But I was just creeped out. 'Even though your own child has probably gone crazy, why are you happy and not saying angry things towards me?' I thought.

"What about the other three? What happened to them?" I asked

The adults just replied, "What are you saying? They've been at home all morning. Ume-chan, if you learn anything from this, it's not to go up that mountain alone again."

Ah, so that's what it was, huh? It had become 'he went up the mountain alone.' Taro and the others were probably locked away in their grandmother's storehouse or something because they'd gone mad. Understanding that, I said nothing.

Two or three days later it was time to go back home with my parents. I never saw Taro or the others again. Even amongst all the people who came to see us off, Taro and the others weren't there.

My grandmother is still healthy even now as I'm in my 20s and I go to visit her with the change of the seasons. The village people are still kind, Taro's parents still act the same, and Taro and the others are still nowhere to be seen. When I asked about them I heard that Hanako got married and moved to Tohoku, Taro and Jiro both started working at the same company, and then both of them moved overseas.

When they were in high school, the three of them supposedly went to school in Tokyo. Whether that was true or not, ever since that incident I never saw them again.

I didn't know what the white eyes and sticky substance were. What Magagami-sama was. Where Taro and the others were. The 'old lady Kichizu' that Taro spoke of didn't exist in the village and I still don't know who she was. In all the years since that incident, nothing has happened to me, and there haven't been any changes.

I haven't seen the white eyes or sticky substance since either. I asked my parents and the villagers about it further, but they just said, "It was probably just a dream. You went up into the mountain alone and came down suffering from heatstroke." "Pond? I don't know anything about that, first time I've heard of it."

When I asked the kids who used to talk about rumours of the pond the same questions they just calmly answered, "I don't know anything about a pond."

Strange religious activity

* * *

This happened to my 15-year-old brother when I was 18.

It was past 12 a.m. and that day there had been some light rain. My brother's room was at the end of the second floor, about 10 metres away from the road. He was reading a book when suddenly he could hear something coming from the road outside. *Don... don...*

Thinking it might just be the rain on the roof, he didn't think too much of it. But as time went on, it felt like the sound was getting closer, so he opened the curtain and had a look outside.

There was a small truck that seemed to be missing its trailer. It was driving really slowly, like the speed of a person walking.

What was strange about it though was that none of the lights were on, and it was surrounded by a group of people.

It seemed like that earlier noise was this truck. There were about six men and women around it. They were all wearing some kind of cloth on their heads.

After confirming that the truck had passed by, my brother came to my room and told me about it.

When I heard, I was like, "Why didn't you come and tell me sooner?!" and rushed to his room, but of course, the truck was gone.

At the same time, I'd also heard the sound from my room. At first, I thought it was just the rain hitting the roof, but… after a while, I thought it might have been the sound of a drum from far away. You can occasionally hear the sound of drums here during the night, and I was just thinking about how much of an annoyance it must be for the people living nearby when my brother came in.

We live in a small town in Hokkaido, by the way. Around 12 a.m. we only get one, maybe two cars passing a night.

I don’t know what it was, but I guess it was some sort of strange religious group.

Camping at the abandoned station

* * *

Right around this season a few years back, I got a special train ticket for my 18th birthday, so I decided to go on a trip by myself.

The platform was already completely dark when I got there.

"Guess I'll go stay at the net cafe on X Island today, hey~"

I got on the train heading towards X Island, but something seemed strange. It seemed I'd gotten on the train heading in the opposite direction instead.

I hurried and got off, but that just made things even worse. When I looked at the timetable, there were no more trains coming for the night.

It was an unstaffed station surrounded by nothing but mountains and rice fields. It was right in the middle of a local area with very few street lights.

There was no station office, just the platform, so I worried about what to do. I thought for a bit while shooing away the bugs hanging around the streetlight. The bridge leading to the other platform was covered, so I decided to wait the night out up there.

I stepped over the chain fencing off the stairs (for some reason it was blocked off) and went up.

To be honest, it was the first time I've ever slept outdoors. 'I'm worried~ This empty station is scary~ It's creepy~' (just like Inagawa Junji would say). I was scared, but as soon as I sat back against the wall I was overcome with exhaustion and slept soundly till morning.

The sound of sparrows chirping woke me up. When I looked down at the ground around me in the morning light, I was startled.

The area was covered in footprints footprints footprints footprints so many footprints, like I'd been surrounded. They looked like muddy footprints (although it could have been something else, haha).

The prints weren't those of a shoe, they were more like an animal. In a panic, I checked all my things, but it didn't appear that anything had been damaged.

Just… I wonder what that really was, hey~?

Old house on the railway tracks

* * *

This story happened to the younger brother of one of my mother's friends about 20 years ago.

This younger brother started living alone in a rented house by the railway tracks of his hometown. It was a small, old single-story house, and because there was just a fence separating it from the tracks, it was extremely cheap.

There were few trains because it was the countryside, and hardly any passed during the night, so he wasn't very concerned about the noise.

Then one night, a few days after he moved in, he was woken by the sound of footsteps on the gravel outside.

He thought about getting up to see whether it was a burglar, but the house was still locked securely so he wasn't worried. He was tired from the day's work so he went back to sleep.

A few nights later he heard the same sound again.

He was just going to ignore it again, but then he realised something strange. It was more like the sound of someone crawling across the gravel rather than walking on it.

Feeling something strange was up, he peeked through the curtain in the direction of the sound.

A few metres away there was a man missing the lower half of his body crawling across the gravel. He was going around and around on the same spot. The younger brother let out a scream of surprise and the creature turned in his direction.

Panicked, he closed the curtain and hid in bed. Before he knew it, the sound outside had stopped.

Zusha...

The sound was coming from inside his room. He timidly peeked out from underneath his futon in the direction of the sound. It was right there.

It was the upper torso of an old man, grinning as he crawled towards him. Terrified, he could do nothing but tremble inside his futon as he waited.

When morning arrived, the sound disappeared.

Every now and then the old man would appear again, but as he did little other than crawl around, the younger brother continued to live there for another two years.

Apparently, there was an old man who suffered from dementia that lived nearby. He was hit by a train and killed.

I went there myself a few years ago. The house is still there, although no-one lives in it now, so it's falling apart.

Something unfamiliar in the binoculars

* * *

A-san liked birdwatching, so he got in his car and went to the nearby mountains like he often did. He was observing the birds in the early morning forest when, for a brief moment, he spotted something unfamiliar in his binoculars.

He looked over with his naked eye, but perhaps because of the distance, he couldn't really see anything. A-san looked through the binoculars once more and shuddered.

On the other side of the lens he could see a strange figure, what appeared to be a clump of moss on human legs stumbling around clumsily. The upper body was as though its head and arms had been shaved off, its legs pale in colour, and it was covered in mud.

Having gazed upon something he shouldn't have, A-san shivered. But then he noticed something that made him run and never return to the mountain again.

That strange thing in the distance was walking slowly with an unsteady gait, but without a doubt, it was heading right for him.

HAUNTINGS

I'm glad we didn't go into that villa

* * *

This is a story about when I nearly ran into a ghost.

It happened when I was a university student. Just before the summer holidays, I found a part-time job at a holiday resort with a few of my classmates.

Even though it was called a resort job, it was at a now-declining summer resort "cleaning a holiday house."

For two nights and three days, food and accommodation were included.

Five of us from our class, three guys and two girls, decided to go.

The manager of the resort met us when we arrived at the closest station and took us there by car.

Although it was old, it was a rather large Western-style resort with a garden and a pool. It was a really nice place.

But while we were all carrying on, like, "wow~ wow~" only one person, A-san alone, was quiet.

She was, in general, a quiet person, but on the way she had been having fun like the rest of us.

I wondered what was wrong when suddenly A-san's phone rang.

She answered it.

After finishing her conversation, she turned to all of us.

"I'm sorry. That was our professor, he wants us all to return right away. There's an academic meeting soon, so it's become a little inconvenient… I'm sorry we came all this way, we'd like to cancel the part-time job."

The old man faltered at her sudden words.

"I need someone to work today. Do you have any friends who could come instead?"

"Sorry, I think that would be difficult as well," A-san asserted decisively.

I was about to ask just what was going on when beside her B went… "Oh yeah! The professor asked us to do some work! The deadline is tomorrow so we have to get back!"

"I'm sorry. I'm terribly sorry. We'll be going back now. We'll walk to the station so there's no need for you to escort us back." A-san grabbed the other girl's hand and pulled her along as she started walking.

"Well, if you'll excuse us. We'll be going now!" At B's prompting, I also bowed and left.

I took a quick look back and the old guy was just standing there, looking at the holiday house.

"Hey, what did the professor say?" I asked A-san as we walked back to the station.

"I'll tell you once we're on the train," she said without revealing anything.

B also silently nodded his head.

We got on the train, and after we passed about two stops A-san finally told us.

"I'm sorry. The professor didn't really call, I lied. Just, that holiday house was scary. I thought we shouldn't stay there…"

"What the hell," I said.

Then B muttered absent-mindedly, "You guys didn't see it, huh? It was at the bottom of the pool, right? There were jars and mannequin arms all over the place weighing something down."

"Huh?" A-san let out a puzzled voice.

"Hmm? A-san, isn't that why you refused to go?"

"No. I refused because there was a woman with a sickle standing near the window…"

According to A-san, the window was fixed with *shimenawa*, rope used to ward against evil. The woman inside had white eyes, and with all her might was trying to cut the rope with her sickle.

As soon as we heard that, we all agreed that it was for the best that we didn't stay there.

The person constantly watching from the opposite window

* * *

Please listen to my story from when I was a university student.

When I was in university, one of my female friends said she was having trouble with a peeping tom. There was a guy constantly looking through her window from the apartment building opposite her.

For the last two days, whenever she went to look out the window the guy was there looking at her.

"That's creepy. I'm gonna go and let him have it!"

I went into her place all puffed up and ready to protect her.

Her bedroom was at the back of the apartment, and from the window, you could see the apartment building behind hers. However, when I opened the window, the parking lot was spread out below and the other building was a little further away.

"Ah, he's looking over here again…"

I couldn't see very well so I took a closer look, and indeed there was a guy in the opposite building looking right this way. He appeared to be sitting.

"Wow, there really is. But, I mean, is he actually looking this way?"

"He isn't? But he's been looking over here for the last two or three days, so it's creeping me out…"

I thought he'd be peeping on her from somewhere closer, so I could yell at him from the window, but it didn't seem like I'd be able to do that from here. It was a little far away.

I turned to face the guy and shooed him away with my hands but there was no reaction.

"What a strange guy… Do you want me to go over and tell him it's creeping you out, so stop looking this way?"

"No, it's okay, I'm too scared. Thanks. I just won't open the window for a while longer."

That night, things ended up going pretty well so I stayed over.

After that, I came to visit her often, and that guy was always there watching.

But what was strange was that even in the middle of the night, he was watching with the lights off, and in the morning when we opened the window, he was still sitting there looking at us.

I'd had enough, so I was gonna go over and say something to him, but my lady friend was scared, so we called the police instead. The police listened to our story and said they'd go check it out.

After that the guy's curtain was closed, so I figured the police must have given him a warning. I should have called them sooner.

I started dating that girl, and then about two or three months later, she got a visit from the police.

Apparently, there was a suicide in the apartment building across from her, and it was that guy that was always looking at her room.

She'd previously called the police about him, so they just wanted to ask a few questions.

I was there when they questioned her, and apparently, the guy had a rope tied around his neck and then up over a pipe in his loft area.

We thought he was constantly looking this way, but in reality, he was just hanging there, already dead.

Instead of freely dangling, he'd done it in such a manner that he just appeared to be sitting down from afar.

I got shivers up my spine when I heard.

My girlfriend was also scared, so that night we went to stay in a hotel. She was too scared to turn off the lights, but we tried not to think about it too much.

The next day I told my friends about it at school.

"Blah blah blah~ The police came~ Apparently it was suicide~"

"No way!? That's scary, hey."

"Right? She couldn't be there anymore so we spent the night in a hotel."

"But then who closed the curtain?"

Another shiver ran down my spine as I heard that.

That's right. After I called the police, the curtain was closed… I quickly called the police and told them the same thing.

According to the officer I spoke to, they went to the room but there was no response, so they just went back to the station.

"Was the curtain really open? We thought he was just looking over from a gap," the detective said.

Did I get it wrong…? I thought about checking with my girlfriend, but then thought better of it.

He came to play with a smile

* * *

When I was a child, my parents worked the night shift. I was lonely, so I had trouble getting to sleep.

Just as I would be about to fall asleep, the edge of the *shoji* door would always open and there would be a small shadow looking at me. But rather than being afraid of it, I wanted to be its friend.

Day by day, the small shadow got closer and closer, and before I knew it, it was right by my pillow (I always fell asleep before it got close to me).

I couldn't see its face in the darkness, but I knew it was a boy around the same age as me (4 or 5-years-old). At first, we never spoke and kinda just played, but then we started to chat as well.

Perhaps we had an unspoken agreement, but I never told my parents. I thought that if I told them I was playing and not sleeping, I'd get in trouble. And for some reason, I was able to see in the dark, so we were able to play with toys, play tag and so on.

When I started elementary school, I made lots of friends. Perhaps because we played so much at lunchtime I was better able to sleep at night, so I stopped seeing the shadow.

Even though I played with my new friends, I was also concerned about my night-time friend, so one day I got into my futon and waited for him to appear.

For the first time in a while, I heard the *susu* sound of the *shoji* screen opening again. He was smiling (I could tell in the dark) and had come to play.

I was so excited to see him again after such a long time, and while running around the room my arm got caught on the light string. I accidentally pulled it.

Underneath the light, I saw him for the first time. He was a child but looked like an old man. He skin was wrinkled, and he barely had any hair (what was there was white). It was the first time I'd seen a person like that before.

He seemed embarrassed and uneasy and hid behind the *shoji* screen.

I ran into the hallway to chase him. He was heading towards the entrance with a really tall woman. As he turned the corner he waved 'bye bye' to me and then was gone.

I remember feeling incredibly sad.

His mother had come to pick him up. I was all alone again. My mother never slept with me. Even though I was just a kid, I was jealous.

I waited for him the next night, but he never came again. I got used to the sad nights without him, and in time I was able to sleep better again.

One day at school I lost a game, and as a punishment, I had to reveal a secret. I didn't have anything particularly good to reveal, so I decided to tell them about the late nights I spent playing with that boy.

“No way, you’re lying,” everyone said to me coldly. I didn’t know why they wouldn’t believe me.

‘They’re just jealous, that’s why they’re saying those things,’ I thought. In actuality, I thought these events had been a totally normal thing.

They asked me what his name was, where he lived and so on, and I realised that I didn’t know anything about him. I couldn’t answer so they branded me a liar, even though it was true.

I was upset. I wanted to see him again and ask him lots of questions and have them believe in his existence, but he never appeared again. I prayed and hoped, but he never came.

For a while I was branded a liar, and the other kids treated me like I was a freak. I was cut off from my classmates. But even so, I was later able to enjoy my high school life and then university.

Eventually, I became a working adult and started drinking more and more.

One day I suddenly got a really bad headache, and I was lying in bed when I saw this old sweets box. I remembered it from somewhere.

I forgot about getting medicine and, following my memories, I looked through the box. I pulled it out of the TV stand, and when I opened it, it was full of old black and white photos.

Forgetting my headache for the time being, I looked through them. He was there. There was a photo of him in the arms of his mother, the woman who came to pick him up that time. For the first time, I realised that he wasn’t a real person (for a long time I had innocently believed he was).

I asked my parents about it, and they said he was a relative. He died from a terrible illness. He had once lived on the land that my current house stood on.

Even though playing with him as a child had been so fun, the moment I realised the truth it was terrifying.

In the end, I went to visit his grave and give him my thanks for everything he'd done.

I accidentally answered

* * *

Aren't there times when you're alone where you feel like someone's calling your name? They say you're not supposed to answer, right? Well, I've accidentally answered before. When I did, it called my name again. Then it started getting closer and closer.

When I realised that I was alone, I could already hear the voice in the next room. There was no way it was going to end well.

"It's calling me again!"

The moment I thought that my phone rang, and I nearly wet myself. But, in the end, it seemed like that phone call saved me. It was like as soon as the phone rang, the presence ran off somewhere.

By the way, that phone call was from a friend. "I had a really bad premonition, are you still alive?"

Ever since then, I pretend not to hear anything and make sure not to answer. I don't especially feel any mental burden or anything, I'm fine, but every now and then I still hear my name being called out.

If it turns out I'm ill without even realising it, well that's pretty scary in and of itself.

The ex-girlfriend who became a ghost

* * *

I have a brother who's eight years older than mc. You could say he's a good-for-nothing dumb-ass. He's flashy and loose with both money and women, but for some unknown reason, he's still popular.

When I was 15 he was rarely home, but when he was, there were always female boots sitting in the entranceway. I often heard the sound of women sobbing in his bedroom (they weren't indecent voices or anything though). I would hear my brother interrogating them with a threatening voice, "Where's the money?!"

Again?! I felt bad for them, but I was scared of my brother turning on me so I couldn't say anything. I couldn't do anything but go to my room and pretend I didn't see anything.

Then one day when I got home from school, there were once again some ladies' boots in the entranceway. From my brother's room I heard a woman crying, and his angry voice scream out, "Get out! We're done!"

The woman started crying hysterically, so much that I wondered if someone nearby might call the police. Then I heard, "Die! Die!" The words rang out clearly throughout my room.

Three days later, at around midnight, my brother came running into my room. He was white as a sheet. He turned on the lights and TV. I was pissed at this sudden invasion of my room that had disturbed my sleep. We had the type of relationship where, in general, even if we were home at the same time, he would never come to my room. We would communicate via texts. So to have him suddenly burst into my room, I could do nothing but feel anger.

"What do you want? Get the hell out!" I snapped. He didn't snap back at me, just said with his pale face, "Let me stay here a bit, please!"

"I'll tell you why later!" he said, looking like he was about to cry.

I wanted to know what he would 'tell me later,' so I reluctantly allowed him to stay; as long as he promised to tell me why. With the volume on the TV turned down, my brother spent the rest of the night reading a *JUMP* magazine lying on my floor.

As morning came, I asked my brother about why he came into my room looking so shaken, and he told me his story. As he was sleeping on his side, suddenly something grabbed onto him from behind. Whatever it was, it was cold and clung to him for dear life, breathing into his ear, "Haa, haa."

He went to turn his neck at this sudden, vivid feeling, and when he saw it he began to shake. That crying ex-girlfriend was stuck to him like a lizard. He shook her off and came running to my room.

He was too scared to go back to his own room, and being in the living room alone was no better. He was worried she might come after him again so, he said, that's why he came to my room.

So it wasn't… a ghost?

I started to ask my brother whether the memories of last night had stirred up his fear again when he called his ex-girlfriend. Luckily she was actually alive, but when my brother was driving his car after that, he would often see glimpses of her in the rear-view mirror, or when he was standing by his car in the parking lot he would see her silhouette in the window glass. Sometimes when he was out eating with friends they even saw her reflection in the restaurant window.

Incidentally, the night my brother came running into my room he smelled of female perfume, although he didn't seem to realise it himself. It smelled a lot like the fragrance coming off the boots that were sitting in the entranceway that time his girlfriend was over (I don't know if was deodoriser or not).

Along with these strange happenings, my brother was also troubled by terribly stiff shoulders. However, it all came to an end around half a year later. Then, three years later, we all returned together as a family to our parents' family home in Hokkaido. Unlike our parents, who were looking forward to meeting our relatives again, we just drove along the dark Hokkaido night roads. It was the perfect atmosphere for some ghost stories, so I started to touch upon my brother's ex-girlfriend when suddenly something brown ran across the front of the car with incredible speed.

We immediately stopped, and I went to see what it was. Something like a weasel was lying still on the road.

'Ah, so this kinda stuff really does happen in the countryside.' I remembered the stories my relatives told me about animals jumping out suddenly onto the road. But my brother said that it wasn't a weasel. His ex-girlfriend had run in front of the car.

"I hit my ex-girlfriend," he began to mutter and tremble.

The rest of the way back we were silent. With a terrified expression he picked up speed, and like he was trying to escape from something, we returned to our busy relative's house.

The old man's ghost on the park bench

* * *

This happened when I was in the fifth grade. It's a true story that, even now, I still find a little strange.

I was on my way home from school, and there was an old man sitting on the park bench. He was grasping at his chest.

"Are you okay?" I called out to him.

"Get the medicine from my bag, would you?" he asked me. There was a bag on the ground nearby, so I took out the medicine and a water bottle and handed them to the old man. After he took the medicine he said to me, "Boy, you're very kind. Don't forget how to be kind to people when you get older."

I was so happy that a grown-up praised me, so I ran straight home to tell my mother about it.

When I did, she was like, "The park over there? Did you give him the medicine and an old water bottle?" (I told my mother about the medicine but said nothing of the water bottle).

"I did," I replied. We went back to the park to find the old man, but he wasn't there. It turned out that when my mother was a child, she had the exact same experience.

Later, I found out that a long time ago an old man died while sitting on that park bench. In his personal belongings, they found medicine and an old water bottle.

My daughter is now in the fourth grade. She goes to the same school I did. I've mentioned this story to her and asked her that if she ever has the same experience to ask the old man his name.

If we can find out his name, I'd like to go and visit his grave with my mother and daughter to pay our respects.

I was shocked when I saw the news

* * *

I was really into fishing when I was in junior high school and often went to the ocean to catch things.

One day, despite the strong winds, I left early to go fishing. I lived about five kilometres from the beach. On the way, I saw a strange old lady. She was carrying a basket on her back and was wearing these old work pants like you see women wearing in old stories.

As I passed her on my bike, I felt this strangely uncomfortable sensation. I turned around and suddenly she was nowhere to be seen.

'Huh, a ghost?!' I thought. I was still just a young junior high student, so I suddenly lost all interest in fishing and returned home.

That same day, around lunchtime, I was watching the local news when my usual fishing spot appeared. Someone had been swallowed up by a wave and their whereabouts were unknown. I was shocked.

If I'd continued on my way, I could have been swallowed up too… Maybe that old lady saved me…

Daitoa Tunnel

* * *

This story happened when I was a university student.

At the time I was a bit of a brat, and I often went to visit various ghost spots.

One day, one of my friends told me, "Apparently there's a ghost tunnel close to here."

I immediately gathered up a bunch of friends and on the weekend we set out for the tunnel. I had no idea there was one so close-by.

The tunnel was about a 10-minute drive from town. It was rather large and we couldn't see the exit. A soft wind and strange sound from deep within the tunnel blew towards us.

Above the tunnel, there was some writing that I struggled to read. "Daitoa Tunnel, Constructed Showa 17th Year 3rd Month 5th Day."

For some reason, the bricks at the edge of the tunnel had collapsed. There was an iron fence, but whether someone had tried to kick it in or not, the middle was mostly crushed. We decided to enter the tunnel through there.

I looked at my watch, it was 11.30pm.

I don't know whether the tunnel was originally used for steam trains or not but the roof was stained black. Only the bricks of the side walls were still in good condition, considering the place had been abandoned for quite some time.

At first, I was a bit nervous, but then we all relaxed, and as we started to play around, that's when something strange happened.

Suddenly the light from my handheld torch went out.

I didn't know whether it was broken, or if the batteries were dead, or if I'd just handled it badly, but I hit it a few times. It showed no signs of turning back on. It was a little creepy.

While everyone stood there petrified, a strong wind suddenly blew from deep in the tunnel. My friends scrambled to escape.

As for me, I stumbled over something as I tried to run and landed flat on my backside. I tried as hard as I could to escape, but it was like I was overcome with paralysis. I couldn't move.

Then, from somewhere ahead, I could hear faint footsteps. Oh, thank god… the tunnel was still in use and one of the workers has come to check on something…

Or so I thought, and when I thought about it later, the iron fence was there to keep people out, so it was highly unlikely the tunnel was still in use.

While this was happening, the footsteps slowly got louder and louder, and finally I saw the silhouette of a person. Sure enough, the 'person' that appeared wasn't a worker. There was a woman wearing an air-raid hood, a man missing half his face, and a half-mummified man with his eyeballs hanging out.

I tried to run, but my backside hurt so much I couldn't even get up. I couldn't do anything but crawl backwards. Slowly they began to close the distance between us, and just as they were right in front of me, my finger touched something. It was the thing I tripped over when trying to escape.

It was a skull within a steel helmet.

Normally you would think something like that would be terrifying, but I didn't know what to think anymore. I lost my composure.

I don't know why, but instinctively I felt like the skull belonged to the 'people' in front of me.

"It's this, right? You want this?" I said suddenly. I don't know why those words came out, but I thought it was the only thing that would help me.

The result was even better than I expected.

The terrifying faces of the 'people' started to change right before my very eyes. They became actual 'people.' A man in his 20s wearing glasses, a man with a sash across his shoulder, a female university student with her hair in braids…

It was like they were alive.

Then I heard someone calling from behind me. My friends had worked up the courage to come back into the tunnel to get me. Surprised, I turned back around, but they were already gone.

My friends had already alerted the police that I hadn't come out of the tunnel. The police and people from the town hall got involved, and it became quite a big thing. Well, we'd trespassed in a restricted tunnel, so of course it did. Of course, my parents were also quite angry about it. Afterwards, I heard more about 'Daitoa Tunnel' from them.

Daitoa Tunnel was completed in the year following the outbreak of the Pacific War. In commemoration of the start of the war, it was named after its official name, "Daito A Sensou" (The Greater East Asian War). The reason it became a ghost spot was because there was an incident there during the war.

A 10-car train, five of which were carrying soldiers going to war, was attacked by an American military aircraft. The train was attacked just outside the Daitoa Tunnel and derailed inside. In addition to machine gun fire, four rockets were fired, three of which hit the train. It went up in flames and overturned inside the tunnel walls. The one rocket that missed hit near the entrance of the tunnel. The fallen down bricks near the entrance of the tunnel were because of that rocket.

In the end, many people burned to death, and those who survived were trapped inside the airtight space of the tunnel only to die from smoke inhalation. Of the 500 staff and passengers on the train, only 54 people survived. The time was 11:30 p.m., August 14th in the 20th year of Showa. The same time we went in.

It was a horrible tragedy, but because it happened during the crisis of the war, over time people started to forget about it. I believed those people came out because they wanted more people to know about what happened there.

Daitoa Tunnel is dangerous for children playing in the area, so discussions about knocking it down have popped up several times. However, each time it does, more and more troubles start appearing and so work is suspended.

After the incident, a large memorial monument was put in place and the remains of the deceased were also gathered for proper burial and handling. After this, another attempt was made to try to demolish the tunnel once more. No more ghostly apparitions were seen. The demolition went smoothly, and the tunnel was destroyed. Now only the memorial monument remains.

Suspension bridge

* * *

This story is about the time two of us went to a certain suspension bridge that was featured as a ghost spot in an occult magazine.

We arrived at the suspension bridge late at night. It was the end of the rainy season, so the bridge was covered in a rather thick fog.

We stopped the car in front of the bridge and planned to walk the rest of the way. I got out of the car.

However my friend, the driver, just kept looking at the bridge and refused to get out of the car.

Friend: "It's kinda creepy… No way. Sorry, this time I'm just gonna stay here."

We'd been to ghost spots together several times, but this was the first time I'd ever seen him so scared.

Me: "Huh? You're gonna wait here all alone? Stop thinking about just yourself, hey."

Friend: "… Nah, I'm gonna stay here."

Me: "Okay, well I'm gonna go then."

I decided to leave him there and began walking towards the bridge. As I looked behind me, the car seemed to get swallowed up by the fog. It was like I was entering another world. The car felt so far away. I wondered if my friend was looking at me and thinking the same thing. While pondering this, I continued to walk forward. But then…

My friend suddenly sounded the car horn and started flashing the headlights.

"Huh? What's going on?"

Thinking something might have happened to him, I ran back.

Friend: "Get in!"

Me: "???"

Friend: "Hurry up and get in!"

I got into the car without knowing what was going on.

My friend quickly turned around and drove away from the bridge.

Angrily I asked, "Hey, what's going on? You scared me."

Friend: "Just now there was a small girl standing between you and the bridge."

Me: "Wha… huh?"

Friend: "There's no way a small girl would be up in the mountains this late at night, you know…"

Me: "… Yeah, I guess. Thanks, you saved me."

Friend: "I mean, I felt something, you know? As soon as I saw the girl. It was like she was warning me not to go near the bridge… She's the one who saved you."

Me: "You say it was a girl… How old was she?"

Friend: "First or second grade of elementary school, I guess… We should be grateful to her."

Me: "I'm grateful but I'm not into little girls."

Friend: "Haha."

Me: "I wonder what would have happened if I kept going."

Friend: "… I dunno."

Me & Friend: "…"

My comment about not liking little girls should have changed the atmosphere in the car, but it didn't. We continued home in silence.

I said goodbye to my friend, and when I got home, it was already after 6 a.m. The next day I got a call from him.

Friend: "Hello? Are you okay?"

Me: "Yeah, I'm fine."

Friend: "… Okay, that's good."

Me: "Did something happen?"

Friend: "No, as soon as I got home I went to bed, but then I had a dream that was exactly the same as last night."

Me: "When you saw the little girl?"

Friend: "Yeah. The little girl was there, and I was honking the horn and flashing the lights trying to get you to come back."

Me: "Okay…"

Friend: "But unlike last night you didn't notice and kept walking towards the bridge."

Me: "What happened to me?"

Friend: "Then I woke up…"

Me: "What… Well, I guess it was a pretty big thing to happen right before bed, so it's not really that strange that you'd dream about it."

Friend: "It would be nice if that was really all there was to it… I wonder if it's some kind of hint…"

Me: "…"

Friend: "…"

Silence filled the air.

It seemed to go on forever but also last just an instant.

However, what broke the silence wasn't the voice of my friend or even my own. There was a faint voice, deep in the phone, and yet despite that we both heard it very clearly.

It was a girl's voice.

"You should have crossed over."

After that, my friend and I went to be purified, and he never dreamt about the little girl again. Of course, he never saw her again in reality either.

You got divorced?!

* * *

A friend from my class at university contacted me about having a reunion, but I was just about to head overseas for work so I told him I couldn't go.

My wife–also from the same class–and I got married soon after we graduated. She was also busy with work so she couldn't go either.

I thought it was a pity, but that was the end of that. I went overseas for work but when I arrived at the airport on my return, there was an incredible amount of mail waiting for me. "You got divorced?!"

According to them, my wife appeared at the reunion, saying she was now able to make it and revealed to everyone that we recently got divorced.

I quickly called her and asked, "Hey, did you go to the reunion?" but she replied, "Huh? No, I didn't."

I asked the reunion organiser and everyone who went what exactly was going on, but they replied that it was just like they had told me.

Something felt off, so we organised a day where we could all get together. When everyone saw my wife's face, they all looked surprised.

Apparently, something was slightly different with her.

When we looked at the photos they'd taken at the reunion, an entirely different woman was in the pictures. Everyone was like, "What, this wasn't her! It's wrong!" They were scared.

"I didn't even notice when the photos were developed," they said.

On the day of the reunion, they even thought, "Something's a little different, but it's been a few years so I guess that's to be expected." It was the same face when they got the photos developed.

Several of them exchanged phone numbers with her but when they tried to mail her, they got "This phone number is not in use" or "MAILER-DAEMON" in return.

The whole thing was strange, but the people that had exchanged numbers with her were especially terrified.

But, nothing in particular happened after that again.

If you're going to kill yourself, why don't you sleep with me first?

* * *

Man: "Your shoes are off, you're going to jump, aren't you?"

Woman: "Like you said, I'm just about to jump. What's it to you?"

Man: "Oh good!"

Woman: "I'm sorry?"

Man: "I mean, you're going to kill yourself, right? If you're planning to jump from here."

Woman: "That's right."

Man: "If you're going to kill yourself, why don't you sleep with me first?"

Woman: "I'm sorry?"

Man: "You don't often meet people who are about to kill themselves."

Woman: "…"

Man: "And yet I'm lucky to just happen across such a beautiful woman."

Woman: "Um, can I jump now?"

Man: "You heard what I just said, right?"

Woman: "I did. You asked if I wanted to have sex with you."

Man: "Heh, that's right. That's my only goal. Don't worry. I don't have the slightest intention of stopping you from killing yourself."

Woman: "Can you just go now?"

Man: "I don't have anywhere to go. If there was, it would only be between your bosom."

Woman: "Can I jump now?"

Man: “Why?!”

Woman: “Look deep and ask yourself that.”

Man: “Come on. I don’t have any right to stop you. Just perhaps let me ask you a single question.”

Woman: “Just one.”

Man: “Were you wearing white panties three days ago?”

Woman: “… What?”

Man: “‘Why does this strange man know what colour panties I was wearing?’ That’s what your face looks like right now.”

Woman: “What the hell is wrong with you?”

Man: “Heh, I’m just some ordinary guy who can’t get any unless he pays for it.”

Woman: “I wasn’t asking that.”

Man: “So why do I know about your panties? That’s simple. For the last week now you’ve been trying to jump from the roof of this apartment complex. Right?”

Woman: “So you’ve been watching me since a week ago?”

Man: “To be precise it wasn’t you but rather up your skirt. You were getting ready to jump and kill yourself, but you always stopped right at the last moment, hey.”

Woman: “…”

Man: “Let me tell you, a week ago when I looked up at this building I was surprised. Like, ‘Ah, panties!’”

Woman: “So the first thing that caught your eye was my panties?”

Man: “Of course it was. I mean there aren’t many opportunities to see a lady’s panties.”

Woman: "You really know how to talk to someone about to kill themselves."

Man: "It's the other way around. It's because you're about to silence yourself that I can say all these things to you."

Woman: "So what was it, you want me to sleep with you?"

Man: "Heh, if you like I can sleep with you."

Woman: "No thanks."

Man: "Huh. You really are quite a difficult person."

Woman: "I'm quite normal. You're the strange one. Even in the world after death, there's no-one that would sleep with someone on their first meeting."

Man: "For sure. It's too sudden."

Woman: "If you understand, then good. Well then, see you later."

Man: "Why are you trying to jump again?"

Woman: "So I can die."

Man: "Wait. We haven't slept together yet."

Woman: "I have no intention of sleeping with you."

Man: "Right now, yeah?"

Woman: "For the rest of my life."

Man: "That's why you can't end it right now. I haven't finished talking. Actually, there's something I really need to ask you."

Woman: "What is it?"

Man: "Why aren't you wearing a skirt today?"

Woman: "What are you trying to say?"

Man: “Heh, when you look up towards the sky from the bottom of this building you can see it shining brighter than the sun. Your panties.”

Woman: “Just how much do you like panties?”

Man: “It’s the thing I most look forward to these days. And so why?”

Woman: “No reason. I just didn’t feel like wearing a skirt today.”

Man: “So what you’re saying is that sometimes you don’t wear a skirt?”

Woman: “That’s what I’m saying.”

Man: “Well, could I have you go and get changed into a skirt for me then?”

Woman: “If I had that much time I’d just kill myself without delay.”

Man: “Why are you in such a rush to die?”

Woman: “Because I want to die.”

Man: “You can do it, can’t you? I mean, in the end you’re going to die, anyway.”

Woman: “What do you mean?”

Man: “Once you decide to die, doesn’t that create some leeway in your heart?”

Woman: “Leeway?”

Man: “I mean, whatever happens now, you’re going to jump. You can end your life whenever you want, so whatever happens, you can feel relaxed and at ease, right?”

Woman: “It’ll all become naught, it’ll all be ended… the result has been decided.”

Man: “Which means you can let most things go, right?”

Woman: “For sure. I can see where this is heading.”

Man: “So, sleep with me.”

Woman: “In the end, it was all about that, huh?”

Man: “Do you not want to sleep with me?”

Woman: “Am I okay for you?”

Man: “Good job answering a question with another question!”

Woman: “It’s better than your words and conduct. But yeah…”

Man: “Oh? Have you finally come around?”

Woman: “That is correct. It’s probably not a bad idea to be useful in the last moments of my life.”

Man: “I’m glad you’re able to grasp the situation so quickly.”

Woman: “Of course. I’ll alert the police.”

Man: “Fu…”

Woman: “I’ll say this now. It’s not a threat.”

Man: “I see.”

Woman: “This is how the world is. If a woman like me reported you, you know what’ll happen, right?”

Man: “Ah, you’re so naive.”

Woman: “I’m naive?”

Man: “You planned your death. You’ve gotten all your affairs in order, yes?”

Woman: “Well…”

Man: “You’ve cancelled your phone, prepared a will and such, that’s more than enough evidence that you planned to commit suicide. And I mean, if you cancelled your phone you can’t really call the police, can you?”

Woman: “Ah…”

Man: "So, in the end, the only choices you have are, you can sleep with me and then die, or you can alert the police and hang around in this world some more."

Woman: "Both are hell."

Man: "So, what's it gonna be?"

Woman: "…"

Man: "If you're quiet I'll be gentle."

Woman: "Aaaahhhh!!!! Someone, help me!!!"

Man: "What?!? Even though you're gonna kill yourself you're screaming for help!?"

Woman: "I'm going to get rid of you and then I'll kill myself."

Janitor: "What happened!?"

Man: "!!"

Woman: "There's this really weird pervert…"

Janitor: "Why are you barefoot?"

Woman: "Huh? Oh, no… I just wanted to feel a little free…"

Janitor: "You wanted to feel free."

Woman: "I… I did. It's, uh, I was imitating that singer, cocco."

Janitor: "I'm sorry, but could I get you to come down from the rooftop now?"

Woman: "…"

Janitor: "Before you know it more and more dark thoughts keep surfacing these days."

Woman: "I understand."

Janitor: "Thank you."

Woman: "Okay."

Man: "Wow, that was a surprise."

Woman: "Aah! Do… don't scare me like that."

Man: “Oh. That’s the first time you’ve looked shocked at me.”

Woman: “… I’m sorry?”

Man: “Oh no, not at all. At any rate when you screamed out, and that lady came I freaked out.”

Woman: “That’s the janitor.”

Man: “I hid without thinking.”

Woman: “You hid?”

Man: “Hmm? You didn’t notice?”

Woman: “I was preoccupied with the janitor.”

Man: “When she pointed out your shoes you got flustered, hey.”

Woman: “… Shut up. Putting that aside, how did you hide anyway?”

Man: “Huh?”

Woman: “There’s nowhere you can quickly hide behind here.”

Man: “You should be familiar with the sight from the top of the fence here.”

Woman: “I should… Oh, right.”

Man: “Did you finally realise?”

Woman: “You managed to hide quickly behind the rooftop fence?”

Man: “Correct. Although it may be small, it was a great place to quickly hide behind.”

Woman: “…”

Man: “Wait, where are you going?”

Woman: “I’m leaving.”

Man: “Hey hey hey, why?”

Woman: “The janitor asked me to.”

Man: “When you leave here, what are you going to do?”

Woman: “For now I’ll return to my apartment.”

Man: “Eh? You’re not going to die?”

Woman: “…”

Man: “I see. So it’s like that.”

Woman: “What are you smiling for?”

Man: “Now you’ll go back to your apartment and together we’ll…”

Woman: “No!

Man: “No?”

Woman: “To start with, why would I even invite you into my apartment?”

Man: “… So, you prefer to do it outdoors then?”

Woman: “Before I kill myself I think it would be better if I killed you first.”

Man: “So you’ll become a criminal?”

Woman: “It’s all the same in the end isn’t it?”

Man: “If so then why don’t you sleep with me?”

Woman: “I’m done with this conversation.”

Man: “We’re on the elevator but what floor is your apartment on?”

Woman: “I’m not telling you.”

Man: “I’m gonna find out now, anyway.”

Woman: “Well what floor are we on now?”

Man: “The first. So your apartment is on the first floor?”

Woman: “No. Now I’m heading out for a bit.”

Janitor: “Hey. You going out now?”

Woman: “Yes, going to get an early dinner.”

Janitor: “I see. It’s dangerous out there so be careful on the street come night-time.”

Woman: "I will. I'm feeling that right this very minute. I'll take care."

Man: "Hang on, you're leaving the apartment?"

Woman: "As expected I can't go back to my apartment now."

Man: "Why?!"

Woman: "Asking why in this situation, you're amazing."

Man: "I mean yeah, I'm a guy who has to pay for it, but if there's a technique that can satisfy a single woman…"

Woman: "Die."

Man: "You haven't been very kind to me since we first met, have you?"

Woman: "It's better than you asking me to sleep with you. I mean, please go kill yourself."

Man: "And now advising me to kill myself. Furthermore, we're at McDonald's now."

Woman: "I'm eating here today."

Man: "Huh?"

Woman: "I don't care if you join me, but I've made the decision to eat here."

Man: "What about eating at home?"

Woman: "No."

Man: "Okay, I get it. But I'm not gonna eat anything."

Woman: "Are you sulking?"

Man: "It's just, hey. At a big franchise like this…"

Woman: "Uh huh. Well, I'm going in. I've fully decided. You're not going to eat?"

Man: "I'm not hungry."

Woman: “Then go get me a seat. I’m starting to see why you’re a virgin.”

Man: “… You’re getting more and more cheeky now. Isn’t that a little much?”

Woman: “You’re the last person I want to hear that from, Mr can’t get any unless he pays for it.”

Man: “…”

Woman: “…”

Man: “…”

Woman: “Why are you suddenly so quiet?”

Man: “Never mind, hurry up and eat.”

Woman: “You want to go back to my apartment that much?”

Man: “No. Doesn’t matter if it’s your apartment.”

Woman: “Nowhere is good for me.”

Man: “Look just hurry up and eat, please.”

Woman: “Why are you rushing me so much? This is my last meal.”

Man: “Your last meal is McDonald’s. You’re gonna regret that when you die.”

Woman: “Yeah, Freshness Burger was probably a better choice. And I mean I don’t even like McDonald’s, anyway.”

Man: “… Then why did you come here?”

Woman: “I wanted to check something.”

Man: “What do you mean?”

Woman: “You’ve heard the saying ‘Hunger is the best sauce,’ right? I think that saying expresses precisely the fault in all humans. Because we’re hungry, food tastes good.

Man: “Ah, I think I see what you’re trying to say.”

Woman: "Knowing that this is my last meal I wanted to know if anything would change. If it does change, then it makes my death after this feel all the more real."

Man: "So how does the hamburger taste?"

Woman: "I don't know. I feel like it might be better than usual, but it also might not be. Perhaps I don't want to acknowledge that it tastes differently. I don't know why I'd think that way though."

Man: "I kind of understand how you feel."

Woman: "Don't say such gross things."

Man: "Now now, there's no need for that. Now listen."

Woman: "… Go ahead."

Man: "You don't want to admit that anything and everything could change with a single feeling. Right?"

Woman: "…"

Man: "As someone who is about to kill themselves, that's not something you want to know. That single feeling that glittered until yesterday, that your intention to die could be shaken."

Woman: "That I'm going to die is a matter of fact. That hasn't changed, even now."

Man: "No. I think if that were so you would be able to enjoy your last meal. With only a hundred yen burger your own will disappeared. Isn't that scary?"

Woman: "This is a Big Mac, it's not 100 yen."

Man: "Stop missing the point."

Woman: "Hmph."

Man: "While we're at it, there's a part of you that thinks it might be nice to sleep with me. Isn't that so?"

Woman: "No. That's the one thing that won't change even if I die. This fault in humans seems to come out only when it's convenient. But there are things in the world that don't change. My feelings are immovable."

Man: "You're amazingly stubborn."

Woman: "I am. My will is firm like a stone."

Man: "You have no sense of humour, do you?"

Woman: "… I'm not here to make you laugh. And stop making me talk about such strange things."

Man: "Strange things?"

Woman: "Yeah. I can feel people looking at me."

Man: "Even though you're about to die you're worried about whether strangers are looking at you?"

Woman: "Sh-shut up. I'm leaving here right now."

Man: "It's your last meal, you don't need to eat it like that."

Woman: "…"

Man: "You suddenly started devouring it, and now you're not eating it at all… You're all over the place."

Woman: "Would you please be quiet."

Man: "You ended up taking quite a lot of time to eat that, didn't you?"

Woman: "Because it was my last meal. It's only natural. Are you complaining?"

Man: "Not at all. Rather than that, I'd prefer to talk about what's happening after this."

Woman: "I have nothing to talk to you about. And how long are you going to hang around, anyway?"

Man: "Are you not planning to make use of my good intentions?"

Woman: "Good intentions?"

Man: "Before you die I'm trying to send you to heaven in bed."

Woman: "I can send you to hell if you'd like."

Man: "Ahahaha that's impossible."

Woman: "Yeah, I think so too… You're really strange, you know."

Man: "My courting behaviours?"

Woman: "Can we just please talk about something else?"

Man: "What's strange then?"

Woman: "Everything, everything is strange. A normal person, when faced with someone about to kill themselves, would ask them why first, right?"

Man: "What? Do you perhaps want me to ask you why?"

Woman: "N-no. Don't get the wrong idea."

Man: "If it's why you won't sleep with me then I'll listen."

Woman: "You just keep bringing that back up, don't you?"

Man: "Well even if I listen to why you want to kill yourself it doesn't mean you'll sleep with me."

Woman: "You're so persistent!"

Man: “Talking seriously, even if I ask why you want to die it’s not very interesting, is it?”

Woman: “Not interesting…”

Man: “I mean I can guess. I’m not terribly interested in it though.”

Woman: “You don’t care what you say, do you?”

Man: “Not really. Because it’s true. For me, I have more interest in your reasons to live than your reasons to die.”

Woman: “My reasons to live?”

Man: “I think your reasons for living are far more ambiguous than your reasons for dying. And more so than your reasons for dying, there are so many different things. If I’m gonna ask you something it would be that.”

Woman: “My reasons for living… Well, just because, I guess. I’m not dead. Somehow I’m alive and so I’m living. Something like that, I don’t really have a reason for why I’m alive.”

Man: “But isn’t that okay too? The reason that you spend your whole life looking for but never find. That reason that even if you die, you won’t understand. Isn’t that a beautiful thing?”

Woman: “… Are you indirectly trying to stop me from killing myself?”

Man: “No, not at all. In the end, my only goal is your body.”

Woman: “You keep bringing that up at every chance! There really are things in this world more painful than death.”

Man: “I’m sure there are. But in this world…”

Woman: “There are people worse off than me who are still doing their best. Are you really gonna say that same old crap to me?”

Man: “Wow, is this that so-called cold reading?”

Woman: “There’s only so many things you can say to someone about to kill themselves so anyone could guess that.”

Man: “I suppose that’s true, yes.”

Woman: “It’s strange to look relatively at such misfortunes. What does my unhappiness have to do with anyone else’s unhappiness?”

Man: “You are entirely correct.”

Woman: “You agree with things so quickly.”

Man: “I do. That’s what I said, isn’t it? I have no intention of stopping you from killing yourself. I would like to have a physical relationship with you just once, and that is more than enough for me.”

Woman: “There’s nothing I can say.”

Man: “Huh? You mean you will?”

Woman: “Of course not!”

Man: “You’re scary. Aren’t you starting to get a little too violent?”

Woman: “That’s your fault!!”

Man: “Okay, I get it. Let me ask just one question so we can all cool down.”

Woman: “You’re just gonna tie it into something dirty again aren’t you?”

Man: “No, not at all. This time it’s a serious question. After you die, what are you gonna do?”

Woman: “… What do you mean?”

Man: “Heh, exactly what I said. Think about it.”

Woman: "Even if you say that I still don't know what you're getting at."

Man: "What I'm saying is, what are you going to do after you kill yourself? I'm asking you to find out why you're looking forward to killing yourself."

Woman: "So, you mean the world after death? Well, there certainly seems to be a life after death and the existence of ghosts, doesn't there?"

Man: "For sure. I think there's merit in considering it."

Woman: "So, what will I do once I die, huh? Seems like I'd be able to do lots of things. Ah, but then there's also whether you go to heaven or to hell."

Man: "Surprisingly, the more you think about it the more you can't stop, right?"

Woman: "But even if I do think about it nothing will change."

Man: "Well, it's connected to raising your desire to kill yourself."

Woman: "I suppose so. Hmm, if I die I'll find a dreamy boyfriend."

Man: "You're going to fall in love after you die?"

Woman: "Yes. I'm gonna find a dreamy ghost boyfriend. Then I'll be happy. If I do that, it'll be proof that killing myself wasn't a mistake."

Man: "Seems fun."

Woman: "It's what you suggested, isn't it?"

Man: "I guess so."

Woman: "I don't know anything about heaven or hell though, so let's just stop thinking about that right now."

Man: "Okay."

Woman: "What? Do you want to say something vulgar again?"

Man: "No. I was just thinking that it seems most people really do think that way, huh?"

Woman: "Think that way? About what?"

Man: "Haven't you ever wondered about it?"

Woman: "… Uh, about whether ghosts are real or not? Is that what you mean?"

Man: "No. Whether ghosts exist or not, I think that they do. Probably. Putting that aside, haven't you ever questioned it? I mean ghost photos exist, right? Don't you think those are really strange?"

Woman: "I have absolutely no idea what you're talking about."

Man: "Well there are lots of different reasons as to why people die, so I can't say for certain. Haven't you ever heard stories like this about ghost photos? 'The ghosts of people who kill themselves will appear in photos taken where they died.' Don't you think that's strange?"

Woman: "Not really. If they have a strong grudge or something they'll appear, something like that."

Man: "Okay, well let me ask you a question. After you kill yourself do you really think you'll want to appear in photos? Suicide is the result of wanting to be released from the existence of being a living person."

Woman: "… Well, everyone's different."

Man: "But if, like you, you die and tie yourself to another ghost and become happy then you can't take pictures together, right? Even if you do appear in a photo, you'll just show up in a way that terrifies people."

Woman: "Could you just say what you want a little more clearly? I have no idea what you want to say."

Man: "It's just a question towards what everyone freely believes. You die and become a ghost. Well sure, that's fine. The problem is after that. You become a ghost and you can see other ghosts. You couldn't see them when you're alive but when you die you can. Why do people think like that?"

Woman: "Even if you become a ghost, you can't see other ghosts…?"

Man: "Strange, isn't it? There are people who don't believe in ghosts. But there's not a single person who doesn't think that once you die you won't be able to see other ghosts."

Woman: "So, what are you trying to say? Are you threatening me with that to stop me from killing myself?"

Man: "Don't make me repeat myself. I already told you I don't have any right to stop you. I just wanted to get the ball rolling on this stagnating question."

Woman: "I don't especially care about your question."

Man: "Really?"

Woman: "Don't make me repeat myself."

Man: "Ah, you're copying me."

Woman: "You copied me first."

Man: "Well then you're copying someone else."

Woman: “Probably.”

Man: “I also felt this is an important question for you which is why I said it. Don’t you think it’s something someone who’s about to die should think about?”

Woman: “Whatever happens after death, I don’t especially care.”

Man: “Well then while you’re alive let’s think about it.”

Woman: “Okay… Wait, why are we continuing this conversation again?”

Man: “Because. While we’re talking like this, there’s no need to sleep with me.”

Woman: “Ha… Has anyone ever told you before?”

Man: “Told me what?”

Woman: “That you’re persistent.”

Man: “…”

Woman: “You’re thinking about it with a really serious face. You’ve heard it a lot, haven’t you?”

Man: “No. You’re the first.”

Woman: “I don’t need your lies.”

Man: “It’s the truth.”

Woman: “Yeah yeah. Then, what were we talking about?”

Man: “Hmm? You feel like talking now?”

Woman: “Because you won’t tell me.”

Man: “You sure do say tricky things.”

Woman: “Shut up. If you’re gonna talk, then talk. I’m going to kill myself you know.”

Man: “Yeah yeah. I know.”

Woman: “…”

Man: "Why do you think people are scared of dying?"

Woman: "I have no idea."

Man: "Think about it a little."

Woman: "Instinct."

Man: "Instinct?"

Woman: "Humans are the only creatures who fear death. Animals just instinctively try to live."

Man: "You have no romance."

Woman: "Don't say that so happily."

Man: "I thought females were a little more… 'sparkling' than that."

Woman: "You want someone who's about to die to say romantic things with a sparkle in their eye?"

Man: "Ahaha, yeah I see."

Woman: "Well what is a romantic reason to fear death then?"

Man: "I dunno whether it's romantic, but to stop wondering about things is the same as dying, I think."

Woman: "There might be a reason for that."

Man: "Our daily lives are just full of mysteries and questions."

Woman: "To live thinking like that must be fun, yes."

Man: "Yeah, for sure."

Woman: "… You're thick-headed, aren't you?"

Man: "Huh? What?"

Woman: "You heard me. And this conversation is going nowhere. Just tell me what you're thinking."

Man: “Okay, okay. Why do people who have never died fear death? In reality, I don’t think we fear death itself that much.”

Woman: “Then what are we afraid of?”

Man: “What comes after death. In actuality we somehow know, don’t you think? What happens after death?”

Woman: “After death?”

Man: “Yeah. We vaguely know what’s ahead. Something even more painful than what we feel in life awaits us in death.”

Woman: “That’s no laughing matter”

Man: “No, it’s not. You don’t want to live anymore so you kill yourself, but something even more painful than that awaits you after.”

Woman: “You say that surprisingly with a smile.”

Man: “I’ve probably been doing that since the start, haven’t I?”

Woman: “Yeah. You’re the first person to ever smile like that while talking to me.”

Man: “Get out. You’re making me blush.”

Woman: “You’re also the first person I’ve spoken to that’s pissed me off this much. I hate people who talk like they know everything.”

Man: “Ah, me too.”

Woman: “I’m talking about you!”

Man: “You don’t have to say it, I do know.”

Woman: “People like you are the absolute worst type of people for someone like me.”

Man: “From the point of view of someone about to kill themselves, a man who stops that is like a *shinigami* (god of death), right?”

Woman: "… And you just keep talking with that arrogant attitude like you know everything."

Man: "Because even though you're trying to escape from reality you just keep holding it back."

Woman: "I really hate people like you. You take something trivial and then keep on nagging about it, it pisses me off. I hate people who look at you with pity as well. And people who mistake being a busy-body for kindness are also the worst."

Man: "And yourself?"

Woman: "… I don't want to think about it."

Man: "And me?"

Woman: "You threw that in there well. I also hate you."

Man: "What!? Why?!"

Woman: "You really can't be questioning that!? I hate everyone. People who are happier than me and people who are more miserable than me. I hate every person that's alive."

Man: "So that means you don't hate me then."

Woman: "… Huh?"

Man: "Well you just said it. 'I hate every person that's alive.'"

Woman: "What a stupid joke. It's not even funny in the slightest."

Man: "Even if it's not a joke, you wouldn't laugh."

Woman: "If my psychic powers suddenly bloomed now after all this it would be quite annoying."

Man: "The world has become sensitive to lies lately. You'd probably just be called a fake psychic."

Woman: “Then if I wrote books about ghosts they’d call me a ghost-writer, huh.”

Man: “Seems like you want to die more and more, hey.”

Woman: “… Anyway, if you’re gonna lie about such a thing you should have prepared a little more beforehand.”

Man: “Prepared?”

Woman: “When I saw the janitor on the rooftop earlier you hid on purpose, right?”

Man: “That’s right.”

Woman: “If she couldn’t see you, there would be no reason to…”

Man: “Something wrong?”

Woman: “… Right. You hid. The first time I saw the janitor.”

Man: “…”

Woman: “But the second time I saw her you didn’t hide. She said, ‘It’s dangerous out there so be careful on the street come night-time.’ She wouldn’t say such a thing if a man and a woman were together…?”

Man: “Perhaps it was just that you didn’t notice, and I secretly hid.”

Woman: “… But you didn’t eat anything at McDonald’s either. You didn’t go and get us a seat either. Which means the gazes I felt in the store were…”

Man: “You finally realised, huh?”

Woman: “Huh? H-hang on a minute. You mean to everyone around me it just looked like I was talking to myself?”

Man: “I told you, didn’t I? Hurry up and eat so we can leave.”

Woman: “There’s no way I’d understand what you meant!”

Man: “Oh my, are you okay? That’s the most dreadful face you’ve made so far.”

Woman: “I’m well aware that I’ve led a life full of embarrassments… Ah… No, wait.”

Man: “You want to say something again?”

Woman: “If you’re a ghost that means I can’t touch you, right?”

Man: “Well, who knows? Perhaps unexpectedly you can.”

Woman: “…”

Man: “Uh, that look in your eyes is scary… What are you…?!”

Woman: “Wowow… you, you really are see-through…!”

Man: “No no no. Why did you try to hit me? If I were alive, you would have broken my nose!”

Woman: “… Just because. Don’t worry about such trivial things.”

Man: “I happen to think that’s actually rather important.”

Woman: “So why didn’t you tell me right from the start, anyway? Thanks to you, I embarrassed myself.”

Man: “Don’t worry about it. The end is in sight, anyway.”

Woman: “That’s not the problem here.”

Man: “You really are a difficult person.”

Woman: “Shut up and answer my question.”

Man: "Well, I didn't think you'd believe me. If I suddenly introduced myself as a ghost would you believe me?"

Woman: "Well, to start with, you haven't told me anything about yourself other than you can't get any unless you pay for it."

Man: "Ahaha. That was rather careless of me. But even if I did introduce myself properly, would you have believed me?"

Woman: "Of course not. But when the janitor came to the roof you would have been able to explain yourself then, right?"

Man: "Well I got kind of excited… it was kind of like I was alive again!"

Woman: "You get excited even though you're dead?"

Man: "I do, yes. I don't know about other people though."

Woman: "… But why can I see you?"

Man: "Now that I really don't know."

Woman: "Really?"

Man: "You can bet your life on it."

Woman: "Idiot."

Man: "This is the first time for me too, you know."

Woman: "First time?"

Man: "Talking to someone since I died."

Woman: "…"

Man: "How many years have passed since I died? I don't even know. If I were to guess it's probably been at least five years or so."

Woman: "You've been a ghost for a while then, huh?"

Man: “Yeah. But you’re the first person to respond to me trying to talk to them. And you can even see me! It’s a miracle.”

Woman: “A miracle, huh?”

Man: “What’s wrong?”

Woman: “… I don’t want you to get me wrong so I’m just gonna come right out and say it. I really don’t like people like you who are always so cryptic.”

Man: “I’m a ghost.”

Woman: “Shut up. Even though you’re a man, you’re so focused on the little things.”

Man: “Ah ha! That’s a controversial statement!”

Woman: “This conversation isn’t going to go anywhere so whatever, that’s fine. While I’m at it, I’m not really that concerned about you either. However, I do feel a little sad for you.”

Man: “Why?”

Woman: “Because of all the people who could see you, it was me. You have an unrivalled love of talking, even I can see that.”

Man: “Please, continue.”

Woman: “Finally someone can see you and it turns out to be me, a good-for-nothing woman… I feel a little guilty. You would have rather meet someone a little more fun, right?”

Man: “…”

Woman: “But I will say that I only feel just a little guilty, okay. Don’t get me wrong here.”

Man: “… I’m glad it was you though.”

Woman: “I’m sorry? Are you begging me? You’re rather audacious for a layman.”

Man: “Ahaha. Has no-one ever told you before?”

Woman: “Told me what?”

Man: “That your speech and conduct are so forceful.”

Woman: “…”

Man: “You don’t have to think about it so hard, you’ve heard it many times, right?”

Woman: “No. You’re the first.”

Man: “Lies! Although probably not.”

Woman: “I don’t usually speak like this. Like, talking to people is extremely tiring and I can’t really do much other than trifling small talk. I don’t have any friends I can speak my heart to. Before you approached me it was like, well I didn’t care anymore. It’s the first time I’ve ever said such mean things to a person before. I should probably be the one who’s glad that it was you who approached me.”

Man: “What’s this? Are you by any chance trying to make a move on me?”

Woman: “Drop dead.”

Man: “No way. I already died long ago.”

Woman: “… If you don’t want to answer then you don’t have to.”

Man: “Hmm?”

Woman: “How did you die?”

Man: “Oh, suicide.”

Woman: “You killed yourself?”

Man: “Was that unexpected?”

Woman: “I have no idea. Can you tell me a little more?”

Man: "… Well, actually, I used to live in this apartment building."

Woman: "No way, did you die here?"

Man: "Oh my veranda, yes."

Woman: "Did you jump over?"

Man: "No. I lived on the third floor so there was a good chance it wouldn't kill me. So in order to make sure I absolutely would die I hung myself."

Woman: "You hung yourself…"

Man: "It's more reliable than jumping. If you're going to jump you want to make sure it'll kill you."

Woman: "Why did you kill yourself?"

Man: "For a similar reason to yourself. But to put it simply, I wanted to go somewhere that wasn't here I suppose."

Woman: "Heaven?"

Man: "Or perhaps Hell. But when I opened my eyes after hanging myself I was in despair. For some reason, I was in front of this apartment building. At first, I didn't even know if I was dead or not. I felt like I'd just become a see-through person rather than a ghost, and furthermore, being a ghost is rather inconvenient."

Woman: "Inconvenient?"

Man: "I can pass through doors and things but I can't pass through walls."

Woman: "Ha. That's unexpected."

Man: "I thought that maybe I'd be able to fly as well but I can't. I wondered if I would appear in photos so I tried as well."

Woman: "Did you appear?"

Man: "I don't know. I've never been able to check. I've also tried entering the female hot springs."

Woman: "… Should I be hearing this story?"

Man: "Surprisingly, I couldn't pass under the shop curtain."

Woman: "What do you mean?"

Man: "I don't know the cause. But if there's something I thought I couldn't do while alive, then I can't do it now either."

Woman: "That's strange."

Man: "Also, I can't sleep or anything. But it's not such a big deal. The biggest shock was that I didn't see any ghosts other than myself."

Woman: "You're saying that you've never seen a ghost, but how would you even know what a ghost looks like?"

Man: "True. But I've been screaming ever since I died. 'Is anyone out there dead?' and so on."

Woman: "And no-one's replied to that yet?"

Man: "Yeah. I've frequently been to ghost spots, deep forests, suicide spots and such."

Woman: "And you never met anyone?"

Man: "Nope. That's when I first realised. If you become a ghost, you can't see other ghosts. When I realised that I wanted to die just as much as the first time."

Woman: "So you're saying that people who like to chat shouldn't kill themselves?"

Man: "… Hmm, didn't I tell you yet?"

Woman: "Huh?"

Man: "I absolutely hated talking to other people when I was alive."

Woman: "…"

Man: "I understand the meaning of the saying 'the eyes are the window to the soul' now."

Woman: "You noticed, huh?"

Man: "For just a moment they were like, 'No way, he's full of crap.'"

Woman: "And I understood the meaning of telepathy."

Man: "Ho ho."

Woman: "And also the meaning of 'the eyes are the window to the soul.' But don't go misunderstanding me now."

Man: "You don't have to be embarrassed."

Woman: "Yeah yeah."

Man: "Well it's natural you would think so. But it's true. I didn't have any friends, let alone have any relationships with the opposite sex…"

Woman: "Well considering all of that you've been rather smooth when talking to me."

Man: "Since I died I've approached many people."

Woman: "You said just before that you hated talking to people, right?"

Man: "Yes. But as the years go by, there's nothing to do. Even if I pass by someone I once knew, they don't notice me. The only thing that's ever noticed me is probably a camera."

Woman: "…"

Man: "Ever since I died it was the first time I felt such a way. I wanted someone, anyone to notice me. I wanted to talk to someone. After I died, I tried talking to all sorts of different people. Like the old guy sitting on the park bench staring off into space, or the young kid playing in the sandpit. I even tried barging into a group of very clearly violent young men, but of course, none of them noticed me."

Woman: "That's gotta be painful, huh?"

Man: "Yeah. But the times our conversations meshed I was really happy. Or when I'd call out and someone would turn around and look just by chance."

Woman: "That's so sad. So then when you approached me as well…"

Man: "No, that was a little different. For the last six months now I stopped trying to talk to people."

Woman: "So why did you talk to me?"

Man: "Because you were trying to jump."

Woman: "…"

Man: "For the last week I've constantly been trying to call out to you. But no matter how I tried the sound of your crying drowned out my voice."

Woman: "So each time I couldn't jump you saw me crying, huh."

Man: "I sure did."

Woman: "You really do piss me off… But somehow I understand you."

Man: "You finally understand me?"

Woman: "Someone who could communicate with others normally wouldn't try to stop someone in such a way."

Man: "Surely. I really did mean to say something a little more decent. However today my voice finally managed to reach you. It was a little rash, but I was so happy my heart soared. I wanted to dance, like, 'She heard me!'"

Woman: "So you've been saying whatever the hell you want since the beginning."

Man: "Yes. I never even dreamed that I could be so eloquent."

Woman: "If you had just tried to lecture me like a normal person I would have jumped."

Man: "So that means my way of persuading you was correct."

Woman: "What persuading? Didn't I stop myself from killing myself?"

Man: "Yeah but it was all right in the end, wasn't it?"

Woman: "What are you saying?"

Man: "Huh?"

Woman: "The course I'm pursuing hasn't changed."

Man: "Isn't this the part where you listen to my story and then change your way of thinking?"

Woman: "I'm sorry but I'm not going to be saved thanks to you. But I am thinking about delaying matters."

Man: "Delaying?"

Woman: "We talked about so many pointless things today, I'm tired. So, I'd like you to come back here again at 11 a.m. tomorrow morning."

Man: "Huh? What are you going to do?"

Woman: "Today I'm going to sleep."

Man: "Oh, okay."

Woman: "I'll say this right now, please don't follow me."

Man: "… You saw through me, huh?"

Woman: "I'll see you again tomorrow. Good night."

Man: "… Good night."

< The next morning >

Man: "Man, it's such a long time, huh."

Woman: "What are you on about so soon?"

Man: "The nights are so long since I died."

Woman: "I had a dream."

Man: "You're lucky."

Woman: "I'm not going to tell you what happened though."

Man: "I don't want to hear it. More than that, I want to know what you're going to do now. That's quite a big bag you've got there."

Woman: "We're going to the apartment you used to live in."

Man: "I'm sorry? W-what do you mean?"

Woman: "When I asked the real estate agent about it I quickly figured it out which was your room. And someone will be moving in soon, so right now it's still empty!"

Man: "No, I didn't mean…"

Woman: "Shut up and come with me."

Man: "…"

Woman: "… Even if I try to pull you along I can't touch you, hey."

Man: "Because I'm see through."

Woman: "But please come with me."

Man: "Okay."

< The apartment the man lived in >

Man: “Wow, they cleaned it up. It’s really nice now.”

Woman: “It’s cleaner than my place.”

Man: “But there’s nothing here.”

Woman: “Yep, there’s nothing but us here.”

Man: “…”

Woman: “So what are your thoughts?”

Man: “To be honest, seeing this room again doesn’t really bring up any feelings.”

Woman: “Even though you used to live here there’s nothing?”

Man: “Perhaps you were worried about me so you brought me here? If so, I’m sorry…”

Woman: “I’m not very good at being concerned about other people.”

Man: “Yeah, I know that.”

Woman: “I brought you here because I wanted to see it.”

Man: “Where are you going?”

Woman: “… Perhaps the only place that hasn’t changed is right here?”

Man: “Ah, I see.”

Woman: “I wonder what the veranda is like?”

Man: “Hmm, it hasn’t changed that much. Ah, but it looks like they changed the fence. However, the biggest thing that hasn’t changed at all is the view.”

Woman: “This is the view you always saw, huh?”

Man: “Yeah. Just a plain old view you can see anywhere.”

Woman: “But it’s a view I wanted to see.”

Man: “…”

Woman: "It really is nothing special, huh."

Man: "Are you disappointed?"

Woman: "I don't know. But since being here I just haven't really felt it yet."

Man: "Felt what?"

Woman: "That this is the place where you died."

Man: "That's just the way it is."

Woman: "I put a few offerings in my bag for you."

Man: "I'm glad. But if you leave them here, they're just going to be in the way."

Woman: "That's true. So why don't we drink them together?"

Man: "How?"

Woman: "I brought various things. There's a small can of juice."

Man: "Wow, that's a lot."

Woman: "Would alcohol have been better?"

Man: "No, I never really drank much."

Woman: "Me either. When I drink I quickly feel sick. To escape from reality, I drank *Black Nikka* whiskey, and it made me so sick I just wanted to die again."

Man: "You really want to die, huh?"

Woman: "There are plenty of people out there who want to die, I'm sure. Probably."

Man: "People who want to die, hey."

Woman: "… Yes, I'll hold this can for you so please try putting your lips to it."

Man: "Okay, this juice, right?"

Woman: "Yes, go ahead."

Man: "If somebody saw this I wonder what they'd think."

Woman: "At least one person would laugh, wouldn't they?"

Man: "They'd be laughing at you."

Woman: "Shut up. Hurry up and drink."

Man: "Uh… Okay, let's see…"

Woman: "I'm also gonna have a drink."

Man: "…"

Woman: "Haha, how strange. Your lips are all puckered up."

Man: "Well I can't do anything other than this. Looking at it from this side you're the strange one."

Woman: "Dinner last night probably looked a little something like this, huh."

Man: "I dare say."

Woman: "… How was the juice?"

Man: "It was probably good."

Woman: "…"

Man: "How was it?"

Woman: "Just what the hell are we doing?"

Man: "You and I are enjoying a delicious juice."

Woman: "'Delicious' makes it kinda sound like you're still alive."

Man: "… It does, doesn't it?"

Woman: "Well, shall we go?"

Man: "Where are we going next?"

Woman: "The roof, of course."

Man: "What are we going to do there?"

Woman: "Don't worry about it, just come with me."

Man: "… Okay."

< Roof >

Man: "So what on earth are we going to do here?"

Woman: "You don't know?"

Man: "Too many things come to mind."

Woman: "Is that so?"

Man: "Hey, hey…!"

Woman: "Don't scream out so loud when all I've done is climb onto the fence. You're the one who said it, right? You have no right to stop me."

Man: "I did, but…"

Woman: "It's not good to lie."

Man: "It's better than killing yourself, I think."

Woman: "… You seem to have misunderstood me. I'll say it again. It's no good to lie."

Man: "I'm not lying. Everything I've told you is real."

Woman: "No, you're lying."

Man: "About what?"

Woman: "You really don't know? Or are you just slow?"

Man: "Hey, you don't have to be so…"

Woman: "My underwear."

Man: "… I'm sorry?"

Woman: "I said, my underwear. When the janitor came yesterday, you should have realised. Underneath the fence, there's a protrusion where a person can hide. You should have realised then. Looking up from the bottom of the building the protrusion is in the way so there's no way you could have seen up my skirt."

Man: "…"

Woman: "So? Am I wrong?"

Man: "No, well, it's just like you say it is."

Woman: "If you just throw any colour out there you have a good chance of guessing correctly, right? And even if you're wrong, it's not a problem."

Man: "… Uh, we came here just to confirm that?"

Woman: "It's very important, don't you think?"

Man: "Well, I wouldn't say it isn't important."

Woman: "For me, it's a question of whether or not I could get married."

Man: "Get married?"

Woman: "… Would you like to hear just one of my dreams?"

Man: "One of your dreams? Okay, go ahead."

Woman: "Until I entered university I wanted to die in some dramatic way."

Man: "You're a strange lady."

Woman: "I know. I think so too. Did I want to get close to people who enjoyed the end of the world and die, or did I want to die sacrificing myself to save another? I yearned for something like that. Rather than exposing the sad state of my life, it would be better if I just killed myself. I really did feel that way. Well, until yesterday I did, anyway…"

Man: "You mean putting your life on the line? It's painted such a beautiful way in fictional worlds, isn't it? Perhaps you were influenced by things like that?"

Woman: "Yeah, kinda like… something more important than my own life?"

Man: “I think so.”

Woman: “Yeah. That’s probably what I was after.”

Man: “Before I died I longed for the same thing.”

Woman: “And now?”

Man: “Don’t make me say it. The heroes in fiction encounter circumstances where they put their life on the line just by accident. In the past, I also drew a line between who I really was and who I thought society wanted me to be. But now no matter how disgraceful or wretched a person may be, I have sympathy for those who really want to live.”

Woman: “Like the bad guys in manga who would sell their own friend to save themselves?”

Man: “Yeah, something like that. I wonder why? Why are people like that drawn in such a bad light?”

Woman: “Because they’re wretched and sad?”

Man: “People who throw their lives away are the ones that people like, right? Sorry, I’m just grumbling now.”

Woman: “I’ve seen a glimpse of your real personality now.”

Man: “How embarrassing.”

Woman: “… But I do understand how you feel now. Just a little.”

Man: “I’m glad.”

Woman: “Before I said I had a dream last night, right?”

Man: “You did.”

Woman: “I had a dream where I became invisible. For some reason, I was a junior high student again. Even as I was running down the hallway, no-one took notice of me. Even as I got on the bus I didn't have to pay any money. It was like no-one was looking at me. At first, I was filled with this sense of superiority, like, you're all jealous, right? But slowly it all just became a big bluff. I just wanted someone to call out my name… this is what I thought in the dream."

Man: "That is undoubtedly an invisible person, yeah."

Woman: "But I didn't think about saying anything lewd."

Man: "It's like I've been doing strange things since I died, isn't it?"

Woman: "It's not?"

Man: "I can't deny it."

Woman: "See."

Man: "You seem somewhat happy."

Woman: "It's your imagination. My life is wretched and sad. So much I want to kill myself."

Man: "… But even so, if you keep on living there's bound to be something good ahead."

Woman: "You say that but what if my life ends without anything happening? I'll just feel even more like why didn't I die sooner?"

Man: "I suppose. 'If you live good things will come' is an irresponsible thing to say. However, I will say that if you jump from here, nothing good will come of it. Nothing."

Woman: "Everyone who kills themselves knows that. You were the same, weren't you?"

Man: "…"

Woman: “That’s right. Even if you don’t commit suicide, we all end up in the same place. Everybody dies someday… right? One day I’m going to die too.”

Man: “Hang on. I know I’m being persistent but if you jump from here…!”

Woman: “You’re too late. Oomph.”

Man: “…”

Woman: “I jumped off the fence.”

Man: “… In this direction, yes.”

Woman: “I didn’t lie. I never once said I’d jump to the ground.”

Man: “… No, you didn’t.”

Woman: “Yes, the end is clear. At any rate, I don’t have to die here, but someday I will die. So it’s probably not so bad to go on with my wretched and sad life. You said it yourself, right? ‘Once you decide to die, doesn’t that create some leeway in your heart?’”

Man: “I said that?”

Woman: “You did, very clearly. Everyone dies in the end so I decided to go on living a little longer. For just a little longer I’ll live and make a few more wretched memories.”

Man: “… You might regret that.”

Woman: “If so, I’ll just die now.”

Man: “You’ll probably regret that too.”

Woman: “Then I’ll choose to go on living and regret that.”

Man: “You’re a strange person.”

Woman: “You’re the last person I want to hear that from. Because of you, I’ve decided to keep on living.”

Man: “You say such cruel things.”

Woman: “It’s true.”

Man: “I’m okay with it but when you talk to other people you should think about what you’re going to say a little more.”

Woman: “I’d say the exact same thing to you.”

Man: “Ahaha. I can’t really talk, can I?”

Woman: “I don’t want to admit it but we’re kinda similar, aren’t we?”

Man: “… What’s with the hand?”

Woman: “A handshake. I don’t like you.”

Man: “Huh? Didn’t you say you only hated people who were alive?”

Woman: “You’re an exception.”

Man: “I see. For the first time in my life since I died, I’ve been rejected. How sad.”

Woman: “Yes yes, I know.”

Man: “… How am I supposed to shake your hand?”

Woman: “Stop worrying about the tiny details. Just grab my hand.”

Man: “… Okay.”

Woman: “Fufu… it really is strange.”

Man: “Ahaha. Your hand’s a little see-through.”

Woman: “Don’t misunderstand me, okay. I don’t like you.”

Man: “You’re so stubborn.”

Woman: “I’ll never lose to you.”

Man: “I wonder.”

Woman: “… Thanks to you, who I don’t even like, I’ve decided to live a little longer.”

Man: “That sounds like something you’d say.”

Woman: “But thank you. I’m very happy I was able to meet you.”

Man: “… No way, don’t do it.”

Woman: “?”

Man: “You’re making me want to live again.”

Woman: “Well then one day I’ll come to you so happy that you’ll want to die again.”

Man: “I wonder when that will be?”

Woman: “I don’t know. I’ll just say while I’m alive.”

Man: “I’m looking forward to it.”

POSTSCRIPT

This story ends here. What follows may be a little redundant. But I’ll just say one thing.

I’m still alive, even now.

Cherry blossom tree

* * *

When I was in the sixth grade of elementary school, I used to travel by train to cram school in order to prepare for my junior high entrance exams. I would return home with one of the cram school kids who lived in my neighbourhood, so even if it was dark I wasn't scared. Cutting through the park on the way home was quicker, so we always passed through it.

One day we were passing through the park at around 9 p.m., like always, when we saw a woman in blue standing underneath the cherry blossom tree in the corner of the lot. I didn't take much notice of her, but then my friend said something strange.

Friend: "Isn't that person awfully tall?"

The woman was standing there, looking down, and from far away her head appeared to be quite high off the ground. I was intrigued, so I went towards her and then I realised something. The woman was floating in the air. She was hanging from a large branch by a rope. I was so scared I couldn't even cry out. My friend and I ran to the police box near the park.

The officer was kind and calmed down the two crying children that had come running into his station. After we finally calmed down and explained the situation to him, he took us home rather than back to the park.

I heard from my parents the next day that when the officer dropped us off, he asked our parents to bring us back the following day. So, that day I went back with my parents, and my friend and his parents were also there. We all went to the park together.

The large branch of the cherry blossom tree was cut off at the trunk. Exactly one year earlier a woman in blue had hung herself from the tree and committed suicide. The part of the branch the rope hung from started to rot, and so no-one else would be able to hang themselves from the tree again, the branch was cut off at the base.

Rumours of a ghost began while the branch still existed, and even after it was cut down people would still enter the police box to report “a woman in blue hanging from the tree.” The police officer apparently told our parents this. We were only children, so in order not to shock us too much he told our parents to try to hide that part from us.

When I grew up, I experienced my first bout of sleep paralysis, and following that I started to experience strange things every now and then. I asked my parents if there was anyone who could purify me when they were like, “Well, actually…” and told me this story.

I thought it was my imagination, but I remembered finding someone hanging. To this day I can’t forget that scene, but I’ve otherwise lead a life without the ability to see ghosts.

By the way, I’ve had myself purified since then and I also received a protection charm so nothing like that has happened ever again.

When I fell asleep with the curtain open

* * *

It was a summer night when I was in the second grade of high school.

That day I had a club game and was really tired, so I hurried to finish dinner, shower and get to bed.

I went to my room, and as soon as I hit the bed I was overwhelmed by drowsiness, so with the curtains still open, I fell asleep.

Not closing the curtains before I fell asleep was a big mistake.

Despite the fact I was tired, I woke up in the middle of the night for some reason.

The room was quiet, not a single sound.

My attention was drawn to the open curtain, and I tried to get up to close it.

… But then I noticed something strange.

I couldn't move.

"Crap! Sleep paralysis?!" I thought and struggled with all my might.

But my body wouldn't move at all.

On the contrary, my body felt even heavier, and I could feel someone looking at me from somewhere.

At that time my eyes were still facing the window.

I could feel a gaze coming from that direction.

"This is not good…" I thought. I tried to look away, but for some reason, my eyes kept returning to the window.

Then I saw something floating outside.

It was a person's head. There was nothing below the neck.

My room is on the second floor, so it was impossible for someone to be looking in through the window.

I struggled even harder to look in a different direction.

But it was no use.

Then the severed head looked at me.

His forehead was split, his hair a mess, it was like the blood covered head of a warrior fleeing the battlefield…

At that point I lost consciousness, and when I opened my eyes again, it was morning.

Since then I always make sure to keep the curtains closed when I go to sleep.

I saw a girl standing in the distance

* * *

I sleep with my feet facing the north, and around midnight I suddenly woke up. I don't know exactly what it was, but something in the northeast of my room, the area where the wall meets the roof, attracted my attention. As I stared at it, it felt like I could see a woman standing in the distance even though I was inside.

She had her back to me. She had long black hair down to her backside and was wearing a red dress. I was alert and conscious, but I'd also just woken up, so I just kept staring at it. Then the girl turned around and looked at me. She smiled so wide it was like her mouth was being torn apart. As soon as she did, I lost feeling all throughout my body. Everything around me felt wrong. I was so scared my entire body broke out in a sweat and I forced my eyes closed. Next thing I knew it was morning.

I went and told my older brother about what happened and he told me the exact same thing happened to him the day before. We both sleep with our feet facing the north and in the middle of the night, our eyes opened. When we stared at the corner in the northeast of the room, a girl was standing there (she apparently looked the same except she was wearing a black dress for my brother). Then when she slowly turned around, 'rip!' In an instant, her grin seemed to rip her mouth wide open and then we both succumbed to sleep paralysis.

We were terrified that we had the same experience without the other knowing about it, but since then nothing else has happened.

How I came to see ghosts

* * *

I'm gonna write about my story now. I'm not very good at writing, so if it's hard to understand, sorry. I've already moved out of home and live alone now, but this story is from when I still lived there.

The first time I felt some sort of presence was when I was around five years old. When you're a kid you tend to sleep with your parents, right? On this particular day, the three of us were asleep on the second floor.

I can't exactly see ghosts, but when conditions are right, I can kinda see things just a little. But it's more like every now and then I just suddenly see something, and then it's gone.

Continuing on.

So, then I heard footsteps coming from the first floor. Sometimes they're the footsteps of an adult, sometimes a child. When it's an adult they're slow, like, *gishi... gishi...* When it's a child, it's like they're running around, *petapetapeta.* But it's not like I'm the only person who hears these footsteps. Seems my parents can also hear them quite clearly.

Me: "Hey, aren't those footsteps downstairs?"

Mum: "Ah, you can hear them too? That's your great grandfather."

Me: "Huh? … But sometimes they're children's footsteps."

Mum: "Oh, those are from your father's big sister."

Me: "Eh… really…?"

I asked more about it the next day.

Our house was built close to 100 years ago. It went from my great grandfather to my grandfather to my father. So, apparently, the adult footsteps belonged to my great-grandfather. My great-grandmother, grandfather, and grandmother are all still alive.

As for the child's footsteps, my father had three other brothers and sisters, but his oldest sister had a weak heart and died not long after she was born. So those footsteps are hers, they said.

Having heard all that, I wasn't scared at all, and life went on as usual. But as I became more aware of the footsteps, I also started to experience sleep paralysis more and more.

The next part of the story jumps to when I was a junior high school student. Until I entered junior high, every now and then I heard things, but it was more like I was just imagining things. Nothing terribly big happened so I'll just leave all that out.

By the way, by the time I entered junior high, my younger brother and sister were born. Seemed like they could hear the footsteps clearly too.

At the time I shared a room with my brother. On this particular day, I went to bed first while my brother was playing games in the living room. So, I fell asleep first. I still remember the dream I had clearly to this day. I probably won't ever forget it. Below is what happened.

It was in a back street I knew well in my hometown. But there were no colours, the world was monochrome. Suddenly I realised I was holding someone's hand. I looked, and it was one of my childhood friends. We were walking and talking about silly things. I think we'd been walking for a while when suddenly my friend was like, "What's that?" and pointed behind us. I was like, huh? And turned to look.

It's difficult to describe what was there, but if I were to describe it roughly in a single word, it was like a 'shadow.' But the shadow was standing independently, it had no owner. It was a 'shadow' standing perpendicular to the ground. Maybe saying a black figure was standing there would be easier to understand.

So, as I looked closer, I could see it was kind of wriggling. It was kinda like the noise you see on a TV. My friend kept looking at it when suddenly it starting coming right for us. It moved by teleporting. It wasn't like it just closed the distance in an instant. It would disappear and then reappear slightly closer.

I was overcome with this strange fear. 'I've gotta get away. If I'm caught I'm done for,' I thought.

"Run!" I screamed. I took my friend's hand, and we ran. But the shadow kept getting closer. As it got closer, I realised it was muttering something. This too sounded like TV noise, I don't know if they were actual words or just sounds. Even that I couldn't really make out.

The shadow got closer and closer.

It was right behind us.

Then right as I was thinking, 'Ah, we're done for,' I opened my eyes.

When I opened them, I had sleep paralysis. To be honest, although I've had sleep paralysis before this one caused me the most panic. I'd just had that dream, after all, it was too much. Of course, when you have sleep paralysis your body can't move. I could only move my eyes. I was just looking around the room, but nothing was there and eventually, the sleep paralysis passed.

Afterwards, I just lay there, doing nothing, wondering what had just happened. Then, for some reason, something near the door started to bother me.

I was scared, so I turned my back to the door and decided to go to sleep. Just as I was about to fall asleep, I rolled over and accidentally looked at the door. As I rolled over and looked at it, I was once again attacked by sleep paralysis.

But in the end, there was nothing actually in the doorway. Nothing was there, but I could still hear the noise? voice? of that shadow. I didn't know whether I was still dreaming or not. All I knew was that I was scared.

This was my second sleep paralysis in a row, so of course I was scared. On top of that, I could sense the shadow from my dream. I decided I wasn't gonna sleep again that night and tried to stay awake until morning. I turned on the lights, put on some music and tried to gather my thoughts.

I've heard that sleep paralysis is when your brain is awake but your body is asleep. 'Am I tired?' I thought to myself. Even if a junior high kid says they're tired, it's not really a thing of terrible importance, right? While I was thinking about it, suddenly my eyelids became really heavy.

'Oh no, I'm gonna fall asleep,' I thought and tried to open my eyes wide, but then I realised something strange. My eyelids wouldn't lift up. You're probably thinking, "What is he saying?" Even though I was trying to open my eyes, they wouldn't listen and just kept closing.

No, I think everyone's probably had an experience like that, where you reach the limits of your drowsiness. But this was entirely different to that. It was like someone was pushing my eyelids down purposely. Like someone had their fingertips on my eyelids and was forcing them down.

No matter what I did, I couldn't fight it. They continued to close. I started to panic. Then, the moment they closed, I again fell into sleep paralysis.

Without a moment's delay, I opened my eyes. But my body wouldn't move. I could only move my eyes. Unconsciously I was looking for that shadow.

There it was.

He was in my room. He was between my bed and the door. That thing from my dream was here.

[This was my second sleep paralysis in a row]

Sorry, in the text I'd only had sleep paralysis once.

I'm writing as I remember so it ended up like this.

Well, by this point the fact I'd given up on sleeping wasn't wrong.

Continuing on.

I could definitely sense it just out the corner of my eye. But it didn't try to come any closer. Then I realised that this sleep paralysis wasn't because I was exhausted.

After a bit, the sleep paralysis passcd. The shadow disappeared at the same time.

I don't know if it was because I was so terrified or not, but at the time I just stopped thinking. You'd think that normally I'd go into the living room and tell my brother about what happened, but at the time I didn't think of it. It's like those guys in horror movies that lose their cool and end up dying first.

Anyway, I couldn't think about anything other than how to avoid sleep paralysis again. The answer I came up with, and it wasn't a concrete plan, but I decided not to look at the door again. Basically, I'm an idiot. So, in agreement with myself, I turned my back to the door and lay there with my eyes open.

In my head, I was just thinking, what was that thing? What would have happened if it caught me in my dream? What about my friend?

Sleep paralysis.

Sorry. I'm not very good at writing so I'll try to make things neater. In trying to keep things short I wrote things a little differently to how they actually happened. I'll sum it up quickly. I noticed some things I need to fix.

The shadow: I first saw it in my dream. I only felt it in reality when I had sleep paralysis.

I wrote that when I broke free of sleep paralysis, I felt something strange near the door. That's wrong. The sleep paralysis continued, and it happened another six times before morning came.

Writing that it happened six times would just drag the story out so I shortened it and changed it a little from what actually happened. I write without bothering to collect my thoughts first so this is what happens. Sorry.

What really happened was the first time I had sleep paralysis I felt something. In the text, it was before the second sleep paralysis. The second sleep paralysis was, in reality, the third time it happened. And during my second sleep paralysis I just strongly felt something from the door.

Okay, continuing on.

'This time I'm not gonna have sleep paralysis again,' I thought to myself and turned my back to the door. Not long after I felt something pulling my shoulder. I freaked out and tried to resist it, but it got stronger. I couldn't stop it. It grabbed my shoulder and forcibly turned me over.

Then sleep paralysis again. This time I forced my eyes shut. I couldn't fight the paralysis. Only my eyes would work freely. 'I didn't wanna look for that shadow again. I don't need to see anything strange,' I thought.

I kept my eyes closed. But it didn't feel like the sleep paralysis was gonna break anytime soon. My body just felt like the sleep paralysis was tightening even further. 'That's strange, before if I waited it just went away naturally.'

So I went to open my eyes just a little. That's when it happened. Against my own will, my eyes flew wide open.

That thing was right beside me. It was right beside my face, looking at me. Even though its face was just black like its body, I could somehow feel that it was peering at me, like I was looking into its eyes.

Then I lost consciousness, and it was morning.

After that, I was better able to feel what I guess is ghosts? I wrote in the thread title that I was able to see ghosts, but really I was able to strongly feel them, and only sometimes I can see them. Various things happened after that. If you wanna know more, I'll write them down.

Sorry it was so difficult to understand. Anyway, if you have any questions, go ahead.

42: In general, a ghost is the spirit of a dead person that's appeared, but isn't what you saw more like a yokai? Why did you think it was a ghost? Do you have any proof?

43: >>42 No, I don't. Maybe it was a type of yokai. Having said that, I don't see any real distinction between ghosts and yokai. I didn't believe in either until this point, so I never thought about it.

44: What happened to your friend?

45: >>44 I was a bit embarrassed to ask, but nothing happened to my friend. Well, of course nothing did.

46: Ah, you're back from the toilet, hey? Welcome back.

47: >>46 I wasn't in the toilet, haha. I was working. There were no customers, so I went out for a bit to see if I could get anyone to come in. Then things got busy, and I wasn't able to return, haha.

48: >>47 Is that so? I thought you were gone for a while but you were just working. Can I ask something?

49: >>48

Go ahead~

50: So, some of my friends say they often see ghosts. I can't see anything though. Is it true that girls can often see ghosts?

52: >>50 I can't answer definitely, but there are a lot of girls around me who say they can see ghosts, I think.

I can see sometimes, but they say there are a lot of conditions you have to meet before you're able to see things. After all this happened, I went to see a monk at the local temple and that's what he told me.

54: >>52 Thanks for answering. So a lot of girls can see, huh? I wonder how it starts? I can't see anything at all so you're ahead of me. I'm jealous.

55: >>54 No, it's nothing special, really. There's no merit in being able to see things.

As for how it starts, it's a long story and would become a sequel, but I can write about it if you want.

56: >>55 Tell me. That way I can become friends with girls who see ghosts!!

57: >>56 So you don't want to see ghosts, you just want to become friends with girls who do huh, haha.

Okay, well I'll continue then.

So, after this happened I went to see the monk at a nearby temple. First of all, I live way out in the countryside. Like when I'm going home from school and the old ladies see me they're like, "Hey, welcome back!"

Everyone in our neighbourhood is friendly I guess.

The day I went to see the monk I was also coming home from school on my bike. The monk was just out for a walk. And as always he was like, "Hey, welcome back!" (laughs)

Me: "Hey old man, I'm back!" (laughs)

We just randomly met by chance.

I told the monk about what happened. I also told him about the strange things I could feel since that day. I also told him about the footsteps I could hear since I was a child.

"There's always been something in our house. I've heard footsteps ever since I was a kid, and apparently they're from my great grandfather and my dad's sister. I never thought they were scary. Maybe it's just my great-grandfather or aunt playing tricks?"

I said something along those lines to him, I think.

59: >>57 Shut up!! These days girls who see ghosts are spoilt!! I wanna be spoilt by guys too!!

60: Then the monk was like, "That shadow isn't your great-grandfather or your aunt. That's for certain." If it was, they wouldn't do anything to try to hurt me. When I heard this, I got goosebumps.

So, what was that shadow then? Was it really something scary?

He said he didn't know exactly what it was. All he had to go off was my story, so that couldn't be helped.

Then the monk was like, there's one more thing. If both your great-grandfather and aunt didn't enter heaven and are hanging around your living family, they're nothing but negative energy. The longer they hang around, the more negative energy they'll gather, and the easier it will be for them to become evil spirits.

But if we go and properly attend to their graves and altar at home, they should be able to ascend to heaven, he said. If we do all this properly, it's just a matter of time.

Finally, I asked him why I was sensitive to ghosts now. He replied, "It's because you've had experiences before."

When you come into contact with something not of this world, you become more visible to other ghosts as well. I think the same thing. I was like some kind of death note. So, that's why I don't go to ghost spots and such. If I don't bother them, they won't bother me. But this time it wasn't from me trying to bother them, they were the ones hassling me.

However, according to the monk, it was to do with the house. It had something to do with what I'd felt since I was a small child.

After all that, I still don't know what the shadow was. Well, outside of the times I see things nothing really happens, so whatever.

51: You might be possessed though. It's a bit scary that you're suddenly sensitive to ghosts. Sure it's a story from a while back. But you still feel things now, right?

53: >>51 Really? I only see things, though. I've never had anything unfortunate happen. It's a bit late to be purified now anyway, haha.

65: Really? Is that so… What's it like to see things, anyway?

66: >>65 Every single time it's scary, haha. I do my best not to look so they won't bother me.

67: You get scared, huh?! Well, there's no way you can protect me then!!

70: Actually, there was a time where my parents saw the same thing. Some black hazy figure. According to them even though it was just a shadow, they could understand whether it was a boy or a girl. And even without eyes or a nose or mouth, they could feel its line of sight.

Also on highways and such, it appears out of nowhere. For a moment they think it's a person and try to avoid it, but then they become calm and are like, no, it's a highway… These things happen quite a bit, apparently.

I have a friend who's a monk in training. He says the shadow is a type of evil ghost. That black hazy thing is in no way any good. Afterwards, my parents did several purifications and haven't seen anything since, however…

>>1, you should be careful as well.

Kitsune possession

* * *

I have a friend who was born in a temple and will succeed it once his father passes away. It's not like he can see ghosts or anything, but he sometimes comes into contact with strange happenings.

Some time ago, one of his friends lost the use of his hand. He went to the doctor but they couldn't find any reason why. My friend found that to be strange, so he told him to say a Buddhist prayer, but for some reason, his friend was unable to.

"Maybe you're being haunted by a ghost? Come to my temple," he told him and forced him to come along.

When he got there his face contorted like a *hannya* mask and he began screaming out, "No!! No!!"

My friend called out to him from the temple in encouragement, and they forcibly dragged him up there by rope. Kicking and screaming, he was surrounded by about 10 monks as they recited a prayer for him.

After that he recovered, like nothing had ever been wrong. He could use his hand freely again. It's still pretty common to become possessed by a kitsune in this area. It's quite a big problem.

Our terrifying experience in the abandoned house

* * *

This happened during the summer of last year.

My close friend's grandmother died, leaving her house in the countryside empty, so he invited three of us (A, the friend who invited us, myself and B) to stay at her place for two nights as a kind of holiday house.

This house was separated from the main manor. When A's family went to stay for Buddhist services and such they would always stay in the main manor while the other house was only ever used for guests.

So, because the main manor was still kept in the same state as when A's grandmother was alive, it was decided we'd stay in the detached house instead.

It had a small kitchen, bathroom, and toilet. In addition, there were two Japanese-style rooms. It was more than enough for three guys and it wouldn't cost anything, so we had absolutely no complaints.

It was about an hour drive from Tokyo along the coastline, right in front of the beach. We immediately ran for the water like idiots (haha).

That night we started drinking and had a BBQ, and while chatting about trivial matters we fell asleep.

During the night I woke up needing to pee.

I shone my miniature torch on A and B, who were snoring, and made my way to the toilet.

The toilet was at the other end of the hall from the Japanese-style room.

When I looked there was light shining out from the frosted glass door of the toilet.

I figured someone had gotten up to use it and forgotten to turn the light off, so I turned on the hallway light and went towards it.

Without any suspicions at all, I turned the doorknob.

Hmm? It was locked and wouldn't open. I rattled the doorknob several times, but it refused to open.

I was half asleep, so I knocked and asked, "Is anyone in there?" But there was no response.

I just wanted to pee and get back to bed already, so I knocked again, complaining that whoever was in there needed to get out.

Then something moved behind the frosted glass.

Finally, I thought, but then suddenly my mind cleared and I realised both my friends were asleep in the other room. No-one was in the toilet.

'If I stay here, I'm gonna see something I shouldn't,' I thought.

I hurried back to the room and, without turning the lights on, I shook the other two awake.

I quickly told them everything, but maybe because they were still half asleep they were just like, "A scary story, huh? Whatever…" and "You woke me up for that?"

What was this? Even though I was trembling with fear, they were acting like it was nothing. But the fact that I was no longer the only one awake was still somewhat of a relief.

Just as A was getting up to turn on the lights, complaining the whole time, there was a sudden BANG from the hallway. The three of us froze.

We went silent. From the hallway, we could hear the sound of a doorknob being turned.

The sliding door to the room had been left open, and in the light coming in from the hallway, you could clearly see how terrified the three of us were.

Then B said, “I’ll go and have a look. It’s probably just some hobo,” and holding his pillow went to exit the room. There was nothing else we could do, so also holding our pillows, A and I followed him to the hallway.

We could still hear the rattling doorknob. In the distance, we could also hear the roar of the waves.

At the end of the hallway, light was definitely shining behind the toilet door.

The knob… was moving.

Suddenly, with incredible speed, B ran screaming towards the toilet. It scared the crap outta me.

While the knob was still rattling he screamed, “Cut that shit out!” and “Get out here now!”

I was dumbfounded, but then suddenly the toilet light turned off.

Surprised, B stopped moving.

A had turned off the toilet light.

We continued standing there like that. B’s hand was still on the toilet doorknob. “Hmm?” he said and opened the door. “Hey, it’s open.”

Light from the hallway shone in. There was no-one in there. There was nothing in there but the toilet. The window was slightly ajar, but there were bars on it so no person would be able to pass through.

Waves crashed and bugs chirped.

After a period of silence, A was like, “We’re just half asleep. Plus, we were drinking.” B and I agreed and laughed it off.

A returned to the room and B handed me his pillow, saying he was going to pee first and went into the toilet.

I needed to go as well, so I waited in the hallway, but then suddenly all the lights turned off. B in the toilet and A in the bedroom both screamed in terror. Of course, I did the same.

“… die for me …”

A low, fragile voice, neither male nor female reverberated throughout the entire dark house.

We panicked. I think B was the most scared.

We quickly turned the lights back on, but it was no good. The three of us were crying.

We wanted to leave immediately, but we’d been drinking so we couldn’t drive. Despite that, we didn’t want to be in that room either.

The main manor was no good either. With nowhere else to go we waited on the beach until morning, and when the sun came up, we returned to the room.

Whether it was because we’d calmed down or the lack of sleep or what but we were unusually calm. We searched the toilet from top to bottom.

But there was nothing strange there. When we asked A about it he said he'd never heard anything strange about it either.

In the end, we had no idea what happened, but we never wanted to go back there again.

Public toilet

* * *

I was going home at around 2 a.m. when my stomach started to hurt, so I dropped by the toilet at a nearby park.

There was a story that a homeless person had committed suicide at this park, so in general, I would never go there late at night, but on this particular day, there was no way around so it so I went in.

It was dim and eerie, the walls dirty and covered in graffiti. The toilets gave me a chill and, even though I was scared, I somehow managed to finish my business.

Afterwards, I realised there was no toilet paper. There was nothing else I could do, so I decided to go and get some from the female toilets. I pulled my pants up and went outside.

The female toilets are built so you can't see in from the outside. From the entrance, you can't see anything. If there was someone in there, I'd look like a pervert, so I yelled from the doorway, "Excuse me~ Excuse me~"

There was no answer, so I nervously peeked inside. Something immediately felt off. I don't know if it was someone breathing, but I could sense a presence. It also felt like someone was staring right at me. Looking around, I could see two stalls in the back. The right was open, but the left was closed. But it wasn't locked. There was no mark saying it was in use.

‘Hmm?’ I thought, tilting my head. There’s definitely someone in there. They must be pushing against the door to make sure it doesn’t open.

But it was strange that they wouldn’t answer. It was even creepier that they were sitting there without making a single sound so I hesitated to go in.

I thought about it for a bit. Perhaps there was a lady doing her business inside and she was too embarrassed to reply.

She doesn’t want anyone to hear anything, so she’s just sitting there frozen, I thought. So I went to sit on a bench outside the toilet and decided to wait.

Five minutes passed and still no one came out. I’d done my business without wiping, so as time passed it was kind of gross. Determined, I called out into the female toilets again.

“Excuse me~ Can I borrow some toilet paper?”

There was no answer. Nervously I looked inside again and, to my surprise, this time the right door was open and the left door was closed. The person inside must have moved. In the open stall I could see about eight toilet rolls stacked up inside. As I saw that the blood drained from my body. Ah, they want me to go in there. They’re trying to tempt me in. It was likely all the toilet paper had been taken from the male toilets and they were waiting for someone to come get it.

The realisation terrified me and I just stood there blankly. Then, from inside the closed stall, I heard a deep voice like that of an old man.

“I’ve got some toilet paper.”

Giiiii

The door slowly began to open, and the moment I saw inside I took off running.

To this day I still can't erase from my mind the horrible, rolled back eyes I saw from that gap.

OBON

My competitive dead mother

* * *

This story happened when I went home for Obon.

I put down my parents' favourite things while alive on their altar and went to bed. That night they appeared by my pillow.

It had become a custom at Obon so I wasn't scared, I'd just always say, "Ah, welcome back~" They'd smile and then disappear. It was always this way.

But this year my father had a strange expression on his face. My mother kept prodding him with her elbow, like she wanted him to say something.

I looked at them for a bit but it didn't seem like they were going anywhere, and as my mother kept hitting him I took pity and asked, "Is there something you want to say?"

He opened his mouth…

"Gonna cry."

"Agitated."

"Embarrassed."

"Your mother keeps poking me."

He went on like this for 10 minutes.

It started to piss me off. "Dad, if you can't say it then Mum should!" After she elbowed his side really hard, she whispered hesitantly, "We're tired of the sweets you left at the altar and would like different ones."

When I asked what they wanted her eyes lit up like a child. "I want whatever's popular now!"

"I'm okay with what we have now..." my father muttered, but he fell silent again after my mother elbowed him once more.

When I pressed her for a more concrete answer, my mother replied, "I'll leave it up to you. But I don't want to lose to OO-chan." I couldn't understand what she said.

I asked her what she meant and apparently, amongst the spirits of the dead, they took great pride in the offerings they received. It seemed my competitive mother had taken a blow to her ego.

"This year I wanna win!" she half-cried, so I gave her the caramels I got as a souvenir from my friend.

Although, to be honest, I think caramels had already past their prime.

But now every year when we meet each conversation starts with, "This year, how would you like...?"

Even in death, my parents are rather carefree.

Why my family has two altars

* * *

There are two altars in my relative's house. The one on the left is for my grandfather and the one on the right is for his nephew who died at a young age. The strange thing is though that when we visit for Obon, the door to the altar on the right is always closed.

I wanted to know why they had two altars when they're so big and bulky, so I asked my relative and she told me.

My grandfather was an active firefighter. He loved helping people and would go out of his way to do so. In a way, you could say he was the good kind of busybody. He had a niece and nephew that he dearly loved and he often took them to a nearby river to play.

Perhaps it was because a lot of rain fell upstream, but suddenly the waters rose and his niece nearly drowned. He jumped in to save her and was able to safely reach the other side of the bank.

While his niece and her family were happy his nephew pestered him, "What about me?" With a smile, he said, "If I happen to be there at the right time I'll save you too," and patted him on the head.

A few years later, his nephew got trapped in some deep water in the river. My grandfather, who was there with him, told his niece to get help and jumped into the water. He rushed to save him but he was getting on in years. Even though he managed to reach his nephew, he couldn't keep holding him up and drowned. His nephew was saved by some other people.

While the family was happy he was saved, they mourned my grandfather's death. His nephew, however, showed no signs of being particularly sad. As he got older, he even started to dislike welcoming him for Obon. His parents scolded him but he retorted sharply, "It's his own fault for being too weak and dying."

After that, they continued without him, but shortly thereafter the nephew also died. He was late returning from school one day, so they went out to find him. He was on the riverbank alone, facing the water, smiling cheerfully. Even slapping him across the face did nothing, he just kept on smiling and laughing.

After he was hospitalised, he did a complete 180-degree turn and lost all emotion. He stopped eating and within half a year he passed away.

After that, his mortuary tablet was placed next to my grandfather's, but come the morning they would find it lying on the tatami mats. They also frequently heard the sounds of banging coming from the altar room. They went to see a monk about it and he suggested they separate the altars.

"But it's Obon, the least you can do is open his altar doors," I said, but when I did my relative just faintly smiled and said, "I don't want to light any incense sticks for my brother at the same time."

Obon will be here again soon. More than their half-hearted attempts at maintaining the family altars after death, I'm more scared of the family themselves.

Cursed second hideout

* * *

This story happened at my father's house in the countryside when I was a kid.

If you want to put it politely, you could say my father's childhood home is surrounded by the beauty of nature. Another way to put it is that it's in the middle of absolutely nowhere.

There are snakes and—although I've never seen them—bears as well, and when I go there for the summer holidays it really teaches me the many meanings of the word 'nature.'

This particular story happened when I was in the third grade of elementary school.

Our family went to stay with my grandparents for a week during Obon. I'd play with my two older cousins (the older brother, A, and the younger brother, B) from morning till night. As it got closer to us leaving, I'd get darker and darker from all the sun tanning I did.

Although you would think I would have played more than enough by then, it wasn't enough, so the day before we were to go back home I asked A and B, "Do you wanna go someplace even more fun?"

At A's suggestion, we decided to go to the 'Second Hideout.'

This 'Second Hideout' was a place just as you enter the mountains, what seemed to be the remains of a building built by a religious group. The land was surrounded by wire fencing, but the entrance only had a loose chain, so it was easy for children to get inside.

With nobody there anymore it had gone to ruin. The wire fencing was falling apart, and the ground was covered in weeds. There was a parking lot and asphalt road leading out, but there were so many fallen leaves you could barely see the ground.

It was a one-story concrete building. White paint was peeling off the walls and all the doors and windows were closed with storm shutters. Each one was padlocked.

A and his brother got in via the back where a fallen tree had broken through a sliding door.

I followed them in and the first thing I saw was like a small assembly room. There was a curved skylight so the entire room was bright. There was a long flat altar and an object of worship shaped like a penis. Being stupid kids, we laughed at it. We swung it around, threw it at each other, tossed it around like a rock, all sorts of stupid things…

We searched the building and played for a while but the sun was setting and it was getting dark so we decided to go back. Just like how we entered A went out first but as he did he suddenly screamed, "Look down! Whatever you do, don't look up!"

"Huh?" I thought. But I continued to look at his feet as we tried to leave the grounds and along the way we passed by someone.

If I were to describe him in a single word, it would be "blue." I only saw his feet, but they were those of an old person, an unnatural shade of blue. I think it was like those old 500 yen notes, or more recently like the same shade as Natsume Souseki on

1000 yen notes, they stood out as something like that.

I got scared thinking that someone like that was standing so close to us so I did my best to stick to A and B as we walked. A kept repeating, “OO-san please help us,” over and over like a chant. B and I were half-crying, clinging to the elder A, just wishing we could get out of there.

We hurried along and finally reached the exit facing the asphalt road. I wanted to run, thinking we were finally free, but as I started to lift my head once again A screamed, “There’s two of them! Keep your head down!”

I was surprised that A noticed I’d looked up without even turning around, but I’d never heard him speak like that before so I quickly looked back towards the ground.

After walking a little while longer I could hear the sound of the wire fencing swaying, and what appeared to be A making his way through the gap. A’s feet were shaking like crazy. After A exited, he held his hand out to us still inside the grounds but it was shaking. We soon realised why.

There really was another one there.

I only glimpsed the feet, but unlike the old guy earlier, this was a young woman. There was a tear in her ankle running a few centimetres upward, and the flesh behind it was blue as well.

A was still saying whatever prayer it was he was chanting. Every now and then his voice got shrill, and it was probably extremely difficult for him, but having brought us younger kids here it felt like he was doing his best for us.

Both B and I clung to A, and holding hands we could do nothing but follow behind him. When we reached the mountain trail, A was still repeating his prayer, and every now and then he'd say to us, "There should be another of them, keep looking down!"

As we got close to the end of the trail, I felt a sense of security so I looked ahead and there was nobody standing there. I was relieved. But, of course, it wasn't over yet.

The last person was standing about four metres above the trail. She was kinda blurry, floating there, with a hairstyle and kimono you don't see these days. She was blue and half-smiling as she stared at us. I was so scared I clung to A and he soon realised what I'd seen so he helped carry me along.

As the sun disappeared we finally reached our grandparents' house. Our worried grandfather came to greet us, asking whether I'd been injured. A explained what he saw and that he'd properly prayed as we came back. I remember the family going into an uproar. My grandfather and father ran about in a hurry, taking an offering off somewhere, and then my uncle who came later also went off after them. My grandmother, mother and aunt all remained in the house. Bawling, our grandmother wouldn't let go of A.

B and I had no idea what was going on. However, that night A broke out into a fever and he started crying that he might die. Our grandmother came and took him to another room to sleep.

The next morning we all went up to a gravesite slightly up the mountain-side to pray. A also came, his father carrying him on his back as his fever came down. I didn't know whose grave it was, but it was old. Quite a large stone made up the base. Perhaps it was our family's patron god, but seeing as there was no shrine—it was just a regular grave—I had no idea.

I saw A again at my grandfather's funeral after we hadn't seen each other for quite some time and we spoke.

"If I'd been done in by those guys, I would have gone crazy and killed you. I did everything I could not to succumb to it. You're from a branch family so you can't be possessed, but if B had seen them, it would have been a different story," he said.

'Our family is cursed?' I wondered, finding it all just a little bit terrifying.

He saw his dead father during a test of courage

* * *

On this particular day, the children's association was holding a test of courage for the kids at A's temple, and as part of the young person's association, both A and I participated as helpers.

Akemi-san and I were to play the ghost roles. Akemi-san was Yuuta-kun's mother. Her husband had passed away in a car accident. She wore white clothing and drew a line of blood from her mouth. Getting into the role she opened up her kimono a little and said, "This way really sets the mood, don't you think~"

Akemi-san was in her late 20s. The whole look was very risque and both A and I fell for it.

Taking some mosquito coils and a torch we went to our places. A told the kids some scary stories and then finally the test began. I could hear the sounds of children crying and screaming from far away each time Akemi-san jumped out to scare them. Just as I was finished with the last group, Akemi-san came over.

Akemi: "Did Yuuta cry?"

Come to think of it, I realised Yuuta-kun hadn't come, and I turned pale.

Me: "He didn't come…"

Akemi: "What?! But, he passed by me!?"

Confused, we went back but Yuuta-kun wasn't there. We ran and searched the entire course but he wasn't anywhere. Akemi-san was half-crying.

When we got back to the temple, however, A was holding Yuuta-kun. We were relieved. Crying, Akemi-san asked Yuuta-kun what happened.

Yuuta: "When I passed you, daddy was there, so we talked."

According to A, "I heard voices behind the main building so I went and had a look and Yuuta was sleeping there."

Akemi: "Yuuta, what did daddy say?"

Yuuta: "Um, he said to take care of you."

Akemi burst out crying at those words.

A: "Well it is Obon. He probably came to see if Yuuta is being a good boy or not."

Yuuta: "No. Daddy said he was going to get revenge."

We all froze.

A few weeks later, I heard that the company of the assailant that had killed Yuuta's father in the accident had finally been forced to pay back all the damages they had been holding off on. From the bottom of my heart, I wish him happiness in the next world.

The bundle of black hair in the floor chair

* * *

This is a true story that happened to my aunt five years ago during Obon.

My aunt works at a hospital dealing with certain beauty treatments. Obon is the time she makes the most money, so she works without holiday. She got divorced from her husband and now lives with her parents.

Her parents left for a few days to visit graves and such, so she spent her time coming back from work at night and heading back again in the mornings. Her floor is covered in tatami mats and in the corner she has a Buddhist altar. Behind the sliding doors, there's an old, prestigious three-sided mirror that her mother uses. It's a perfect Japanese-style room. In the evenings, it's gloomy and so a little creepy.

One night, my aunt was looking for a hair clip or something. Without any hesitation, she searched above the mirror, in the drawers and such, and then she opened the cover of the legless chair in front of the mirror. Inside was a bundle of long, thin black hair coiled up neatly. Startled, she pulled it out, and it was over a metre long. It was clear it wasn't a wig. It looked like it had been cut clean off with scissors. Of course, neither she nor her parents or anyone had grown their hair that long. Everyone in the family had thick, frizzy hair, so there was no way it could be any of them.

She was creeped out, so she immediately threw it in the rubbish and went to lie down. However, she was unable to sleep and went to work like that the next day. When she returned from work, she turned the TV on while doing her skincare routine. An old Japanese horror movie was just beginning.

'Wow, they're so young,' she thought as she watched. She didn't remember too much of it but those who know it will probably understand. The name of that movie was *Kurokami* (black hair). Did it have something to do with the happening the night before? She wanted to think it was just a coincidence but she couldn't. She was so scared she thought she might go crazy.

She was home all alone. It was also Obon, which just made her even more scared.

When her parents returned, she asked them if they knew anything about the hair but they had no idea. She also tried asking their relatives but no-one knew anything. Of course, neither did I.

First and foremost, my aunt had used that chair for a long time so there was no way it hadn't been opened at least once. But who put the hair in there? And besides that, just whose hair was it?

What turned off the apartment's self-lock?

* * *

I don't believe in ghosts, but I have experienced something strange in my life just once.

It happened four years ago.

I was living in Kobe and working for a security firm. I was working the night shift during Obon when we got a call.

"There's something strange with the entrance auto lock at this newly constructed building." My partner and I rushed over.

'Was there a thief?' I wondered, but when we checked it out, there were no signs of foul play. According to the residents, the door opened of its own accord. Thinking it was just a fault in the mechanism that controls the lock, I went to investigate it. However, there was nothing wrong with it. I wondered whether I should call the electric company when suddenly there was a noise behind us. *Batan!*

When we turned around, the door was open even though no-one was there. Both my partner and I were shocked, and then the machine started going *pi pi pi*.

"Hey, take a look!" my partner said. The console for the auto lock showed "302." I got chills. There was nobody there but us…

A few days later, I became curious about who lived in 302. I checked it out, but nobody lived there. However, a little while later my partner told me something. He knew the person who used to live there. He died during an earthquake when the apartment he was living in collapsed.

So, perhaps during Obon he was feeling nostalgic and had come to visit his old apartment, he said.

The heirloom we couldn't bring out

* * *

In my family, there are three treasures that we call heirlooms. I don't know if they have value to anyone but us.

The first is our family tree. Our family tree goes back over 400 years, written over several scrolls and kept in Paulownia boxes.

The second is a katana. A long time ago one of our ancestors received it as a gift from his lord.

The last one is a mirror. It's not so much a mirror as it is an antique polished piece of metal. It's like something you'd see in a Japanese history book and fits in the palm of your hand. This also sits in a very fine Paulownia box.

There is a particular way these three items must be handled. Only the family patriarch of that particular generation may remove the family tree from its box. The sword could be sold for a considerable amount of money but it must never be sold. The family head must also clean and maintain the sword once a month. The mirror must remain enshrined in the family altar and every day it must be checked to see it is safe. It must never be taken off the family lands. Not even the family head may remove it from its box.

The rules are something like that.

This story is about that bronze mirror. If it's really true…

The bronze mirror has a strange shape. A round mirror part sits on a hexagonal pedestal. Even if you look into this mirror, perhaps due to the rust or small scratches on it, it appears to have lost the ability to really reflect anything. However, at two centimetres thick it's rather heavy and feels kind of magical.

When I was in elementary school, my friends and I had a 'rare item you're proud of' competition where we went to the park after school and showed off our treasures. Everyone brought toys, but I took along the family mirror. I told everyone not to touch it, but of course, they didn't listen to me. In the end, it was decided that I had the item most like an actual treasure so I won. I triumphantly marched home.

What was waiting for me at home was exactly what you would expect; a thorough scolding from my father. There was nothing wrong with the mirror, but my father persistently questioned me, harshly telling me off and making me promise never to touch it again. In my eyes, it wasn't like I broke it or anything, so I couldn't understand why I was getting such treatment. However, in the end, I apologised, and that was the end of it. My father forgave me.

After that, I wasn't especially interested in it so I didn't touch it again. Then last year, I turned 20 and my father summoned me. I'd entered university and was living away from home. Wondering why I'd been called I went back. My father asked me to sit in the room with the family altar and began to speak.

To sum up, he told me about the family heirlooms and how to handle them. Our genealogy had roots in *onmyodo*, and the family heirlooms came to us because of our dealing with cursed items. Most items had been donated as gifts to museums and thus few were left.

It was here that my father stopped to take a breather. I was a little fed up that he'd called me for such a boring story, and thinking that he'd finally finished he started again. "Now, let's get to the important part."

Oh, come on, drowsiness was taking over me, but I couldn't do anything but sit and listen to him seriously.

My father took the mirror out of the altar, put it on the table and began talking again. The contents of the conversation were unbelievably separated from reality. I'll sum it up.

So, the reason why this bronze mirror couldn't be taken out. In history, it had been taken out three times, and all three people met disastrous ends. So, why couldn't we take it out of the box?

Because the mirror is a mirror that shows a person's death. Until recently, the taboo about the mirror had been thought to be superstition, but due to events 30 years earlier it was now strongly protected.

30 years earlier… My grandmother died 30 years ago. I'd heard it was an accident, but I was never told the details.

Apparently, if someone tried to remove the mirror from this plot of land, they would meet with disaster. It was passed down that the three people who had tried to remove it had all met horrible fates and died.

The first time it was taken out by a subordinate of Ishida Kazushige during the Sengoku Era. However, after the Battle of Sekigahara and Ishida's death, it was returned.

The second time was during the Second World War. Military police forcibly came to take the mirror away for metal collections and my grandfather watched them get cut down by American machine gun fire.

The third person was my grandmother. This mirror was also a possession of hers. While she was alive, my grandmother treated stories of the mirror's curse as superstition and even took it out to show guests when they came to visit. It was a curious antique mirror that didn't reflect anything.

My grandmother came to Osaka during Obon, and when she was about to leave, she bowed to the family's three heirlooms. When she touched the mirror she accidentally saw her own face reflected in it. She went pale and apparently compared her face over and over with the bronze mirror and the bathroom mirror.

Then she said: "My face in this family heirloom is pitch black!"

My father told her it was all in her imagination. But she had apparently seen something terrifying and couldn't stop panicking. She asked if she could take the mirror to the family temple in Kyoto and have it purified. It would be against the family rules, but if it would make her feel better my father agreed to it.

But, he said, he came to regret it. Why?

Because of that, the bronze mirror was able to manifest its largest ever curse. On 18th December 1985 at 6:04 p.m., an airplane from Hanada to Osaka took off. The mirror was on board…

Translator's note: The flight referenced at the end is Japan Airlines Flight 123, the deadliest single-aircraft accident in history. All 15 crew members and 505 of 509 passengers on-board died.

Detached house

* * *

My grandparents on my father's side of the family have a pretty old house, and with constructions to the house ongoing, there are a few rooms currently not in use. Because it's so old and dangerous my grandmother often tells me not to go near it.

This story takes place when I was in the fourth grade of elementary school during Obon. We're the head house of the family so during Obon and New Year all the family gathers at my grandparent's house. In our family, I'm the oldest child, and including my younger sister, all the other children are either in the lower grades of elementary school or kindergarten. As such, at these times I would be in charge of all the gathered kids.

After the monk would leave we'd put away the sliding doors to reveal a wide open room where all the adults and children would eat together. After that, the adults would begin their party while the children played in another room. It was always this way.

One night at just past 8 p.m. one of my cousins found a flashlight. At first, we turned the lights off in the room and shone the torch on things. I don't know what was fun about it, but we still enjoyed it, regardless.

Before long we started talking about going on an adventure and it was decided that we'd visit the detached house. Normally we were told not to go near it but we were all a little excited and I wanted to show off some good spots to my cousins there so off we went.

I wanted to tell the adults we were going there but of course, I couldn't tell my grandmother. I told my father, who by this stage was drunk out of his mind, and he was like, "Okay, take care~"

I went ahead first holding the flashlight, then behind me was my younger sister and cousins all gathered closely together.

We went down the hall beside the Western-style room and passed through the altar room. We turned on all the lights along the way and then the glass door to the detached house came into view. The other side was completely black. The torch reflected off the glass door.

When I opened the door I was struck by the smell of old tatami mats and wet wood, but it made me think, "Ah, how Japanese~" From the torch and hallway lights we could see a hallway with wooden boards and a tatami room. There was also a wooden door at the far end of the hall. We didn't know what was behind it.

"Why don't we go inside?" I said, but my cousins were scared and didn't want to go. Of course, I was scared too, but being the eldest I was like, "Well, I'm going to go and open it, so you just wait right here." I told my cousin to keep shining the torch ahead and went on alone.

The floor didn't seem like it had been used, it was dusty and creaked as I walked across it. I put my hand on the wall and slowly walked across to the wooden door. 'I'm scared~ No, I'm not scared!' I thought as I stood before the door. I turned around and my cousins were all huddled together watching me.

"See, I'm fine!" I yelled out and pulled on the door, but it wouldn't open.

"Huh? Oh you have to push it open~" I said in a cheerful voice, and as I pushed the door open it let out a sound much louder than I expected. As it opened, I fell forward and nearly tripped over. At the same time, a cat meowed somewhere and my fear levels reached their peak. I let out a soundless scream and tried to crawl back to my cousins on all fours but the heartless monsters ran off. I slowly made my way to my feet, aiming for the light at the end of the hall as I ran. The wooden door behind me let out another loud sound as it closed.

I ran to the room the adults were in with all my might and my cousins were already there crying. For a moment I was relieved but then my father started going off at me, despite the fact he'd given his okay.

"There was a monster!" my cousins were screaming. It was getting late so it was decided that the party would end there for the night.

After our relatives went home, I asked my sister what happened. She said when I opened the wooden door and it let out a big noise everyone was surprised. Then the youngest kid ran off, and like a piece of thread, everyone else followed. Nobody heard the cat.

"But then," my sister said, looking like she was about to cry, "there was a person beyond the door." Suddenly I was terrified all over again. "But the sight of you crawling on all fours towards us was even scarier." Suddenly I was sad again.

I asked my cousins about it a few days later but they were like, "A dog with big red eyes came running towards us," and "Rokurokubi was there and stretched out her neck!" Everyone's story about a monster kept changing and I couldn't get the real truth. However, one of the boys and two of the girls, my younger sister included, said that a person was there so I was beginning to think someone really was.

"It's Obon so one of your ancestors returned," my grandfather said, trying to comfort me, but I was still puzzled by the sound of the cat. Later on, my grandmother secretly told me about it.

When my father was still a high school student, they were doing some end-of-year cleaning in the detached house. When they opened the glass door, they heard the sounds of "meow, meow" coming from somewhere. They thought perhaps a cat was living under the floorboards but it was crying so much they had to check. There were two cats, however, one wasn't moving. It was dead.

Thinking it a little creepy, my grandmother chased the crying cat away and then disposed of the dead one. However, the cat continued to live under the floorboards after that. No matter how much they chased it away it would be there again, crying out. At her wit's end, my grandmother called in a contractor and had him block up the floorboards. I asked her if that was really necessary but she replied, "The first time we chased it away I got scratched several times. Since then I've hated cats."

Perhaps the sound I heard that time was the same cat that was there all those years earlier. But cats don't live for that long, and in any case, there's no way under the floorboards now. So did that mean that night we ran into two ghosts? The one of our ancestor (who I didn't see) and that of the cat?

I haven't gone near the detached house since then, but if I do go there again, I'll take a few photos.

The mysterious countryside ritual

* * *

I heard this story when I returned home to the countryside the other day. It was kinda shocking, so please let me write it all down.

There's a custom in our village that after visiting someone's grave we return to the main family house on foot carrying a lantern.

If that were the only thing it would be quite normal but there are various conditions that go along with it.

1. "You cannot extinguish the lantern. If the flame goes out, you must immediately return to the grave and relight it."

2. "You must not run."

3. "The youngest person there must carry the lantern (however in the case of those like babies who cannot carry the lantern by themselves it will go to the next oldest)."

4. "Under no circumstances must you look at the shrine."

The shrine referenced in the fourth point refers to one found on the way to the main house from the gravesite. The road is mostly nothing but rice fields, however, there is an isolated area that looks like an artificial forest where there is a small stone-built shrine.

So what it's saying is that you can't look in the direction of that shrine.

When I was a child, I experienced carrying the lantern and at the time my parents strictly ordered me to follow these rules.

"This lantern helps your ancestor move from the grave to the altar in our house so it must not go out along the way," I was told.

I was just a child, so I was like, "How strange," but I performed my duty.

Then I remembered my mother covering my eyes as we approached the area with the shrine. I just thought she was playing around so I innocently giggled and joked around.

Things continued this way until we passed the shrine and after my mother took her hand away, we continued walking until we reached the house. The flame was transferred to a candle on the altar and that was the end of the ceremony.

I didn't think much about the custom at the time, but after returning home for the first time in years this year I decided to ask my grandmother about it.

"Oh yeah, we never properly told you about it, did we?"

When I heard the true meaning behind the rules of carrying the lantern, I was honestly shocked.

1. "You cannot extinguish the lantern. If the flame goes out, you must immediately return to the grave and relight it."

Like I heard in the past, the lantern acted as an object to guide our ancestor to the house. If the flame went out, they wouldn't be able to follow along.

2. "You must not run."

Because if you run it's easier for 'it' to find you.

3. "The youngest person there must carry the lantern."

'It' targets the weak, so this position places them where their ancestor can most assuredly protect them. In short, the person holding the lantern is the one closest to their ancestor's protection.

4. "Under no circumstances must you look at the shrine."

If you accidentally directly look at 'it' then your ancestor can no longer provide you with protection.

While my grandmother was explaining things the word 'it' popped up several times. I had no idea what she meant.

"What do you mean by 'it'?" I asked her.

"'It's' it. It's the thing in the shrine."

'It' was something that lived in the shrine located in the forest in the rice fields. Supposedly it looked kind of like a monkey with long legs and had been there for quite some time. Usually, it was peaceful, however, during the Obon season, it would turn into something dangerous.

Apparently, it had a name, but it was forbidden to speak it. "You're better off not knowing," my grandmother said and refused to tell me. They don't tell the children about it because then they'll become curious and may accidentally see it.

Now that I think about it, that time when my mother covered my eyes was likely because of that very reason. I'm thankful to her for that now.

My grandmother went on and told me about a time the custom, or rather the ritual, failed.

There was a time where the lantern went out on the way home and the bearer saw 'it' causing the ritual to fail. When that happens someone in the family will invariably meet with an inexplicable accident or even die by the time of the next Obon.

At this point, I started to find the whole thing rather suspicious, but then my grandmother said, "You know F died last year, yes? He was killed by 'it'."

I got goosebumps all of a sudden. At the end of last year, my cousin F-kun died in a car accident. We used to play together a lot as children so I was heartbroken. According to what my mother told me he was driving straight along a nice stretch of road when suddenly he turned the steering wheel and drove into a river where he died. Even now we don't know why he suddenly turned the wheel. The reason why I returned home after so long was because I wanted to light some incense for F-kun.

"So, last summer failed? The person carrying the lantern?" I asked.

"Last year U-chan (a relative's child) was the bearer. Seems like he saw 'it.' He was terribly frightened."

Afterwards there was a big panic, and they tried to have him purified but apparently, it was no good.

In the past, I took part without really thinking anything at all about it, but coming to know the real meaning behind the ritual I was terrified. This time the ritual had already taken place before I arrived so I just went to visit the grave.

I can't do anything but worry about whether this year's ritual was a success or not. Next year, however, I'd like to take part and carefully watch over it.

Closet on the second floor

* * *

I don't believe in ghosts at all, but this story is about one such single experience I had.

I think I was about 20 years old. My grandmother was starting to go senile. She started saying things like someone came to see her during the day, or strangers were calling her on the phone.

When we took her to the hospital, it turned out to be complications from Alzheimer's. Gradually things got worse, as did the things she said. In particular, she started to say things like, "There's someone upstairs," a lot more frequently.

However, when we would go upstairs to investigate, there was, of course, no evidence anyone had been there. The family and I could do nothing but pretend not to hear it.

Then my grandmother became bedridden. One day she was taken to the hospital by an ambulance and a week later she passed away. She was 84 years old. I'll never forget what happened the next year on August 15th.

I was on holidays for Obon and for some reason was giving the house a big clean. At the time, only my mother and I were home. My mother was outside hanging out the washing.

So, while I was cleaning I heard this *gata gata* sound coming from the room my mother and older sister sleep in. At first, I thought perhaps my mother was doing something upstairs, so I didn't think much of it. But gradually the *gata gata* sound got louder and louder.

Then I heard my mother laughing and chatting with someone from the neighbourhood outside. I was covered in sweat from all the cleaning. "Huh? Who's making that sound upstairs then?" I thought.

I went up to the second floor. I thought maybe my sister was back and also doing some cleaning. I made for the room the sound was coming from. Even though I could hear the *gata gata* as I reached the top of the stairs, as soon as I entered the room it fell silent.

Me: "Sis? Are you doing some cleaning?"

As I said this, the small closet started to move. *Gata gata.* Thinking my sister was inside I went to open it. Even now I can't forget the shock that awaited me.

When I opened the small closet at my feet I heard the *kya kya* laughing voices of small children. I was confused. I got down on my knees, and inside I saw three children around four or five-years-old, packed in there eating something. One of them was a girl with a short bob cut. The other two were boys with shaved heads. The three of them were extremely dirty and smelly. What's more, the three of them were looking right at me with big smiles.

When I realised, I took off running downstairs. I ran outside barefoot to find my mother. When I came running outside barefoot and pale-faced, my mother was surprised. But when I explained everything to her she just went, "Huh~?" and went inside.

For a while, I couldn't move. My heart was racing so furiously I could hear it beating on and on and on. A little while later my mother came back outside. Apparently, there was nothing there. She just said that inside the closet was extremely smelly.

That was the first and last time I saw the things that looked like the ghosts of children, but my dead grandmother often said, "There's something upstairs," so I'm not sure if that was somehow related. Did they appear because it was Obon…?

That house was knocked down, so it's not around anymore. I still can't forget that smell, however. It was like the smell of someone who hadn't taken a bath for a month… I wonder if they were the spirits of children who died in the war?

Even now when I go to open a closet, I have to summon up all my courage.

Working the convenience store night shift alone

* * *

This took place sometime after Obon, I think. I was responsible for the night shift so I was always cleaning the fryers, putting out stock and other such things. Working the night shift at our convenience store is a one-man job, by the way.

Then, when I was in the storage room ordering some things on the PC, a false alarm went off. That *ping pong* sound when a customer comes in. I went back to the storefront straight away. “Welcome!” I said, but there was no one there.

Well, we often have false alarms so I didn’t really worry about it. It especially happens a lot in summer when moths come in, I thought perhaps it was just reacting to that? It’s a mystery as to why it also happens in winter without any bugs though.

I’d finished some work, and it was 2 a.m., when customers generally stop coming into the store, so I went into the fridge to put out the juice and sake. You can’t hear anything in there so in order to hear if any customers entered the store I kept the door open as I went about my work. But as we often have false alarms so you can’t really count on the doorbell. Even if a customer comes sometimes it won’t ring and they’ll be left waiting at the front counter.

So every now and then I look out from between the shelves in the fridge to see if there are any customers while I’m restocking. I was restocking the shelves for about 20 minutes, perhaps? I was so involved I forgot to check if there were any customers, so I peeked out from behind one of the shelves and there was a customer right in front of me. He was staring at the *Asahi Super Dry* with vacant eyes. He then locked eyes with me. He looked like a tired, dispirited old guy. I was so scared for a moment I thought my heart would stop.

I was looking out from behind the sake shelves, so I couldn't see the entire store, but I hadn't even noticed there was a customer. 'Crap,' I thought and rushed out. I yelled out, "Welcome!" even louder than usual in the hope that he wouldn't complain.

But there was no one there. I thought perhaps he'd moved behind the shelves or somewhere I couldn't see so I took a look around the store but there was no one there. I even checked the toilet but again, there was no one there.

Hmm? Did I get it wrong? There was nothing else I could do, so I went back to work. My heart rate rose a little though. Perhaps it was a person who had returned here for Obon and wanted to drink an *Asahi Super Dry*?

While pondering that I finished putting the stock out and exited the fridge when, *ping pong*, the bell rang again. Was it a customer this time? I went back out into the shop, and again no one was there. Ah, maybe the person I just saw gave up and went home because they couldn't buy anything. I dunno why I thought that, but I yelled out, "Thank you very much!" as loudly as I could.

I'm still working at that store this year, I haven't left yet. There are still an awful lot of false alarms.

There are so many false alarms that I've taken to watching the surveillance camera to see if any customers are coming into the store. I can see them coming in, but when I go out no-one's there…

When I left my apartment for a few days

* * *

This happened to me recently, it's not a joke.

I like motorbikes, so during the Obon holidays, I took the opportunity to just wander around for a bit. On the evening of the last day, I returned to my one room apartment. For an entire week, nobody was in this single man's room that nobody other than himself enters, and it was extremely humid.

I turned on the air conditioning, took a hot shower, cracked a cold beer and sat on the sofa. Just as I was settling in to rest…!

"Jijijijijijijijijiji."

A strange sound rang out loudly throughout the room. I looked in the direction of the sound and froze.

"Eh?!"

There were around 10 cicadas sitting on my white walls. I guess one of them realised a person was around and suddenly started chirping. Gross. But, I am a man. Like, I'm not scared of bugs or anything. Where did they come from? The vents? I got up and went towards them before suddenly my stomach dropped.

Each and every one of the cicadas was fixed to the wall with a pin. Other than the one cicada that cried out, the rest were already dead. They were completely dried out.

I immediately called the police, but seeing as nothing was stolen they couldn't do anything. They concluded it was likely just the work of some weirdo. It's possible whoever it was entered through a small unlocked window.

(But, my room is on the fifth floor.)

The condition of each of the dried out cicadas was different, which meant it was possible that this person entered my apartment over several days. Perhaps they had also brought the dead cicadas. But there was still an alive cicada, so at worst, the intruder had possibly been in my apartment that very morning.

I was creeped out, so I went to the fridge and threw out everything inside, including the half-drunk whiskey bottle.

The police took the cicadas and pins as evidence.

Do you believe in Feng Shui?

* * *

I'm not a person who can see ghosts, so I'm safe in that regard, but last Obon I had a bit of a scary experience. I couldn't stop feeling *something*.

Last March, both my younger sister and myself successfully got into university, so from April, our parents were living alone. Our father didn't want the house to become a sad place, so he went out and bought a dog. He built a doghouse in the corner of the house and they began raising it.

Once the new school term started, my sister and I both moved to our respective new lodgings. Later, when we returned home for Obon, our mother was wearing this huge cast.

"What did that?" I asked.

"I broke my collarbone in a traffic accident," she answered.

When she was crossing the road in her car, she was hit from the side, and apparently, it would take three months to heal completely. If it were just that, it would be fine. The type of story you might hear anywhere. But in reality, that wasn't all.

"How silly of you. It happened because you were careless!" At the time I was smiling, but little did I know that I'd soon be wrapped up in it too.

Our mother's accident happened in the middle of July, but two months before that our father was also hit from behind. I heard he got whiplash from that particular accident.

Then, when I asked my mother why she had the accident, she said, "OO (my sister) was trying to kill herself, so I was hit on my way to the park to stop her."

For a long time, my sister had suffered from hysteria. This time around, her boyfriend broke up with her right after she returned home for Obon, so in despair, she ran away. Our mother got news of where she was, and on her way to the park was hit from the side.

"This is an unlucky year for our family, hey. You should be careful too, son." As she said that to me she left to start getting dinner ready.

Then, two days later on August 14th. In order to open a time capsule from our elementary school days, I was waiting for my friends. It happened on our way to the school. I peddled my bike as fast as I could, and as I turned the corner there was a red car right in front of me. My memory is a little vague after that, but according to what I heard, I was hit by the car.

I was tossed about seven metres and hit the asphalt. Blood poured out the back of my head and I went into convulsions. Some people living nearby came to help me. I told them where I lived and I was taken to the hospital. In the end, I ended up with eight stitches in my head. It was a serious injury.

When I returned home from the hospital, my friends who opened the time capsule came around to deliver the letter I had written to my future self.

"You're probably already dead, huh? In an accident or something."

I was a second grader at the time. Was this really what I wrote?

Our entire family had been involved in accidents or suicide attempts. My grandfather found it strange, so he came over to investigate and discovered the doghouse in the corner of the room with the household altar, and furthermore, it was facing southwest.

According to a Feng Shui master, the dog house was disrupting the unlucky quarter (the southwest) of the household altar, and so bad luck was trickling in. We quickly moved the dog house and cleaned up the room.

After that, there were no more accidents, but about a year after they got the dog it suddenly died. Did he take all the bad luck with him…? I feel like he did.

The fear I felt at the mountain with my cousin

* * *

More than 20 years have passed. I was in the lower grades of elementary school at the time. My family returned to the lush green fields of the countryside for Obon. With a bug net in hand, I ran around catching bugs with my cousin. He was the same age as me and I hadn't seen him in a long time. There was this sense of space that you couldn't get in the big cities. Before we knew it, we were standing before the mountain behind our grandfather's place.

Me: "There are probably some really big bugs up there."

Cousin: "What are we gonna do if they don't fit in the net?"

Putting aside mutation, it was highly unlikely there would be such bugs, but the mountain was overflowing with life so we held high expectations. The two of us ran around for a while but suddenly my cousin stopped.

Cousin: "Sorry, I need to go to the toilet."

I didn't know why he was apologising but he looked upset about it.

Me: "You wanna go back?"

Cousin: "No, I can't hold it in any longer."

He crouched down in some nearby bushes and pulled down his pants. I could imagine from the sound just how much liquid there, was so I turned around and started playing with the pockets of my pants. I was raised well, so there were tissues in my pocket but I wasn't sure whether it would be enough.

While considering such thoughts, a scream rose behind me that didn't sound like anything on this earth.

Me: "What's wrong?!"

Pushing his way through the grass with his pants halfway up my cousin looked at me with a terrifying expression on his face. His hands and feet were covered in soft, squishy red things.

They were leeches.

They're not especially rare in the countryside, but they were unknown to a city kid. Of course, we were just elementary school kids, so we didn't know anything about them or what to do.

Me: "Hurry up and flick them off!"

I timidly held out a tissue for him. He reached out and grabbed it, but instead of wiping off the leeches he wiped his backside once, twice, and then took off his pants and underwear. From his ankles to his feet, he was covered in dark red leeches, like a spotted pattern. He was absorbed in trying to get them off, but they were too strong and not going anywhere. Lines of blood painted his lower half, he looked like some kind of undiscovered monster.

Cousin: "He… help me!"

He screamed out in panic. Seeing his naked lower half exposed and coming at me I felt incredible fear. I screamed and ran away from my cousin turned monster down the mountain path, heading towards our grandfather's house. On the way, I turned around several times. My cousin continued to chase me with the leeches dangling from his naked lower half. All I could think about at the time was how my cousin that had become one with the leeches would change me into a leech person too.

Me: “Mum! Dad!!”

I dove into the entranceway half crying. While calling out for my parents I went to take off my sandals and then I realised. My feet were covered in leeches. Was I going to become a leech man like my cousin as well?!

I cried. I took my sandals off while crying and ran into the hall looking for an adult. Then I heard a female voice scream out behind me. It was my mother’s voice. I did a U-turn so I could go back to her and then screamed myself. There was a line of small footprints on the floor. They weren’t just any footprints. They were the colour of blood. Was I being chased by some kind of monster?! Something behind me that I couldn’t see was leaving behind bloody footprints while chasing me.

I cut through the guest room and Japanese style room looking for the adults, continuing my escape from the monster I couldn’t see. Of course, it was clearly evident that they were my own footprints, but at the time I didn’t notice and just accelerated my own panic. I ran around the house, leaving tiny bloody footprints behind me wherever I went.

My grandfather’s house was huge. But, of course, they heard all the noise and my uncle and aunt found me. My aunt clung to me while my uncle screamed out, “Lighter! Lighter!” My mother screamed in the entranceway for the second time.

I was surrounded by confused relatives. As we passed through the blood-covered hallway, my mother was in the entranceway with my wailing cousin. The sight of my cousin covered in blood and leeches stirred up even our relatives who lived in the countryside.

As our uncle and grandfather started to burn them, the leeches that had clung so tight dropped off in a funny manner. They took my cousin's shirt off and while he was standing in the entranceway naked the adults thoroughly inspected his whole body for leeches. Without leaving a single one behind, they all fell off.

The adults stood on them as they dropped, and they were washed away with hot water. But my feet and my cousin's body continued to bleed. Even when they put on ointment, the blood didn't stop. An ambulance was called, and along with our parents, we went to the hospital.

When you're bitten by a leech, there's no pain, but they secrete a substance to stop your blood from coagulating, so it becomes difficult to stop it. After that, an annoying itch continued on and on. This soon calmed down after they applied some ointment.

I was okay, but my cousin was bitten all over, and taking into account his small size and how much blood they took, he was kept overnight on a drip. His father decided to stay with him. In his hospital room, he was covered head to toe and bandages and his face was somewhat blue.

Me: "I'm sorry…"

Without saying exactly why I lowered my head.

Cousin: “Thanks for the paper.”

Ah, he was talking about the tissue paper. As we left the room, there were two policemen standing there. I don’t know who called them. I told them all about how we went up the mountain to catch bugs, how he went to poop in the woods, got covered in leeches, the mysterious thing chasing me at home and the adults searching my cousin’s naked body for all the leeches.

The next day, my grandfather and people from the local area went up the mountain with their grass cutting tools and cut away all the grass. Then it was all sprayed with chemicals. The strange smell even reached my grandfather’s house.

In the end, my cousin was in the hospital for two weeks. There was the fact he wouldn’t stop bleeding, but they also checked him for various infections.

When we returned from the countryside to the city, my parents also took me to the hospital to be checked over. At the time, I was more bothered by the needles than any infection.

When I saw my cousin again the next year, we certainly didn’t feel like going to catch any bugs, and we most certainly didn’t go near the mountain.

A while later, our grandfather passed away and left his house to my cousin. I heard that, besides work, he’s also studying leeches. He’s probably using that experience to help protect people from the harm of leeches.

…Or so I thought, but according to my father,

the damage done by leeches in that area has been rapidly increasing. I don’t have any solid numbers, but I have a real feeling that since my cousin moved there, the number of leeches has begun to increase.

Just what the hell is he studying?

BUILDINGS

Laughter and footsteps

* * *

I'm a regular person with no ability to sense the supernatural, but there was one time that I had a ghostly experience. My room in our apartment faces the hallway outside, so it's easy for me to see when somebody passes by. I can clearly see the shadow of people through my thin curtains.

This happened when I was in the first grade of high school. I was studying in my room just before the summer holidays for our end of term tests. It was past 2:30 a.m. and raining really hard outside. I was just thinking about going to bed.

Badum. Badum. Badum!

"Ahahahahaha…"

I could hear what sounded like a small child's laughter and skipping. It sounded like it was near the building elevator nearby, so I thought the family that lived on the same floor was returning from a night out. But what was strange was that I could only hear the sound of the child's laughter and footsteps.

While I was wondering why the parents weren't telling the child off, I quickly turned my light off. When I think about it now, I realise that, for some reason, I didn't want to know why the child was awake, so to escape from the voice I jumped into bed.

Badum. Badum. Badum!

"Ahahahahahaha…"

The voice started to get closer to my room. That's when I suddenly thought, why is it only a child's voice and footsteps? Why can't I hear the parents' voices too? I quickly closed my eyes and waited for the child to pass.

In just a little bit they'll pass! That's what I was hoping for, and just when it seemed like the voice would pass it happened. The voice and footsteps stopped right in front of my window.

…………

A horrible silence descended over my room. The owner of the voice was right there in front of my window. It felt like they were looking directly at me from the 10cm open gap in the window. Whether I was scared or curious, I thought I'd just get up and close the window but my body refused to move.

I slept with my feet facing the window, so I should have been able to get up and go straight there, but my body was like a stone and wouldn't move. Slowly, as I calmed down, I urged myself, "Get up right now, if you look outside it'll all be over! Then get to sleep!!" I don't know how much time passed but before I knew it, the sun was rising and it was time to get up.

Realising it was morning, I jumped out of bed and told mum about what happened the night before. But she was like, "Well, that's pretty common for kids that age, just forget about it." She didn't believe me. Since then, I haven't experienced anything supernatural again but for me, it was no laughing matter and a terrifying event.

Scratching

* * *

I once lived in a one-room apartment with a kitchen. My room was at the end of the second floor, but sometimes I could hear a scratching sound coming from the wall on the side with no neighbours.

At first, I was concerned, but I figured it was just a wild animal so I forgot about it. (In reality, I had seen a flying squirrel around before.)

The first time my girlfriend came to my apartment, the scratching started again. I told her to listen carefully. When she did, she told me to take her to the convenience store right away.

When we arrived her face was blue, and she said, “It looks like you could only hear the sound. I saw a black arm sticking out of your wall. It was scratching, making that sound. It also gave off a rotten smell.”

Of course, I soon moved.

I can’t go back

* * *

I was eating chicken nuggets at home, watching TV when I heard a young female voice call out “I’m home!” from the front door.

“Welcome back!” I replied while watching the TV.

I live alone. I don’t have a girlfriend.

I looked back but no-one was there. I was sure I heard something. ‘Hmm? What is this? Am I imagining things?’ I felt it was strange rather than scary. I cleaned up and went to bed.

During the night my eyes suddenly opened, and I tried to look over beside me. I couldn’t move. For the first time ever, I was experiencing sleep paralysis. I could only move my eyes so while searching the room I felt like there was something in the corner.

The door was slightly open. A round eye was watching me from the gap.

Before I knew it, it was morning.

That night I stayed in the nap room at work. It was only the fifth day since I’d moved into that apartment. But I can’t go back.

I saw someone looking in

* * *

This happened when I was still living at homc. My parents' house is an apartment on the first floor. Both my parents worked, so usually when I got home, no-one was there.

On this particular night, I returned home from work and went to my room to get changed when I saw what looked like someone peeping through the curtain. Shocked, I ran to the living room but then I realised that perhaps the window in my parents' room was open (because it was summer). Nervously, I went to their room and there was someone outside staring right at me. It was dark so I couldn't see his face clearly but it was a man with glasses and a buzz cut.

Gripped with fear I yelled out, "Who… who?! Who are you!?" However, he ran away.

'Man, the first floor really is scary, I'm glad nothing happened…' I thought, and that was the end of that.

Then one day, a few weeks later. I was out with my friends and when I returned home around dawn, I noticed that I'd carelessly forgotten my house key. I didn't know what to do but in the end, I decided to just wake up my sleeping parents and have them let me in. I quietly went around to the back of the apartment and reached out my arm to tap on their window when suddenly I remembered that day and got goosebumps.

The guy I saw that time I clearly saw from the waist up. But even though our apartment is on the first floor the inside is built a little higher. The windows reach your waist from inside the room, but when viewed from the outside they sit at about one and a half metres high. I looked around but I couldn't see anything that looked like you could climb up on. Plus, when he ran away it didn't look like he dismounted from anything.

So what exactly did I see…?

The children playing by the river

* * *

Do you mind if I tell you a scary story?

This happened when I was in the second grade. At the time, our family lived in an apartment next to a river. At night-time, we all slept in the same room.

One night, my father was out, it was just me and my mother. I just couldn't get to sleep and when I looked at the clock, it was already half past two in the morning. As the clock struck, it made a *boooon* sound and any desire to sleep vanished. I got up to get a drink of water and then I heard some voices, like they were having fun.

When I looked out the window, I saw a boy and a girl playing by the riverbed. The girl looked to be about my age, the boy a little younger. They were both wearing really nice clothes, like you might see had they been invited to a wedding.

'That looks fun~' I thought to myself. Then the girl looked my way and waved at me. I waved back.

"A friend~ Let's play~" the boy said as I waved. I suddenly wanted to go really badly, so I said to my mother, "My friends are calling me, so is it alright if I go out to the river and play?"

My mother, who was peacefully sleeping up until that point, suddenly shot up.

"You're just seeing strange things because you don't go to sleep right away!"

She got really angry and told me to get back into bed. When I turned back, there was nobody by the riverbed.

There have been plenty of nights since then where I've been unable to sleep, but I never saw those two kids again.

I hate to think what would have happened if I went to see them that night without telling my mother… when I think about it now it terrifies me.

The white robed goddess of death

* * *

When I was in high school, I caught the flu and had a high fever. I was feeling faint, so an ambulance took me to the hospital. Turned out I had pneumonia and I slept for the next three days straight, but I didn't get any better so I ended up staying in the hospital for half a month.

A nurse came in regularly to change my drip and clean things up, but sometimes a nurse who looked to be in her 30s would come in and, without doing anything in particular, would just hang around and look at my face.

Finally, I was able to eat again and started to get better, and I was able to talk to the nurse. I asked her about the nurse in her 30s who would sometimes come around. Who exactly was she?

"What did that person come to do?" I asked, but the nurse replied, "There's no staff here with that much free time."

"Do you remember how many times she came?" the nurse asked, so I replied, "Five or six times."

"I wonder if she was a part-timer…" The nurse gave a vague answer and then left the room.

Then, one year after I left the hospital. I broke a toe and was admitted again, and by chance, I saw that nurse once more. She was in the emergency hallway, looking at an elderly patient being carried on a stretcher with an expressionless look on her face.

Just as I was thinking it was a little strange, I got goosebumps all over my body. She looked over and noticed me, and then slowly approached me.

"Can you see me?" she asked.

Without thinking, I covered my face with my hands, and in my heart I screamed over and over, "Disappear, disappear!"

After about five minutes, I looked up and she was gone. I thought she was nothing more than a ghost, but perhaps she was really a goddess of death.

I was working part time as hospital security

* * *

This is a story from when I used to work part-time as a night-time hospital security guard.

It was around 2 a.m. and I was taking my scheduled nap as my partner worked the floor. There was no nap room set up, so we were using a room in a separate building that wasn't occupied. The morgue was located in the basement of that building so it was a little creepy, but just as I was getting used to it all 'that thing' happened.

A nap is just a nap, so I never fell into that deep of a sleep, but I had 'that dream.' That is, I was crawling up the stairs. I was struggling to wriggle up the stairs with all my might.

In the dream, I was heading for a particular room, absentmindedly thinking, "Yes, this is it." It was a room I'd seen before. It was the room I was sleeping in right now.

At that moment, I opened my eyes. I was covered in sweat. I wiped my brow. It felt so real.

"What a creepy dream," I voiced to myself.

I wanted to get back to the building full of people right away. But whether I was even more tired than usual that day, I fell asleep again without realising it.

Then, *bang!* The sound of a large metal door closing woke me up. For a moment I had no idea what was going on. I wasn't lying down like I should have been. It felt like both my legs were being pulled down by gravity. Everything was dark. There were only two dim lights.

I was in the morgue.

The sound I'd heard earlier was myself closing the door. There was a dead body lying in the bed before me. It seemed like I'd been called here.

Confused, I escaped back to the other building. When I asked about it later, a man who had lost both legs died there that night. That's probably why he crawled up to summon me.

The girl with three months to live

* * *

In a certain hospital, there was a girl who had been diagnosed with only three months left to live. Two of her friends came to visit, and while her mother was helping her to sit up in bed, they decided to take a photo together. The sick girl sat in the middle and they took a photo.

In the end, a week later she took a turn for the worse and without even reaching three months, she passed away.

As things began to settle down for her mother after the funeral, she remembered the photo she'd taken at the hospital. She went to visit the photo developer to get it but they couldn't find the photo. She asked the photo studio about it but they said, "There was a problem developing it…"

The mother found this strange, and as it was the last photo taken of her daughter, she pressed the photo studio even harder about it. Shaking, the staff member retrieved the photo for her and said, "I think it's better that you don't see it, but please don't be shocked," and showed her the photo.

The three girls were pictured, but the girl in the middle, her daughter, looked just like a mummy.

The mother was very shocked but said she'd take it as a memorial of her daughter and returned home. Even so, the photo was terrifying, so she took it to see a medium and asked her if this was hinting something about her daughter's death.

The medium didn't want to answer her. Of course, the mother pushed her for an answer and so the medium replied, "I'm terribly sorry, but your daughter is in hell."

Strange happening at the abandoned hospital

* * *

I like abandoned buildings and often go looking for them in my free time. I had a few days off and thought I'd go stay overnight in one of these buildings, so I got my camping gear and sake and went to an abandoned hospital for the night.

I arrived around 3 in the afternoon, the sun still high in the sky. After looking around inside for a bit, I heard the voices of some children, like they were breaking things. I figured some of the local brats thought this would be a good area to go crazy in.

It isn't just the passing of time that breaks down old buildings. I wholeheartedly believe that kids and delinquents acting violently also contribute.

I put some distance between myself and the voices, entering one of the hospital rooms and getting my sake out to start drinking.

As the sun went down, it seemed like the kids went home, so I grabbed my lantern and went for a walk around the place.

After walking for a few hours I was hungry, so I went back to my room and got the rice ball I bought from the convenience store, drank some more *shochu*, got in my sleeping bag and went to sleep.

As the night went on, the cold woke me up. The sake had completely worn off, and I was freezing. I needed to pee, so I left the hospital to go do my business. On the way back, I heard laughter.

It was a child's voice.

At the same time, the sound of something breaking reverberated throughout the hospital. It was the same sound I'd heard in the afternoon. I started sweating even though I was cold and quickly returned to my room.

The sound of laughter and things breaking continued incessantly, and it sounded like it was getting closer to my room. Wide awake, I gathered my things and held my breath while I listened.

Before long, the sounds were coming from the next room. The crazed laugh of a child soon changed into screaming. If it were a normal person, the sound would have destroyed their throat. It was like someone being tortured. The scream shook me to my core.

Each time something banged on the concrete walls it reverberated within me. I had no more time to wait. With just the lantern in hand, I took off from the room, not bothering to check if the coast was clear or not.

As I put some distance between myself and the hospital I turned around. I saw what looked like my stuff being tossed out the window. I couldn't see anything in the darkness, but there was no doubt that 'something' was in there.

After that, I never went to abandoned buildings during the night again.

A face in the wood grain

* * *

This happened when I entered the third grade of junior high school. The school desks were made of wood, but no matter which way I looked at it, my desk looked like it had a face in the wood grain. It freaked me out, so when no-one was looking I swapped desks with the girl who sat next to me, Chimura-san. After that, Chimura-san started acting strange.

After school she'd stay behind in the classroom alone, and every now and then I'd see her talking to someone. Our parents were acquaintances and her mother mentioned to mine that Chimura-san was saying how she'd made a boyfriend.

So, in addition to her own lunch, she would make lunch for this boyfriend every day as well. There was no indication of any of this at school and I thought it was a bit strange, but at the time I was at that rebellious age so I just replied, "Oh yeah?" and the conversation ended there.

Before long, Chimura-san's behaviour got even stranger. She stopped trying to go home. Rather than avoiding going to school, she was avoiding going home. She went crazy when her parents and teachers tried to make her go back, and in the end, she was forced to go to the hospital. That was right around this time.

With the weather getting humid, the classroom started to stink of something rotten. When we looked inside Chimura-san's desk, it was full of rotting food. But stranger than that, the face in the wood grain had disappeared. I think it's probably attached itself to Chimura-san now.

The old janitor

* * *

When I was in high school, there was an old janitor who was a little too friendly with the students.

People didn't really complain about cigarettes too much at the time, so you could often see him under some shade on the school grounds with a box of *Seven Star*, puffing away during his break.

"If you smoke menthols, you can't get an erection," was his pet theory on the subject.

"He's always looking at us, grinning while he chews on that tobacco."

Loose socks and short skirts were the fashion at the time, and the girls often said such things about him. They were creeped out by him.

"If you don't want me to look then you should make your skirt longer! Or stop wearing that makeup."

My friends and I were kinda nerds, but while we chatted about our favourite anime, *Macross 7*, we strangely felt a sense of pity for the old janitor.

Then something strange happened towards the end of the summer holidays. One of the girls from the volleyball club's clothes went missing. It became a huge thing, and at a full school morning assembly, the PE teacher addressed it.

"If you come forward yourself, we won't get angry. If you know anything please inform one of your teachers."

A little while later, I heard that the janitor was fired. Apparently, some girl's underwear and skirt was found in his janitor's closet. Right until the end, he proclaimed his innocence.

The school year ended, and it was getting to the time where I needed to think about my future. That's when I heard that the janitor had killed himself. He hung himself at home, leaving behind a note claiming his innocence.

"A person's entire life can change with a single piece of clothing."

My friends and I felt deeply sympathetic for him while we were thinking about our own futures.

Not too long after that, we heard the math teacher's body was discovered strangled to death. In his apartment they found the rest of the girl's clothes, secretly filmed videos and photos. They also found the butts from a box of *Seven Star* cigarettes (The math teacher greatly disliked smoking).

"The old guy's not haunting us and chewing tobacco, is he?"

As one of my friends muttered this I thought to myself, "No, it's not like that at all."

The thing in the basement

* * *

One day, when I was returning home from work, I decided to stop by the store to do a bit of shopping. I think it was just a little after 8 p.m.

Rather than calling this shopping mall a department store, it was more a small collection of shops. But it was convenient for small things like clothes, so every now and then I went there.

It was a six-floor building; the fifth and sixth floors for parking, and then the basement to the fourth floor were shops. At the time, the basement was under renovations so you couldn't enter.

The mall closed at 9 p.m., so when I dropped by at 8, most of the shops were getting ready to close, hanging up their green nets for the night.

After I finished my shopping on the fourth floor, I didn't want to be any further hassle to the shop staff so I hurried to leave. I went towards the elevator at the end of the floor (the elevator was already stopped and waiting on the fourth floor).

I got in and pressed the button for the first floor. I've ridden that elevator many times. It's cramped with no window, the lights are dim, it's slow moving and noisy with a huge mirror in the back. It's not a nice place to be in.

When the elevator started moving, I looked at the buttons and noticed that the light for the first floor wasn't on. The light for the button underneath it, the basement, was lit up.

I figured I'd just pressed the wrong button by mistake so I pushed the first floor again but the light wouldn't come on. It continued down to the basement, currently restricted due to renovations, and the doors slowly opened.

Everything was under construction so it was pitch black, not a single light was on. The only thing I could see was the green emergency exit sign. Of course, there were no tenants there, it was just a wide open space.

It was kinda creepy, so I pressed the button to close the elevator doors and once again tried to go to the first floor, but just as the doors were about to close, I saw something out the corner of my eye.

My eyes weren't used to the dark yet, so I wasn't sure what I'd seen. Whatever it was, it looked like a person running to try to get on the elevator before the doors closed.

So I decided to wait and pressed the button to keep the doors open, but as my eyes began to adjust to the dark I took a better look at what was running towards me. It looked to be easily over two metres tall, yet its head was strangely small and the body incredibly thin.

The figure on the dark floor seemed to have its hands clasped behind its back and was wriggling towards me, as though trying not to fall over.

Scared, I quickly pushed the close button.

Whether it saw that or not, suddenly it picked up speed and began twisting its way over even faster. Terrified, I pushed the close button over and over again.

Finally the doors began to close slowly, and then I got a glimpse of the figure under the light of the emergency exit sign. It was bald, like a monk. And while I didn't see it very clearly, I also remember it was barefoot.

Even after the doors closed, I kept hitting the close button like an idiot, but the elevator refused to go anywhere. I'd forgotten to press the button for the first floor. Quickly I pressed it, and as I did, there was a loud bang against the elevator door, like something hitting it really hard.

I kept hitting the button for the first floor repeatedly, and as soon as it arrived I flew out and ran out of the building. After that, I called my friend to come and pick me up. I didn't tell them anything about what happened.

Mossan

* * *

There's something that appears in the catheter room of our hospital (the place where patients with serious illnesses go to get treated) called Mossan.

Mossan wears pyjamas with blue polka dots and has various appearances such as a middle-aged man with messy hair, a sweet looking young boy, and even a skinny girl, amongst other things.

The one thing they all have in common is that Mossan stands in the corner in those same pyjamas looking at the ground. He doesn't say anything or even move. Before you know it he's there, before you know it he's gone. If he's there, everyone in the room will see him.

When Mossan appears the patient undergoing treatment dies within the next few days. Without fail.

Mossan doesn't appear before every patient who dies, but if he does appear there's no getting around the fact that that patient will soon pass away. Even if the treatment is a success, the patient starts going downhill again.

Apparently, Mossan has been witnessed in the hospital since long ago. They've tried several times to exorcise him but it never works. He only appears three or four times a year but all the doctors and staff in our department are aware of him. Even if he appears during someone's treatment everyone is silent and doesn't react. The only ones who are scared are the new nurses.

The young doctors fall into a terrible slump whenever Mossan appears, but only the head doctor refuses to give in to him. Even though he's the one person who's seen Mossan more than any of us he doesn't believe in his curse.

Even now he's continuing his battle to try to save those who fall to Mossan's charms.

I heard a sound from an empty room

* * *

This is a story from a few days ago.

In our family, there are four people. My father, mother, older brother and me. At 6:30 a.m., my brother had early morning club activities, so he left for school. At 7:45 a.m., my father left for work. My mother drove him to the station, so she was also out. I had to be at school by 8:10, so I took my time getting ready.

Our bathroom is close to the entranceway, directly opposite my brother's room. Around 8 a.m., I went to the bathroom and started drying my hair. Then from behind, I suddenly heard the sound of something falling. *Doton.*

Maybe it was because of the hairdryer but I couldn't hear it very clearly, and the TV was on so I thought maybe it was just the TV program. But it was still a little scary, so I turned the hairdryer off and listened carefully.

Holding the dryer I listened closely. *Zaaaaa. Shaaaa.* I could hear what sounded like something being dragged inside my brother's room. In the mirror, I could see my brother's door was open.

As you would expect, I was terrified, so I left the lights and TV on and went straight to school. Then when I got home in the evening, my mother got angry at me. I told her about what I'd heard.

"Whatever you do, don't tell your brother," she said.

My brother really, really hates ghosts and monster stories… then when my brother got home that night he sat down on a chair in the living room and was like, “Man, I had the strangest dream today!”

“What kind of dream?” I asked.

“Like, when I opened my eyes there was this woman crawling under my bed.”

My mother and I looked at each other. There’s no way it was a coincidence. I was terrified.

The young man's back

* * *

This happened to me just yesterday, so please listen.

My father died the other day and passed on his house to me, but while the location wasn't bad, it was kinda old and too big, so after discussing it with my wife we decided to sell it. Luckily, while we were taking care of my father's effects we found some real estate advertisements and business cards, so we called them and decided on four companies to come and take a look at the house for us.

It was the third of those companies. A stylish, modern looking young man around 30 came to assess the house. He spoke clearly and seemed nice. But his assessment value was 10 000 000 yen higher than the previous two companies. Both myself and my wife had pretty much decided and were about to tell him when he asked if he could take a photo of each room of the house. I agreed and accompanied him, telling him about each room as we went.

I opened the door to the small room next to the family altar and the moment the young man entered I was suddenly struck frozen with my hand still on the door. I've experienced this type of paralysis several times before, but this was the first time it happened so suddenly and while I was standing on my feet. For a moment I was worried it was a serious illness and began to panic when I heard a woman's voice right next to my ear. The voice was mumbling and extraordinarily difficult to hear but it sounded like she was saying, “It hurts.”

It seemed like I could just barely move my eyes, but if I looked at her it might be dangerous, so I looked away into the room, and when I did I saw a woman with brown curly hair and heavy black clothes attached to the young man’s back.

That was scary enough, but her neck was long (about 40cm) and though her back was toward me, her head was facing me and her eyes were rolling about like a chameleon.

It all felt so unreal, rather than looking at it with fear I was more dumbfounded, but as soon as the young man turned around she disappeared and I regained feeling again. Of course, I didn’t tell him what happened and said I wasn’t feeling so well and excused myself.

Afterwards, I investigated the company the young man worked for and when I did… it was full of bad reviews. “Something’s there! Something’s there!” Of course, this morning I called and politely declined their offer.

When the young man turned around, I clearly heard a voice say, “Suffer!” Perhaps that young man or even his company has perpetrated a lot of accidents. Thinking about it until now I haven’t had a wink of sleep, so after I get this down I’m gonna take some sleeping pills and go to bed.

Why that toilet has no mirror

* * *

This story took place when I was a university student 10 years ago.

I was a fourth-year male student at a certain university in Saitama. This university was strong with foreign languages and had calm, gentle school traditions. We enjoyed campus life with both club activities and study.

"Do you know why the toilet in building two doesn't have a mirror?"

One of my seniors asked me this question during the sophomore school training camp. There were six department buildings within the university, and come to think of it, only the toilet in building two didn't have a mirror.

According to the senior, the reason there was no mirror was because 'a person appears that you can only see through the mirror.'

There were other stories also, like "the top half of a woman's body appears climbing up the wall in building two." For some reason, only building two had all these rumours surrounding it.

For a training camp consisting of both boys and girls, the idea of going out to do a test of courage was especially appealing for the boys. It was decided immediately that we would set out in the late night to explore building two.

The mission was "Enter each toilet in building two and look around with the hand mirror borrowed from the girls."

My group was the first.

Of course, the school grounds at night were creepy but there were four of us so it wasn't particularly scary. We went about the mission from the bottom floor doing well, and then as we exited the last toilet on the fourth floor we were relieved that all we had left to do was go back. Then…

While we were heading downstairs, I noticed something strange.

(Hmm? Sounds like footsteps… Were there that many of us?)

The worst case scenario immediately popped up in my mind. I forced myself to remain calm and, looking forward, I called out to the other group members in the most natural voice I could as we continued downstairs.

After everybody replied, I was relieved they were all there, and I turned around. There was very clearly a shadow of someone with long hair behind the last member in the line…

It looked like the girl walking next to me noticed as well.

"Run!!!"

I don't remember much of what happened after that. I think I grabbed the hand of the last person in line and ran downstairs.

Of course, the test of courage was cancelled for the groups following us. The girl who saw the thing with me refused to spend the rest of the night at school, so she got a late night taxi home.

Incidentally, now building two has been destroyed and a new building put up in its place.

It was terrifying, but afterwards, I felt like the ghost situation also created a kind of fun atmosphere, so at the same time, it's also a kind of sad memory.

Toilet

* * *

I was working as a late night security guard for a large building. I was new, so I was paired up with a colleague. It was an extremely easy job. All I had to do was follow a particular route with a torch in hand.

Just when I was starting to think that this would be an easy job with nothing much happening, we approached a toilet at the end of the third floor. As we did my colleague was like:

“I need to go to the toilet.”

I was only new and had no reason to refuse, so I figured I’d go as well and we went in together. It was nondescript, a regular, clean toilet with four urinals and two stalls. My colleague apparently needed to go number two, so he went straight towards one of the stalls.

Even though there shouldn’t have been anyone there at this time, I dunno if it was just a habit or not but I found it a little strange that he knocked first. Of course, there was no answer from the other side and so he grabbed the doorknob. He turned the knob, but perhaps someone really was inside, or the door was broken, but either way, the result was the same.

My colleague gave up and went into the next stall. I’d finished doing my business, but the door that wouldn’t open intrigued me, so I went over to it. When I looked at the knob, I could see the red paint signifying that it was locked from the inside.

Was someone in there…? Did they have a heart attack or pass out while doing their business? Or perhaps a drunk had fallen asleep in there? Hoping it was the latter, I put my ear against the door.

I couldn't hear any snoring. I couldn't hear anything but the awful sound coming from the stall next door. If it were the former it would be terrible, so I started thinking about what to do.

In the end, I decided to have a look over the top of the door. I took a bucket out of the cleaning cupboard and climbed up on it, putting my foot on the doorknob. I lifted myself up and put my hands on the top of the door. Then I looked inside.

There was a dead body; what appeared to be a middle-aged businessman. Taking a closer look, there were small flies all around him. His necktie was wrapped around his neck.

I see. He committed suicide.

But strangely, the dead body didn't smell. Normally in this situation, I think calling the police would be your main priority. I don't know what I was thinking, but I felt like I needed to alert my other colleagues, so I left the one still in the next stall and headed for the guardroom. I didn't rush. I was decidedly calm.

But, if you really think about it, other than myself and the colleague still in the toilet there was no-one else in the building. Of course, there wasn't anyone in the guardroom either. I figured I may as well go back and headed for the third floor.

But there was no toilet there. No matter how much I looked, there was no toilet.

Maybe I'd gotten the place wrong. Perhaps I'd mistaken the floor, so I searched all the toilets but it was nowhere to be found. My memory of the event ends there.

A few days later.

No matter how much I tried I couldn't remember the face of my colleague in the toilet stall. I couldn't remember the face of the dead body either. I couldn't remember where that building was. I couldn't remember how I got home from that building after that, or even the circumstances leading up to the job.

Why didn't I call the police? Why did I go to the guardroom even though no one was there?

Did I ever really have that job? Was I really a security guard?

I've started wondering about these things recently.

There were so many contradictory, doubtful and suspicious points, I thought it had to have been a dream. Only the scene remained clearly in my head.

There's one more strange thing. While I'm sitting here watching TV, telling this story, I'm having this really strong sense of deja vu.

Don't enter that toilet

* * *

This is a story I heard from a friend. Friend A worked delivering goods to a certain building in Shinjuku Station. One of his colleagues told him, "Whatever you do, don't use the toilet in the basement parking area."

However, one day he just couldn't hold it any longer so he went down there. He went to one of the stalls and closed and door and was about to get to business when it happened.

Clang!

Suddenly the knob on the locked door started to shake. Friend A thought someone made a mistake, so he yelled out, "Someone's in here!"

At that moment…

Clang! Clang! Clang! Clang! Clang!

With incredible force, the doorknob rattled, and then something began intensely banging on the door. Friend A pushed against the door with all his might. Then, when he looked down at a hole in the door, he saw a bloodshot eye looking in!

Panicking, he kept pushing against the door as hard as he could, but not long later it stopped, so Friend A ran from the toilet as fast as he could.

When he told his colleague about it several days later, he said, "You idiot. If you go into that toilet it means you're down for it, if you know what I mean."

That basement parking toilet was a famous spot for being picked up in.

Someone's watching

* * *

This is a story from about 10 years ago when I was a junior high school student.

After lunch there was cleaning time, and at the time I was in charge of the teaching materials room. Teachers rarely came to this area during cleaning time so it was popular with students, and when time came to change cleaning areas students always fought over who would get to go there.

Even if you were slacking off from cleaning, it was a difficult place to be found in which is another reason it was so popular. There was only a single door of frosted glass so if someone was coming you would soon see it. For example, if someone came, and we didn't notice it, as soon as the visitor opened the door there were plenty of shelves to hide behind so we wouldn't be found easily. I remember hanging out with a lot of my friends there in just that manner.

Then one day, we met up with something dangerous in that room. As usual, we were playing around in there when suddenly one of my friends yelled out in a small voice, "Someone's coming!" Someone was on the other side of the frosted glass.

We quickly tidied up what we were playing with, picked up our cleaning tools and hid in the darkness of the shelves. We pretended to be seriously cleaning for a while but no matter how much time passed the door didn't open.

Perhaps someone had just been passing by and that was all we had seen…? The friend who had called out also thought that was probably it.

Sticking my head out from behind the shelf I looked in the direction of the door…

"!!!!!!!!!!!!!!!!!!!!!!"

There was definitely someone standing behind the door. But, why? They didn't move, didn't try to enter, why were they just standing there…?

It was then we noticed something was strange about the whole spectacle. The entire door was frosted glass, so that should mean we'd be able to see the shadow of the person's whole body. You could see up to the forehead of even the tallest teacher through it. But we could only see up to the chest of the figure standing behind the door. We all slowly looked up and then let out a small scream.

Above the door was a skylight window, about 2 metres high, and someone was staring right at us. What we saw with our eyes was a regular human. But that height was not normal…

None of us could yell out. We were scared that if we took our eyes off it that it would enter the room, so we could do nothing but keep looking. How long passed while we were like that?

Finally, that person suddenly looked away from us and then quickly disappeared from in front of the door. For a while, none of us could move…

Eventually, the bell rang to signify the end of cleaning time and we heard the sound of students' voices moving towards their classrooms. Little by little, we calmed down and left the teaching materials room, but everyone remained silent.

Even now we don't know who that was, and we haven't heard about anyone seeing whatever 'that' was either. There was nobody in the school at that time over two metres tall, and no matter how much I think about it there's just no way to explain it.

Reunion in an abandoned school

* * *

It scared the crap out of me!

Right around Obon, I returned home for my class reunion, and because the opportunity was there, around 10 of us rented out a classroom from an old abandoned school.

Around 10 p.m., two ladies went to the toilet, but they came running back crying and screaming. We ran out into the hallway to see what all the commotion was about.

Something with really long black hair, I'm not sure if it was a boy or a girl, but it ran like a dog with amazing speed right in front of us before disappearing.

Its long black hair under the dim light of the torch was really, really creepy. Its claws made this *kakakakaka* sound as they hit the floor.

We all screamed and ran for it. Even I shrieked like a little girl. I realised that when I'm really scared, I don't let out a manly "gyaa!!" but more of a "hiiiyaaaaaaa."

We thought it might have been a pervert, so in the end, we called the police and it became a bit of an affair. An officer escorted us to the abandoned classroom so we could gather up our things. Some nosey old folk outside started screaming with all their might, "I told you that school was built on no good land!!"

According to the ladies who went to the toilet, they saw something dark in the corner and thought it might have been a rubbish bag. When they got closer, they saw whatever that thing was crouching there, holding its knees. It was traumatising. They said it even had horns.

Umicchi and Pirorin often look at 2chan so I wonder if they'll see this. I won't be returning home for a while, sorry. That thing was no joke, I don't want to see it again.

Incidentally, the mayor has been keeping the abandoned school around to use as a community centre as part of the school abolition policy.

GAMES & DOLLS

Kokkuri-san wasn't finished

* * *

Amongst my female friends, there is one girl who can apparently see ghosts.

I first met her at a university party welcoming new students but her outward appearance showed nothing strange. I don't know whether she's just really perceptive or not, but her sixth sense is no joke.

When we got lost one time she suddenly stopped in the middle of the road and said, "There's a dead cat somewhere around here."

Just for fun, we decided to have a look for it, and behind a vending machine, we found the body of a dead cat that had been run over and hidden there.

"Since when were you able to see ghosts? What started it?" One day while we were at a coffee shop I half-jokingly asked her.

At first, she avoided the question, but perhaps because I was so insistent she finally broke and started talking.

"Don't regret asking," she began.

Her story:

When I was in the third grade of elementary school, Kokkuri-san was really popular. At the time, I couldn't see ghosts so I didn't believe in it.

But there was a group of kids in our class that were really into it.

The centre of that group was a girl who could sense the supernatural, and each time they played she said stuff like “Kokkuri-san was right!” and “It happened just like Kokkuri-san said it would.”

In all honesty, I didn’t like her very much. And so, I ended up getting into a fight with this self-proclaimed ghost visionary over it.

“She exists!” “She doesn’t exist!” It was a never-ending argument, but then she said, “I’ll show you,” and I went along with it. Well, I was kinda interested to see whether it really was true or not.

Four of us, myself and three members from her group, got together to play Kokkuri-san. We waited for school to finish and then headed for the roof. Apparently, it was the best ‘point’ in the entire school. I kept thinking it was stupid, but I helped them set up. We lined up some unused desks. Then, finally, we began.

While we called out over and over, “Kokkuri-san, Kokkuri-san, please come,” the 10 yen coin moved over to “Yes.”

Everyone got excited that Kokkuri-san had arrived. Seeing them like that, I thought they just looked stupid, so I joked, “Kokkuri-san, Kokkuri-san, please show us a ghost.”

The 10 yen coin moved to “Yes.”

Then everyone took off running.

Me: “… That was it?”

That was a letdown. Like those scenes where someone loudly bangs on the door and everyone jumps, but in the end, it's only a surprise. It's totally different to fear. The story itself felt incomplete.

Me: "Is there more to that story? That can't be all. The ending was weak."

I told her honestly. We didn't usually hold things back from each other.

Her: "Even though I went to all the trouble of telling you that story you give such harsh words. Asshole…"

Even as she said it she was grinning. It looked like that wasn't all after all.

Her: "I went back there the next day and the Kokkuri-san set was gone. I guess a teacher found it and cleaned it up. But according to the rules of Kokkuri-san, the people who called her have to finish by passing the coin over the shrine gate, right? We didn't do that. So, the game hadn't finished."

I got chills. 10 years later, Kokkuri-san was still going. Where did the kids go that called her?

Me: "So why didn't you all get together to play Kokkuri-san again? Then you could all go back and everything would be fine."

"There's no way," she said. Then…

Her: "You see, other than me everyone else is already dead."

There was nothing I could say. She went on, ignoring how I'd been stopped in my tracks.

Her: "Some of them died in accidents, others suicide. They were all different. In the end, only me, the first one to take my finger off the coin is still here. Well, anyway, it's time for me to go. You made me tell an awful story, so this is your treat, hey? See ya."

I couldn't say anything. Because of her, it was likely that her classmates died. I pestered her to tell a story she didn't want to remember. I felt awful. I needed to apologise.

I looked up and our gazes locked. She stopped gathering her things and was looking at me.

Her: "I told you not to, but it looks like you regret it now, huh?"

I nodded. Before I could say I was sorry she continued.

Her: "Okay, well while you're sorry, another thing. Up until elementary school, I had droopy eyes."

She pointed to her own eyes and laughed. While I was sitting there dumbfounded, she cheerfully went "Well then, later!" and left the shop.

Kokkuri-san had been continuing for 10 years.

Her eyes were slanted upwards.

Translator's note: Kokkuri-san herself is an animal spirit, a mixture of a kitsune, dog, and tanuki. The punchline at the end of this story is that the girl who can see ghosts was born with droopy eyes. However, when the protagonist looks at her, he realises that she has slanted eyes. This is a particular characteristic of the kitsune; she's been possessed by Kokkuri-san since the game 10 years earlier.

Our elementary school Kokkuri-san experience

* * *

I wouldn't say I experienced this as much as I was forced to experience it. Apparently, I'm very easy for ghosts to attach themselves to. Those who can see ghosts often look at me and go, "You've done well to come this far, huh?" It's commonplace for there to be four or five people, but sometimes there are also apparently things attached to me that may or may not be ghosts. Anyway, to get to the point of the story, it seems that if you play Kokkuri-san with me, you'll be cursed.

In elementary school, Kokkuri-san was very popular. "Hey, you play too!" I was told, and after school, three boys and three girls got together to play. Just like we do at lunchtime, we put four desks together and in the middle, we put a piece of paper and a 10 yen coin.

"Kokkuri-san, Kokkuri-san, please come."

Something like that, we said the lines you were supposed to say to call her. After waiting 10 or 20 seconds we asked, "Kokkuri-san, Kokkuri-san, are you there?"

The 10 yen coined moved to "Yes."

"No way!!!!" "She really came!!!" I freaked out but everyone else was acting strange. Nobody said a single word or moved a muscle.

'That's strange,' I thought and turned to the girl sitting beside me. All the colour had drained from her face. Her teeth were chattering and drool trickled down as she trembled.

'Oh, this is bad,' I thought, but when I turned to the guy sitting on the other side he was exactly the same. I looked around; everyone except for me was acting strange. They were all staring right at me, trembling. If it kept on like this, I thought something bad would happen, so I screamed out, "Kokkuri-san! Kokkuri-san! Please go home!"

Then the 10 yen coin moved to "No."

I kept saying it and it kept on "No."

Everyone continued to tremble, their teeth chattering. One girl wet herself and started foaming at the mouth. I didn't know what to do. I yelled, "Just go away already you idiot!!!" I kicked the desks into the air. The paper and 10 yen coin flew out the window.

The kids sitting around me fell off their chairs. I was worried, so I went to check on the girl closest to me when suddenly she screamed.

'Wait, what?' I thought. I figured she was scared and held out my hand, but she backed away from me. I don't know if she couldn't stand up out of fear or what, but it was like she crawled away with just her arms. Everyone else slowly moved away from me. I had to say something.

"Hey." The moment I said it…

"Aaaaaaaaaaaaaahhhhhhhhhhhhhhhh!!!!" they all screamed, running over the girl on the floor towards the door. They burst through it and escaped outside. The girl cried out to them in a hoarse voice, "Don't leave me!"

As I got close to her she wept, “Don’t come any closer.” There was nothing else I could do, so I went to get a teacher.

After that, it became a huge thing, and they called an ambulance for the girl. While waiting for it to come, I explained to the teacher that we were playing Kokkuri-san but he didn’t believe me. But not too long later the phone rang.

Apparently, it was the parents of one of the kids who played Kokkuri-san with me so he finally believed me.

All of our parents were called to the school. 10 or 20 minutes later they arrived and everyone hid behind their parents’ backs, shaking.

I asked, “Are you okay?” but they were all terrified. After everyone calmed down a bit they explained. They all said I was the problem. When we started playing Kokkuri-san, apparently some type of mist started coming out of my arms. The moment they saw it, they were paralysed and couldn’t move.

Then more and more kept coming, covering the desks. It started to move from everyone’s fingers on the 10 yen coin and up their arms. They tried to let go of the coin but couldn’t move. The mist felt warm, and it was like it was sucking the power out of their arms. Right as it was getting close to their faces I kicked the desks flying and they could move again. The mist that had been attached to their arms slowly peeled away and came back to me. Well, of course everyone was shocked.

In the end, they didn’t believe us. They thought we were just scared and making things up and left it at that. But just in case Kokkuri-san was banned from school after that. I never spoke to any of those kids after that ever again.

This is a story about being cursed, but aside from me everyone who was touching that 10 yen coin ended up injuring their arms. They broke their arm, they strained it. In the worst case, someone lost a finger. I'm not entirely sure but if I truly was the cause of it, then I really did something terrible.

When we tried Kokkuri-san again at junior high school

* * *

This happened at junior high.

Like everywhere else, there was a period where everyone was fascinated with the occult. Whenever we were free, we'd tell scary stories. I'd also tell scary stories with the guy sitting next to me. Let's call him A-ta.

Before long, we went from scary stories to promising to play Kokkuri-san together. Of course, I was strongly opposed to the idea. If something strange happened again, I'd be in trouble and I didn't want to take responsibility for it.

Then A-ta teased, "You're just scared."

Thinking back on it now I should have just told him in all seriousness "Yes, I am." But of course I was full of pride like an idiot and I went ahead and told him, "Let's do it."

We decided to meet in the classroom after school the next day. I thought at first it would just be the two of us, but A-ta went and invited another male friend and two females to join us.

As everyone quietly went about setting up, I couldn't help but think that something was going to happen again and I got scared. I decided I wouldn't do it anymore. Again they made fun of me, but I was terrified, so I kept telling them I wouldn't do it. Reluctantly they decided to go on without me. I was worried, so I went to the back of the classroom and decided to watch them from there.

They pushed four desks together and sat facing each other like a cross and began playing Kokkuri-san. A-ta was sitting facing me, but he looked strange. With his eyes wide open he kept staring at me. That was the first time I saw a person's face turn pale right before me.

Like that other time A-ta's teeth starting chattering, and he began to tremble. Everyone around him also noticed and began to worry. When I looked carefully, I noticed his gaze had shifted to my feet. Was there something coming out there?

I told everyone to take A-ta and leave without looking at me, just in case. As I did, they turned to look in my direction, so I quickly wrapped myself behind the curtain next to me.

"Hurry up and get him out of here!" I yelled.

They still didn't seem to understand what was going on, but I heard the door open and the sound of footsteps running away so I got out from behind the curtain.

Everyone was gone, only the desks remained. Just like the first time, I kicked the desks and sent them flying. Just in case, I trampled on the paper and 10 yen coin over and over again. After about 10 minutes everyone came back. They all seemed fine, only A-ta looked terribly frightened. They asked him lots of questions, but he just lied and said he had no idea so in the end they all just went home.

A-ta and I decided to go back home together. A-ta really didn't want to, but I told him I'd tell him a secret, so he reluctantly agreed. I told him about the first time I played Kokkuri-san and the terrible things that happened. When I got to the part about the mist coming out, A-ta was like, "No, that's not right. What I saw was like a black *oni*. It came out of you and started crawling towards me."

'What the hell is he saying?' I thought, but he was insistent about it.

"You really need to go see a priest and be purified," he said.

In the end, without really getting anywhere we went our separate ways home. A few days later, however, A-ta was in a traffic accident. Luckily he only sprained his ankle. This time only one person ended up getting hurt so there wasn't a big fuss. A-ta also started to keep his distance from me.

Kokkuri-san

* * *

This story took place when I was a first-grade junior high student.

Kokkuri-san was really popular in our class at the time. In our class there was a group of kids who were a little odd, they said they could see ghosts, who started playing Kokkuri-san. Then, like an explosion, it spread to the rest of the class and everyone started playing it.

I, too, starting playing Kokkuri-san with a group of my close friends. It was so much fun. We asked silly questions, questions about the opposite sex and other pointless things. We had a great time. But the longer you play something, the more boring it becomes. So we decided to play a game within Kokkuri-san.

We started a type of roleplaying game within it. We formed parties called *Genbu* (black tortoise), *Suzaku* (vermilion bird), *Seiryu* (azure dragon) and *Byakko* (white tiger). It was so much fun. To formidable enemies, we'd send thoughts telepathically through the 10 yen coin, and when you levelled up, it felt like you really did level up in real life, too.

Kokkuri-san started to take over everything. When the teacher was away and we had a self-study period, of course, we played Kokkuri-san. Thinking about it now, our class probably looked a little strange with people playing Kokkuri-san all over the place.

Before long, the group that had first started playing Kokkuri-san came out and said, “There’s someone in here that’s cursed,” and they started talking about finding the cursed person. Of course, that cursed person was me.

“You might as well give up, you can’t do anything against us!” Several of my classmates said as they chased me out.

“Hey, hey, quit playing around!” The moment I said it, it happened. Suddenly lightning hit one of the trees outside and it fell. *Baribaribari.* After a few moments of silence, it started pouring down rain.

A few girls screamed. The class fell into a strange silence. Only a few small voices could be heard whispering about how dangerous it was. All at once everyone stopped playing Kokkuri-san. After that no-one wanted to play it ever again.

The turmoil over Kokkuri-san ended there, but of course, for me, it continued. From that day forth it felt like my body was so heavy, like I was constantly under water. Riding my bike felt like I was being pulled by someone behind me.

I managed to get home and open the door, but the moment I did, the clock facing the entrance and some animal horns decoration fell to the floor, *gataan*, in perfect sync like it had been arranged beforehand.

I didn’t want to acknowledge it might be the work of a ghost, so I just went to my room like, “Eh, these things happen.”

The moment I opened the sliding doors to my room the chest of drawers fell over. *Batan!* By now

I was really scared. I didn't know if I should talk to someone about it or not and didn't know who to talk to even if I did want to. With nothing else to do, I started watching TV. It also started going up and down in volume of its own free will, but I just decided that it was broken.

A week passed without going to get myself purified. But during that time these poltergeist-type happenings continued. The biggest thing was things falling over. The TV and stereo were also constantly turning themselves on and off.

My body also felt strangely heavy and it was mentally wearing me down. It was no better at school either. The place where I loved to go and hang out with my friends became difficult to go to and I spent all my time with my face down on my desk.

A few days later it was really starting to get to me, both physically and mentally. Just when I started to think that I'd have to go and tell my parents about everything that had happened, it was like I was suddenly freed of my demons. My body felt lighter; the sensation that until now I'd been floating in the middle of mud was gone.

After that, I felt great, and everything went back to normal. But I really wanted to know why I'd suddenly gotten better. At some point, I went to talk to my closest friend. We had often played Kokkuri-san together and until then had an unspoken understanding not to talk about it.

On our way home from school one day I mentioned how I suddenly felt the heaviness in my body disappear. He said that right about the time I felt freed, he had gone to a shrine to perform some purification rituals and had also done the same for me. I've never been more thankful to my friend in my entire life. Really.

Shrine, sacred tree, kitsune

* * *

About 10 years ago I lived in a place that was so countryside we were surrounded by nothing but mountains.

Near the top of the mountain, we had a small rice field. We weren't farmers or anything; it was just a tiny field that made enough to feed ourselves.

It was located in a basin, however, when you entered the side road it led to the middle of the forest and also a mountain trail (or perhaps an animal trail).

Of course, there were no convenience stores, and as for playgrounds, there was only the temple grounds and forest? woods? near the shrine.

At the time I believed in ghosts and other such unscientific things but I'd never once seen or felt any. I had zero ghost sense, so to speak.

There was a graveyard not even a hundred metres from our house. When I was younger, my little brothers and I used to play there like it was a playground, playing hide and seek and so on. I thought the people there had already passed on to heaven so it's not like they would appear or anything.

So we often went to play at the shrine as well. While my brothers and I were returning from elementary school one day we went to play in the forest nearby and that's when it happened.

There was an animal trail we followed that you could barely even call a path. There were a lot of sacred trees however so we used those as landmarks as we walked.

My two younger brothers and I played tag and hide and seek, and when it was my turn to be *oni* for hide and seek I slowly counted to 10. As I did all the sounds I'd heard up until then, the wind through the leaves, the cries of birds and voices of insects all suddenly stopped, just like that.

'Something's strange,' I thought and called out my brothers' names so I could find them.

It was hide and seek so even if I called out their names it's not like they would answer. With the strange silence, I became more and more worried.

I went and searched all the places my brothers would usually hide and despite the fact I could usually find them easily they were nowhere to be found. Up until that point, there had never been a time where any of us hadn't found each other.

At last, I gave up and yelled, "I don't know where you are! Give me a hint!"

Whenever we couldn't find each other we would clap to give a hint as to our general whereabouts. It was kind of a sign amongst us siblings. However, there was still no response.

I thought my little brothers were having some fun at my expense and it was already evening so I yelled out, "If you don't come out now I'm going home!"

My brothers were very close to me so it was unthinkable that they would let me go home without them. I thought it might get them to come out but again there was nothing but silence.

Did the two of them go back home without me, perhaps?

Under normal circumstances, they would never go home without me, but in the strange silence where I couldn't hear anything but the sounds I made myself I became worried and started to think they might have. Well then I'll just go home too, I thought and started walking back.

I soon became aware however that something wasn't right. I mentioned there were sacred trees that we used as landmarks, right? No matter how much I walked the same sacred trees kept appearing in front of me.

'Am I walking in circles?!' I thought. I picked up a rock and started marking all the trees that weren't sacred as I walked but once again I kept seeing the same trees… moreover the marks I carved into the trees had disappeared.

Quite a bit of time had passed and it wouldn't be strange for it to be dark but dusk seemed to go on forever.

I got scared. Thinking it would be safe near the sacred trees I spent a fairly long time just standing and sitting at the base of them.

I still couldn't hear any noise other than that I made myself and there wasn't a single bug to be found. Not even a single ant.

I was so scared I started crying when something suddenly dropped on the opposite side of the sacred tree I was sitting under. I was so surprised at this sudden sound that wasn't myself, I remember making a small choking sound.

The sacred tree was so big that it would take three adults spreading their arms around it to reach each other, so even as I turned around I couldn't see anything.

I nervously moved around to the other side of the tree. A yellowish, whitish, cream-coloured? kitsune was there, staring right at me.

I've seen plenty of wild foxes before, but this kitsune was a little larger than most.

I was still only little myself so I was afraid of meeting wild animals in the forest with fangs. While looking it in the eyes I slowly backed away.

We lived in an area where bears often appeared so both from home and school I'd been taught to look the animal in the eyes as you put some distance between yourself and it. You couldn't show it your back as you ran away. Even though I was only a young kid at the time, I think I did really well, well enough that if I could I would praise my younger self on a job well done.

However, the kitsune never showed any signs that it would attack. It began walking around the sacred tree with light feet.

I didn't know what was happening, so I just watched it, and after it circled a few more times it stopped and began walking down the animal path I'd followed.

Relieved, the kitsune walked until a certain distance away and then stopped to look back at me. Its tail wagged slowly as it looked at me.

It was exactly the same thing my pet dog would do when it wanted me to follow so I drew closer to it.

As I got closer it began walking again, and as it did, it would look back at me.

It was as though it was telling me to follow it. Even though I had lost my bearings as I followed the kitsune we once again closed in on the sacred trees and everything around me suddenly got dark.

I was surprised but then I noticed we were on the shrine grounds and was relieved. At the same time, my brothers had apparently gone to let our mother know I was missing when I heard, “OO-kun!! (my name)” and she hugged me. I knew she’d been searching for me and she was so scared she refused to let me go so I cried like a baby.

The kitsune I’d followed suddenly disappeared without me even noticing.

The next morning I heard from the shrine priest’s son (my friend) that five foxes were found dead with their necks ripped open around one of the sacred trees.

I wondered if perhaps I’d been bewitched by those five foxes and that kitsune had saved me from them.

Just last week I returned home for spring holidays and in the woods near our house, I saw a kitsune that looked exactly like the one from that time. I remembered what happened and felt like I needed to tell someone about it.

At the time I only intended to tell my mother about it but I wasn’t very good at expressing myself so she didn’t really understand me.

However, the events remain clear in my memory so I thought I’d take the chance to write them down now. I wanted to leave behind what happened to me somewhere for my own satisfaction.

Sorry for using up quite a bit of space. To everyone who read my story, thank you very much.

Hide and seek started out fun after school

* * *

This happened when I was in the second grade of high school.

I wasn't in any school clubs at the time, so after school, I'd always hang out with five of my good friends. That day it was raining, so the students who didn't have club activities left school quickly, but we were having a good time so we decided to play hide and seek in the school.

I-kun lost *janken* (rock, scissors, paper) and became the *oni*, so everyone went their separate ways and hid throughout the school. I'm a coward and didn't want to hide alone in some dark place in the school, so I figured I'd go look for my friend A-chan and hide together with her. I pulled out my phone and asked her where she was.

"I'm hiding in 2-C."

I quickly went to 2-C and in the corner of the pitch black classroom, A-chan was hiding. It was also dark outside and we couldn't see each other very well. We whispered to each other while we hid.

Me: "Hide and seek is fun."

A: "Yeah."

Me: "But it's a little scary."

A: "Yeah."

Me: "… Like a ghost might appear or something."

A: "(whispered something I couldn't hear)"

Although it was dark and I couldn't see very well, A-chan was silent after that and kept looking in my direction. Then the door suddenly burst open and I-kun entered the room.

I: "Ah, found two of you! Who is it?"

A: "No way~ Two people hiding in a dark classroom together is scandalous~" (laughs)

… ???

For a moment I had no idea what was going on. A-chan, who was supposed to be hiding right beside me, was standing behind I-kun. I trembled, my heart beating with amazing speed.

A: "I'm gonna turn the lights on okay~"

The classroom lit up in an instant. When I looked sideways, there was nobody there. I was relieved when suddenly I heard from right behind me.

"I'm right here."

I was so scared I flew out of the classroom. I told the other four what happened. Turned out that when I called A-chan, she'd already been found. The sound of my phone call was all broken up and my voice fuzzy.

However, over the top of my voice, she heard a clear voice.

"Let me play too."

It was the scariest experience of my life.

When we played hide and seek in the forest

* * *

This is a story from when I was in the fourth grade of elementary school.

It was our day off, so I went to the forest with five or six of my friends and we decided to play hide and seek. We met up at school and decided to head out after eating lunch. After we finished eating one of my friends was like, "Should we go now?" so we all headed towards the forest.

We walked for around 30 minutes and then reached our destination. We immediately played *janken* (rock, scissors, paper) and decided the *oni*. From here on out, I'll refer to the *oni* as S, and my other friends as A, F, T and M.

S started counting to 30 so everyone quickly ran to hide. I decided to hide about five metres away from A, F, and T. For some reason M tried to blend in with the trees (laughs).

Before we knew it, it was night-time and the dim forest was kinda creepy. M was the first person found. A, F, T and I saw it and laughed about how quickly he'd been found, despite trying to become one with the trees.

A little after that, we told S to start counting again. Then,

S: "Are you ready?"

Me: "Not yet!"

I said and laughed.

One more time S called out, "Are you ready?"

From somewhere nearby I heard a girl's voice, "Okay!"

"Hmm?" I thought but figured it was just my imagination so I didn't think much of it.

S: "Are you ready?"

Me: "Okay!"

As soon as I said this suddenly a girl wearing red clothes with a red hood appeared right before me. Her face was all messed up, and she had no teeth. She grinned at me.

"Hey, I found you."

.

.

.

When I came to, I was in S's house. When I asked everyone about the girl, they said they saw her as well. A small girl was crawling on all fours towards you, they said. When I heard this, it was the first time in my life I got chills.

After school hide and seek

* * *

This story happened to my father when he was an elementary school student.

After school, my father and five of his friends were playing hide and seek like they always did. If they didn't go home quickly, they'd get in trouble with the teachers so they would make sure to only play one game a day that would finish within a few minutes.

That day my father lost at *janken* (rock, scissors, paper) so he crouched down at the back of the classroom, covered his face with his hands and counted to thirty.

"… 29, 30! Are you ready?"

"Not yet!"

The reply came so my father started counting again.

"… 48, 49, 50! Are you ready?"

"Not yet!"

This time the reply came from further away, so he started counting a little quicker.

"58, 59, 60! Are you ready?!"

"I'm ready."

For some reason, he heard a voice directly above his head. Of course, there was nowhere to hide above him, but more than that it was not the voice of any of his friends. There's no way someone would give away their hiding place on purpose. Usually whenever you called out and there was no answer, then you would go searching.

My father froze. He didn't know how much time passed, but then he heard footsteps running towards him from the hallway.

"Come on, what the heck are you doing!?"

"We got found by the teacher first, ahhh."

"Ahhh."

"Hey, are you listening?"

"OO?" (My father's name)

At that moment my father started bawling, so they couldn't let go of him. He cried not because of fear but because he was relieved that his friends finally came for him. The teacher was shocked, as my father usually never cried, so that day he took him home himself.

A few days later my father told his friends about what happened, and until they graduated there wasn't a single person who brought up playing hide and seek again.

Of course, there wasn't anyone hiding in the classroom at that particular time. So, who was it?

No, rather than who was hiding…

Even though he grew up and has a child of his own now, my father still believes that hide and seek is a forbidden game.

Mizunome-sama

* * *

21: When I was in elementary school, there was a really popular game similar to Kokkuri-san. It was called Mizunome-sama, and it was just a little different to the regular Kokkuri-san.

As for how it was played, first, you had to go to a certain drinking fountain on the school grounds and stand in front of the third tap. This was important. Then close your eyes and say the spell.

Mizunome-sama, Mizunome-sama
Please, please
Show yourself, show yourself
Before me, before me
Please appear, please appear

After reciting those words you touch your left heel, and then your right heel. Everyone said the spell a little differently, but what they all had in common was the word 'Mizunome-sama' and repeating things twice. Then with your eyes closed you drink the water. The moment you open your eyes your body feels light.

Even though your feet are planted firmly on the ground it's like the entire world is floating. It's probably difficult to understand what I'm saying. Even though you should be standing in front of the water fountain, it's like:

(’・w・ `)<!
| |
((’・w・ ` ))~~~susususu~~~(’・w・ `)<!
| |
(’・w・ `)<!

You sway in all directions and suddenly *suuuuuuuuu*~~~ even though you’re not walking it’s like your body is moving freely of its own accord. It’s probably a little similar to how you feel if you spin around when you’re drunk.

But, including the first time I tried it, I’ve only successfully done it twice. After that, no matter how many times I tried, I couldn’t do it again. But as Mizunome-sama became more popular, the water fountain got busy, so it also became more difficult to try it. Having said that, a lot of kids who played Mizunome-sama ended up going crazy so the school banned it. For a while we could no longer use the water fountain and then once a new one was put in we couldn’t play it anymore.

24: >>21 In the spell it says “Please show yourself” but even if you succeed you just feel strange and you don’t see her? Sorry, just wanted to point that out, haha.

Perhaps if you saw her you went mad or felt like you were spinning around?

25: >>24 I thought the same thing at the time but that was the spell. There were other ones like

"Mizunome-sama drink the water" and "Mizunome-sama please show me the way."

To add a little something to the end of that story, myself and some of my friends who fell into that strange feeling went on to be able to see will-o-wisps and black shadows and like hallucinations and such.

But as for any kids who actually saw Mizunome-sama (I don't even really know what Mizunome-sama was in the first place), there weren't any…

But this spell suddenly became popular during the fourth grade, we don't know who spread it though. Plus the kids who went crazy, well we didn't know who they were and no-one saw them at the spot, so perhaps there was another reason for it. At the time we just thought "it is what it is" but now that I think about it, it's really scary.

Translator's note: *Mizunome* translates literally as "drink the water." The -*sama* suffix is added to the names of customers, royalty, gods etc as a sign of reverence. So here they're basically talking about a "drink the water" spirit.

The mysterious Ken and the secret on the second floor

* * *

1: I'm gonna write now, okay. My details (at the time):

175cm 62kg
A regular face
Hobbies: Shogi, aquariums
Never had a girlfriend, only a few friends

Okay, let me write this down.

At the time I was a first-grade university student and living alone so I didn't have much money (my allowance from home was also quite small).

I worked part-time jobs at family restaurants and convenience stores, but I noticed that home teachers got paid a lot better. But registering to be a home teacher on the web is a bit of a hassle, isn't it? So, I got permission from the neighbourhood and started handing out flyers.

I'm pretty sure I had on there that I could teach junior high school students English and Japanese, one hour was 3000 yen, and it had my contact details.

Then a few days later I got a phone call. It sounded like a middle-aged lady.

"I saw your flyer~ Would you be able to come over?" she said.

When I asked her about it she said she was looking for someone to teach her son. She wanted me to come every day and teach him for four hours. I was like, are you for real? That's 12 000 yen a day, awesome! I should have thought it was a little strange she wanted me to be there for four hours a day every day.

6: I get it, they kidnap and kill you on the day, and then demand a ransom. I saw that yesterday.

9: >>6 I saw that too and thought I should start a thread! Because this story happened about four years ago…

11: >>9 Really? Being a home teacher really is a scary job, huh…

8: She wanted me to come the very next day, so the next day I went over. It was in the evening (from about 5 p.m. I think) for four hours, so I ate dinner early and went over. When I arrived at the address, a tiny old house was sitting there. It was also *that* time of day, so it gave off a bit of a creepy atmosphere. Well, it's work… I thought, so I timidly rang the doorbell.

When I did, I heard the voice of that same middle-aged lady from the phone and felt a bit relieved. When the door opened and I saw her, I was at a loss for words.

Her head was full of dandruff. She had dark bags around her eyes. Her grin was horrifying.

Instantly I wanted to go back home, but in the end, money won out.

Old lady: “Please, come in.” (grin)

“Thank you,” I said and stepped inside. I think my voice was shaking.

I asked her where her son was and she was like, this way, and led me into a further room.

To be honest, I was absolutely terrified. I dunno how to explain exactly but the atmosphere the house gave off was really scary.

Reluctantly, I followed her further inside and we ended up in what looked like a child’s room. There was a chest of drawers, a TV, a bed, stuffed toys, toy robots, a study desk… There looked to be a child sitting at the study desk in the back, but when I walked over to it I suddenly realised.

“Hello!” I said as I approached, but upon closer inspection… it was a doll… Not just any doll, it appeared to be handmade. It was about the size of a real child and was even wearing regular clothes. Its face was awful. There were just three dots made of cloth. In *Mario* there are these characters called shy guys, right? It looked just like those.

Old lady: “That’s my son.” (grin)

I turned white. This place was dangerous. Really dangerous.

“Uh… that’s a doll… right?” I accidentally spit out.

That was the wrong thing to say.

Old lady: “Huuuuuhhhhh?!?!?!?! What are you saying?!!! That’s my son!!! Ken-kun!!!!” she suddenly screamed out in a loud voice and began to cry.

This was really bad. She's probably gonna kill me. I don't want to die. I need to end this peacefully somehow and get back home.

"Oh yeah, I know! I know!" I said.

"Ken-kun, let's study!!" When I said this, the old lady started to smile again and returned to normal.

Of course, Ken-kun didn't answer. Why would he? He was a doll after all. Rather than calling it study, I just turned towards the doll and began talking to it. Having to do this for another four hours would be hell. Even taking a break for ten minutes was still painful.

"The be-verb is here, so it becomes this~ This is the conjunctive form, so it's 'u' okay~" I went on like this alone for four hours. The old lady watched from behind the whole time grinning. It was really creepy.

15: That's terrifying.

16: Somehow I managed to pass the four hours.

"Okay, well let's finish it there~" I said to Ken-kun.

There was no reply. Of course not. It was a doll.

Old lady: "Well done~ Thank you very much~" (grin)

While thinking about how creepy her grinning face was, I got ready to go home.

Old lady: "It's already late, so why don't you stay and eat first?" (grin)

No, I ate before I came so I'm alright, I told her. Besides, any food that came out of this creepy house was bound to be awful.

Old lady: "Please eat!!!!!"

She screamed again. It was so scary. She was mad. But I thought she would kill me so I reluctantly accepted. She took me to what looked like the dining room and I sat down in a chair.

She took out a knife and started preparing dinner. When she took out the knife, my heart began to race. I broke out in a cold sweat. She took out a dirty old pan and began to boil something. It smelled like curry.

Ah, curry. I'm glad it's something normal, I thought from the bottom of my heart.

Old lady: "Okay, here you are." (grin)

She put curry onto a dirty plate for me. The spoon was also the type you get free from the convenience store that she was using again.

"Thank you," I said and timidly began to eat. It was just regular curry. Not awful, not great…

Old lady: "Tastes good, I hope?" (grin)

"Yes! It's great!" I said in a really loud voice. I was so scared I may have replied a little too enthusiastically.

Old lady: "I'm glad. Why don't you stay the night?" (grin)

I had no idea what was going on anymore.

17: Why couldn't you refuse the food?

20: >>17 Because I was so scared.

"No, really, that's okay," I answered.

Old lady: “Ken-kun would be so happy~ Please, stay.” (grin)

“No, it’s okay,” I said again.

Old lady: “Please stay!!! You’ll make Ken-kun sad!!!!”

I was scared. But staying overnight in this house was even scarier. The thought of being killed was even scarier than that. I had no choice. I decided to stay. I’d pretend that I was staying and when the opportunity presented itself, I’d run.

It was decided I’d stay with Ken-kun in his room. Having to sleep in the same room as this creepy doll was most unpleasant. She put out a futon for me in his room.

Old lady: “Isn’t it great~? You get to sleep with your teacher tonight~” (grin)

I was so scared.

18: I don’t get it.

21: Isn’t that confinement…?

23: Old lady: “The toilet is next to the dining room, so don’t go upstairs okay.” (grin)

First, I’d wait for the old lady to go to sleep, so I waited patiently in Ken-kun’s room. I lamented that I’d forgotten my phone. If I had that I could call for help. She’ll fall asleep once it gets late, so I waited some more. That was around 10:30 p.m. I had nothing to do, so I just lay there in the futon.

Before I realised it, it was 1 a.m. Looked like I’d fallen asleep. ‘The old lady has to be asleep by now,' I thought, so I got ready to make my escape. I grabbed my bag and began to tiptoe to the door.

One step… another step… Only my heartbeat made any sound.

"What are you doing?"

Uh oh… that's it, I thought. I'm dead.

When I looked over the old lady was sitting behind the dining room door, grinning at me. No way… she's been sitting there watching me all this time…? All the blood drained from my body.

Old lady: "You weren't trying to go home now, were you?" (grin)

I panicked.

"Uwaaaaaaaaaaa!!!" I screamed and ran towards the back of the house. There was no window a person could escape from in Ken-kun's room. I ran up the stairs as fast as I could.

Dotadotadotadota!! I saw a door in front of me. I opened it. It was pitch black. I looked for the light switch and turned the lights on. Everything in the room lit up.

The room was full of nothing but stuffed toys and dolls. It was terrifying!! I was brought to a standstill when suddenly,

"Kyakyakyakyakyakya!!!" I could hear a voice screaming from the back of the room. I looked over and saw something that looked like a person with a really huge head and eyes that looked like they were gonna pop out.

Our eyes met.

"Hyahyahyahyahya!!!!"

It was terrifying. I wet myself. It was disgusting. In a panic, I opened the second-floor window and jumped out. I didn't feel any pain. My fear won out over that.

I ran all the way home. That night I couldn't sleep, and my foot was in so much pain that the next day I went to the hospital and found out I'd broken my left ankle.

Afterwards, I moved away and didn't go there again. I didn't want to go there again. I wonder what it was I saw in that room?

The end.

28: Perhaps it was a disabled person locked up?

32: >>28 I thought it might have been the real Ken-kun. Maybe he was a handicapped kid, and the doll was her way of escaping reality…

29: Wow, that's terrifying, haha.

30: So scary.

33: When I said I moved, I meant I moved away from that town entirely. If you have any questions, I'm happy to answer them.

34: Do you remember where that house is?

37: >>34 Kind of. I forgot the exact address though.

35: In the end did you get the money?

38: >>35 Nope. Returning home safely was more than enough.

36: Was it hydrocephalus ?

41: >>36 Maybe, his head was really, really big. Like it was gonna explode.

39: I'm sure it was really scary, but no doubt it was Ken-kun locked away on the second floor. Was he really there in the dark all that time? He was probably happy to see another person after so long.

42: >>39 The more I think about it the scarier it gets…

44: >>42 I was just kidding. That's the first time in a while I've been so scared. Thanks.

40: I've foooound you~

42: >>40 Quit it…

43: What prefecture was this?

45: >>43 Kanto region.

47: Was it Chiba?

48: >>47 Do you live in Chiba? Never fear! It wasn't Chiba.

51: What an interesting story. Anyway, did you change your phone number?

52: >>51 I blocked her number and changed mine soon after!

55: This isn't something you should read on the street at night. I decided I'm not gonna walk and read my phone anymore.

56: Are there no more questions? Well, I'm gonna go to bed now, if you're gonna be a home teacher make sure you're really careful. See ya.

58: Been a long time since a scary story gave me goosebumps.

22: Man that's scary. But the fact you could make this thread means that you're still alive. I'm relieved.

Do you believe in doll's curses?

* * *

Everyone, do you believe in dolls curses? I didn't until that time…

This happened when I was in the fifth grade. It was the summer holidays and rather than going outside I was just reading manga in my room. Midday was nice and warm so drowsiness snuck up on me and I fell asleep. I'm a dreamer so as usual, I had a dream. Even though it was a dream, I remember everything that happened exactly.

In the dream, I was standing at the top of the stairs on the second floor. In my hand, I was holding a Korean doll with a rattling neck. Suddenly I threw it from the second-floor window and it broke. When I saw the doll I shuddered. The doll I'd thrown was the one my parents had bought me when I was in third grade. I'd broken that doll's head by smashing it in with a rock. My parents ended up throwing it away.

Suddenly the dream changed, and a woman covered in blood was looking at me. I was so scared I woke up, but when I did… I couldn't move my arms or legs and I couldn't scream either. I had sleep paralysis. I got more and more scared and with all my might I tried to move but couldn't.

Then suddenly, the doll I'd thrown from the second-floor window was coming up the stairs, step by step. *Rattle rattle.*

The reason I knew this was because it was a continuation of my dream. When the doll reached the second floor it slowly rattled towards my room. I could feel it getting closer. I was terrified and kept saying over and over in my head, “Don’t come, don’t come!” Suddenly I felt it disappear and I could move again.

I rushed downstairs to my family.

They say a doll maker puts part of their soul into each doll they make. I think the spirit of the doll I broke while playing with it turned into a grudge and attacked me in my dreams. Now whenever I see a doll, I shudder and think it’s going to attack me.

I don’t know when I’ll be attacked next. If you buy a doll, make sure you look after it very carefully.

Japanese doll with an interesting history

* * *

For some reason, lately I've been remembering this strange experience I had when I was a child.

Ever since I could remember until I was a junior high school student every Obon we went to visit my father's family home and would stay for two or three nights.

His family home was in the countryside of Yamanashi where they ran their own business separate from the family home.

We would sleep in another room, but in that room there was a glass rectangular case with a Japanese doll in it. It had short hair and wore a red kimono, and was about 50~80cm tall. As a child, it seemed really big to me.

Even though it hadn't been there before that this particular year it was just suddenly there. I remember looking at it and quickly telling my parents that I thought it was creepy

Its mouth was slightly open, and it had little teeth. Had they been there since the start? I couldn't tell whether it was laughing or angry, I don't really know how to describe its expression.

I think my parents were also creeped out by it but they never said anything.

The next day as I was lazing about by myself I felt this really strong gaze from behind me. When I turned around the doll was there. It was creepy, so I turned the glass case around 90 degrees so it faced sideways and went back to lazing about.

Not long later I fell asleep and had a dream. In the dream, I'd become an adult. With my adult legs and standpoint an endless, unbroken road stood before me. Either side of the road was just hills.

Even though there were no street lights or anything the road was lit up. People wearing tattered rags like farmers from the Edo Period were walking along it. Against my own will, my feet got tangled up, and I fell off the road into the dark hills.

I stopped in an area full of patchy grass and weeds. I couldn't move a muscle. I thought I was dead.

Suddenly I heard a Buddhist prayer. Someone on the road above was saying a prayer for me.

I was so happy. I didn't want to die alone. Just as I thought that my viewpoint changed to the person looking down on the dead body. It was a stranger. Their hair was thinning, mouth open, eyes upturned, they were most certainly dead.

Then I woke up.

I was covered in sweat. What a strange dream, I thought. When I rolled over the doll was looking right at me. It looked like it was smiling. The glass case was still in the same spot. I didn't want to touch it so I left it like that.

The next year the doll was in the guest house again. Its hair had grown.

Its hair reached its shoulders now. Apparently, it was normal for a doll's hair to grow, but to me, it was just creepy. I remember my parents being like, "Wow, its hair is growing~"

I asked my aunt about it. Just what is that doll? Her reply was:

"Ah, that. It hasn't done anything bad, has it?"

I stopped asking questions right there. I just said, "No, it's fine."

That night the entire family ate watermelon and set off fireworks. While we were playing with the fireworks another aunt (who lived by herself and only returned for Obon) idly said:

"A-san is behind you OO-chan (me), how nice of him to come."

My aunt and father's faces froze. "Well, it is Obon," my father said cheerfully and everyone laughed.

Afterwards, I learned that A-san was my great-grandfather. Apparently, during his time the family was very well off, but he was a prolific philanderer who spent little time with his own family, and unable to bear it anymore my great grandmother and her son, my grandfather, ran off in the night and broke off all ties with him.

After that my great grandfather went on to spend his money like water and in the end died alone. The person I saw in the photo that was supposedly A-san was the dead person I'd seen in my dream.

The next year the doll was gone. I couldn't feel its strange gaze anymore, and the fear began to fade, so once more I asked my aunt about it.

"Where did that doll go?"

"It did something bad, so we took it to the shrine."

I didn't find any of this strange.

"What did it do?"

"It was in a case, right? It would get out and walk about freely at night. Well, just that would be fine, really, but in the middle of the night it tripped up OO (my cousin) and badly hurt his ankle."

In short, when morning came they kept finding the doll in places other than its glass case. They kept putting it back but had no clue what was going on.

Despite the fact the glass case was locked, the lock was cleanly broken off. While they were wondering about what was going on, that's when my cousin accidentally saw it.

He was a high school student at the time. He woke up during the night and went to the toilet. He heard a small noise in the hallway. When he flushed the toilet and stepped outside, he suddenly felt a tug on his pants and fell forward.

When he went to look at what his pants were caught on he saw the doll's hand stretched out and holding onto the cuff of his pants.

According to my cousin, he even heard the doll laugh. It wasn't a girl's voice. It was deep, but like something between male and female.

Then he got so scared he passed out. My aunt woke up in the morning and found my cousin with the doll lying on his ankle and his leg in pain. That was just no good, so they took the doll to a shrine and left it there for safekeeping.

They should have done so sooner but the doll was important to my aunt so she felt bad about doing so.

I had another question. Where did she buy the doll? She said she didn't. It was a gift.

Where from? Her friend. That friend had passed away. Which is to say that until that friend died they had looked after the doll and it was their wish that she take it as a memento.

That friend made the kimono for the doll. Why? My aunt didn't know. But the doll originally wasn't her friend's, either. That friend also received it from somewhere else and was asked to make the kimono for it.

Who did they receive it from? Where was it sold? She didn't know anything else about it.

It was quite a scary story to the child I was at the time.

From our parents' chest of drawers

* * *

This is a story from when I was still just an elementary school student and my parents went out leaving me and my younger brother alone.

We were bored, so we decided to play hide and seek.

First, I was the *oni*, so I started looking for my brother. I went to my parents' room and starting digging through the clothes in their chest of drawers when suddenly something grabbed my hand. Thinking I'd found my brother, I grabbed and tried to pull him out.

"Hurry up and get out here," I said, but no matter how hard I pulled the hand he wouldn't come out.

The clothes were in the way so I couldn't see anything. He also wasn't saying anything, so I started to think it was a little strange. Then my brother appeared behind me.

"Big bro, what are you doing?"

I had no idea what was going on. I shook off the hand with all my might and ran out of the house as fast as I could.

It goes without saying that until my parents came home, I couldn't go back inside the house.

Just what the hell was that hand?

A thief? Or perhaps…

Voices playing hide and seek

* * *

Recently, some kids in the apartment complex next door have been playing hide and seek in the evenings. I often hear voices counting, and kids calling out,

"Are you ready?"

"Okay!"

I usually go to the toilet before I take a bath, and the day before yesterday I went to the toilet as usual. As I did, I heard this really small voice from outside the window,

"5, 6."

I figured I'd have a little fun, so in a small voice that they wouldn't be able to hear I went,

"7, 8, 9, 10… Are you ready?"

I didn't hear the girl's voice. Thinking she must have finished counting while I was speaking, I got up to leave the toilet when right next to my ear I heard,

"… I'm ready."

The hide and seek *oni* outside was probably a junior high school kid. The voice I heard was that of an even smaller child.

Of course, the smaller kids also played but around this time of evening, but at least one parent would be watching them, so it was highly unlikely that one of the smaller kids would be able to slip away and hide under my toilet window.

The ground underneath was also gravel, so I'd be able to hear them coming…

So, what was it then?

TRAVELLING

The mountain pass onibi

* * *

On the way from Tokyo to Yamanashi, there's a road called "Wada Pass."

It's a famous mountain pass on the internet with rumours about 'something appearing.' My friend's aunt had a strange experience there.

This aunt's husband liked to go fishing and often went here and there. The two of them were very friendly, so she often went along with him. They drove through Wada Pass several times.

"Wada Pass is kinda scary. Going from Tokyo to Yamanashi is okay, but the return leg is creepy. If the windows are open, I always close them. It feels like something might come inside."

On this particular day, they went to Yamanashi to go fishing and passed through Wada Pass late that night on their way home.

'Aahh, it's the pass soon,' she thought, and when she looked outside, she could see these blue lights shining in the trees.

'Are they fishermen?' she thought and turned her gaze away. But no matter how far the car drove the lights were always in front of them.

"?????????"

It was a bit creepy, so she said to her husband, "Darling, are those torch lights? They keep following us."

"I know," he said. "But those things aren't from humans."

She then noticed the number of lights were increasing. They were in front of and behind the car, like they were chasing it to surround it.

"Darling, go a bit faster."

The aunt was spooked and closed her eyes so she wouldn't have to see the blue lights. It felt like forever before they got over the pass, she just kept praying to herself, "Faster, faster."

Suddenly she felt the car going back downhill.

'We've passed it,' she thought and opened her eyes. Without a doubt, they'd entered the Tokyo side of the mountain pass and were descending.

Fearfully she looked around, but the lights were gone. She couldn't see anything in the darkness of the trees. Relieved, she noticed that she'd broken out in a cold sweat.

"It didn't look like that often talked about plasma or anything. It seemed like it was alive…" she said, unsure of what they really were.

The sky seemed strangely red

* * *

The other day my new car was delivered, so I decided to take it out for a spin and went to the nearby mountains. Even though they're nearby, I've never driven there before so I enjoyed the new road for a while.

Then the road started to get smaller, and on the side of the road I could see lots of little shrine gates (about 30cm high), and ropes tied around trees, and the sky started turning this strange colour of red.

I started talking to the person in the passenger seat, "Isn't it scary? Maybe we should go back, haha." "If you weren't here I'd be so scared," and so on.

I was driving alone. No-one else should have been in the car, but I was undoubtedly having a conversation with someone.

Then, no matter how much I drove the road just continued on and on and I was getting more and more scared. I didn't want whoever was next to me to notice that I was scared (I was probably embarrassed about it) so I acted like nothing was wrong and kept on driving.

Eventually, the road started to widen again, and I arrived back in the residential area. At the same time, the fog cleared from my mind and I realised how strange the whole situation was so I took a different road home.

Yesterday I drove through that same road during the daytime but without seeing any of the shrine gates or the long narrow road. I arrived in the residential area soon after.

I wonder if that was another dimension? Either way, I promised myself to never drive that road at night again.

I was desperately job hunting

* * *

This happened around this time last year when I was job hunting. I was on the train heading towards the city for the information session of a company there. I was standing near the door when I saw something like black gas floating between people.

At first, I was like, what the heck is that? But when I took a closer look, I could see it had something like a face. I felt it could be dangerous, so I did my best not to look at it. Its face kinda looked like a little more human-looking 'Ochonan-san' from the manga *Fuan no Tane*. Its eyes were rolled back, like they had no focus.

Of course, it appeared no-one else in the train car could see it. After it appeared my stomach started to feel queasy and it was cold. I couldn't put up with it any longer so I got off along the way, but as I was leaving, I briefly turned around and saw the black thing was at the next door, holding onto the back of another job hunter around the same age as me. While looking down from the top of his head its mouth was opening and closing like that of a carp.

Then, not too long after that, there was a suicide on that train line. Even now I make sure not to use that line anymore. I have no proof that the person who committed suicide was the same person, but in any case, that black thing was the real deal.

The hanged woman

* * *

Three years ago I went to Hiroshima with a few of my friends during our summer break from university. We didn't particularly have anything we wanted to do there or even decide how long we'd stay, it was just a lazy holiday.

There was no special reason why we chose Hiroshima. But after going we were bored after a single day, so that night at the business hotel we were staying in we discussed whether we should go home the next day or not.

In the end, we decided that we'd come all this way so we may as well stay a little longer. We rented a car (we went to Hiroshima by shinkansen) and decided to go for a drive.

So, the next day.

Well, we didn't have a destination in mind so we just drove around (the driver was my friend; I don't have a license), ate some terrible lunch, hung out by the river, it was really a rather pointless drive.

And then on the way home, we got lost. It was getting dark, there were no people around, and everything went to shit.

Everyone was in a bad mood and when it seemed like a fight was about to break out my friend suddenly screamed and slammed on the brakes. Surprised, I asked him what happened.

My friend said while shaking, “I looked in the rear-view mirror and saw a woman hanging by her neck in the back seat.”

The woman apparently had a rope around her neck (supposedly really tight) and that rope was attached to the hand-hold (is that what it’s called? The thing you hold above the window). She was hung while the car was driving, it seemed.

We panicked, so I don’t remember much after that but somehow we managed to make it back. It was a horrible memory.

Last year, I read in some book that the woman my friend had seen was really killed in an incident in Hiroshima. She wasn’t hung, she was choked to death. But the criminal wasn’t sure if she was dead, so just in case they tied a rope around her neck. While she was like that they drove around in the car.

Well, whether what my friend saw was really related to that, I don’t know (I didn’t see it after all).

That’s what happened. Sorry for so many words.

Tunnel story

* * *

My friend heard this story from the owner of a hairdressing salon, A-san. A-san had absolutely no ability to sense ghosts whatsoever, but she liked horror stories. She often listened to scary stories from her co-workers and customers, but one day she heard about a rumour of something that would appear in a nearby tunnel.

It was your standard, “If you go into the tunnel, turn off your lights and honk the horn~” story. She mostly didn’t believe it, but the tunnel was nearby so she figured she’d go check it out, anyway. But going alone would be scary, so she asked one of her older male friends who could sense ghosts to come along with her.

At first, he was like, “It’s no good to play around with these things for fun!” and refused her, but A-san said, “Well then I’ll just go by myself.” So he reluctantly agreed.

The tunnel was located in the mountains where even the locals wouldn’t go at night. At night-time, it was pitch black. A-san drove there while her friend sat in the passenger’s seat. If her friend felt it was actually dangerous, they’d just drive off immediately, it was sort of like a test of courage.

As they slowly drove along the pitch black road, the tunnel came into view. Before they entered the tunnel, her usually bright friend went suddenly silent. A-san repeatedly asked him, “Is everything okay?” He just replied, “Yeah, maybe.”

Despite getting scared she went into the tunnel and stopped about halfway as the rumour instructed. If it was true, when she turned the lights off here… the story would continue, but…

Friend: “Wait, don’t turn off the lights.”

There were no lights in this narrow tunnel in the middle of the mountains, so all they could rely on were the lights from the car.

Friend: “Exit the tunnel.”

A-san hurriedly stepped on the accelerator and the car took off.

But he didn’t mention if he could see anything chasing them, or if he heard any voices. So without going too fast, they exited the tunnel. But his expression was still harsh. On one side of the dark mountain road was the mountain range, on the other side a river. Her friend, who was silent even after exiting the tunnel, quickly said in a tense voice, “Hurry up and go faster!”

She floored it, and somehow they arrived in a residential area. Her friend said everything was okay now, so they pulled into the parking lot of a convenience store. A-san was terrified.

A: “What happened?”

Before they entered the tunnel there was apparently a man and a woman standing on either side of the entrance. A middle-aged man and woman. It appeared they were looking at the car, but it didn’t seem like they would do anything. Every now and then there were ghosts who just stood around, so her friend didn’t bother to warn her about it.

However, once they stopped the car inside the tunnel he could see the couple coming towards them. They were just walking, but they were heading towards the car. These sort of things are never good so, so he said, "Exit the tunnel."

It would have been nice if they'd just given up there, but then apparently the couple started chasing after them.

If they were bound to the tunnel, then when they exited they'd be able to escape, he thought, but they kept on chasing, and finally caught up to the car.

Friend: "Hurry up and go faster!"

While muttering about something, the couple were peering into the car from the driver's side window and the passenger's side window. A-san couldn't see anything, but apparently, she broke out in a cold sweat and couldn't stop trembling. As they picked up speed, they shook them off so her friend said it was okay now.

Friend: "If there's something in your car that you don't remember, rubbish or something, quickly throw it away. Don't open it."

It seemed the couple had died in an accident or a natural disaster. They were probably looking for their son or someone. Her friend said that they were probably around the same age as the couple's son.

After, well I can't say that A-san or her friend got sick and died or anything. A few days later it was as if nothing happened.

When it got light the next day and A-san went to take her car for a drive, she noticed there was a small vinyl bag attached to her back car door. She couldn't see what was in it very well, but there was something black or brown coloured inside. Without looking at what was in it, she quickly threw it away.

What would have happened if she did open it? Or if she'd followed the rumour exactly and waited inside the tunnel, what would have happened?

Territory

* * *

My ex-girlfriend has the ability to see ghosts and is the type of person who regularly sees them daily. Even when we were hanging out at her place, she would suddenly say things like:

GF: "My grandfather's watching us from the veranda upstairs~"

… Talking about her grandfather that passed away a year earlier, or while in restaurants:

GF: "Takashi… Do you see the old guy sitting in the chair just there?"

… She'd ask suddenly, but I couldn't see anything at all.

Me: "There's nothing there, haha. If you're trying to scare me it's useless."

Whatever she said, I'd just sidestep the issue. But this particular day I couldn't do anything but believe her.

One day we went for a drive around Osaka in her car. We went to Tennoji, talking about what we would eat that day when suddenly she stopped the car. We were behind the T Zoo. It was a dark alley without any shops.

… When I thought about it, I wondered why she drove into such a place.

Me: "Hmm? What's wrong? What happened?"

I asked but, she didn't reply. She just stared out the window and ignored me. Then, suddenly:

GF: "Over there."

She said, pointing to something ahead. A gate rose into the air in the darkness, and beside it, lots of gaudy banners waved. It was like the playhouse of a public theatre.

GF: "There's a girl standing over there. Can you see her?"

She said, pointing to the right side of the gate.

Me: "I... I don't see anything. Are you sure you aren't just imagining things?"

That was a lie. I couldn't see the exact shape, but I could definitely see something there. Some vague light. Because I was unable to see clearly, my girlfriend described it to me.

It was a woman, around 30 years old. She was wearing a blouse, standing by the edge of the gate. She seemed to exude an evil aura. I wanted to get out of there quickly. I went to tell my girlfriend as much. When I did, she suddenly looked frightened.

GF: "She's here... what should I do... this is bad..."

Me: "What's wrong?"

GF: "That woman, she's not there anymore... Now... she's sitting in the back seat..."

Without thinking, I went to turn around but suddenly:

GF: "Don't!! Whatever you do, don't turn around!!"

She furiously stopped me and I froze. She started to move the car forward slowly. At the same time, she opened all the car windows. Apparently, that would make it easier for the woman to leave. She continued up the road slowly. She didn't say a word.

I closed my eyes and waited for everything to pass. Somewhere, 50 cm behind me, something that didn't exist in this world was there. Just thinking about it made it difficult to breathe. Hurry up, hurry up and leave…

GF: "Kyaaaaaaaaaaaaaa!!!!!"

She screamed and slammed on the brakes. The impact brought me back to the present. Breathing raggedly, my girlfriend was face down on the steering wheel.

GF: "She's gone… she spun around the car and went out your window… but she's still behind us…"

I couldn't take it anymore. I looked in the side mirror. She was definitely there. Her cold, emotionless face. She floated there for a few seconds, then like the white noise on a TV she faded away into the darkness and was gone.

GF: "I think we entered her territory, so she came to chase us out… Wow, that was scary…"

A few days later she told me as such.

By the way, apparently there's a graveyard behind that theatre, but it scares me so much I've never been there again. Since I broke up with that girlfriend, I haven't had any other experiences like that so I think I can't see ghosts anymore.

Strange woman in the night

* * *

This happened seven years ago. I had a lot of overtime at work and was driving home late one night.

I passed underneath the freeway and as I emerged there were guard rails on either side of the road.

There was no sidewalk beyond the guard rails, just dense weeds growing taller than a person, but there was a pale-looking woman dressed head to toe in navy blue standing there.

I was driving slowly because I was tired so I looked at her like, "What is she doing in such a strange place at this time of night?"

She was holding a large piece of cloth like a white sheet, kinda like she was holding a baby? She brought the baby closer to her lips and was muttering something as she looked at me.

The rest of the sheet drooped into the weeds near her feet, the whole thing was very strange. When I glanced up at her face, my eyes met with hers, looking at me wide open (her expression was terrifying!).

It scared me so I stood on the accelerator and the moment I passed her I looked into the rear-view mirror. "Huh, what's going on? No way!"

The woman pitched forward over the guardrail and in the rear-view mirror I could see her mouth open wide as she stared at me.

All the blood drained from my body.

I like cycling

* * *

I like cycling. I'm usually busy with work so I can't go every day, but when I get a day off, I like to go riding to distant places or up the mountain-side.

Last Golden Week I returned to my family home for the first time in a while and I decided to bring my bike along with me. What opened my eyes to cycling was that for the first time I was living alone and that my current house was so far from my family home. It was my first time seriously cycling on the roads I was so used to from my youth.

The day after I arrived back home I got up early and went for a ride. It was sunny, and the air was clean; I had a great time. As I was riding up the mountain-side, I discovered a small stream on the side of the road. My water bottle was empty so I figured I'd fill it up and go home, but out the corner of my eye, I noticed a shrine gate made of trees. No, rather than trees I'd say it was made of branches strung together, it was that small. When I went for a closer look, I saw a small stream flowing underneath it.

"What's this?" I thought and went to leave, but suddenly I felt something tugging at my clothes. My jersey was caught and accidentally pulled the shrine gate down. While wondering just how fragile the gate was, I fixed it and when I tried to leave, I heard a voice.

"Hi."

It wasn't a muffled voice either, I could hear it very clearly.

I turned around in surprise but no one was there. I apologised to the shrine gate without thinking and quickly descended the mountain.

When I think now about the voice, I heard I realised it was probably actually saying "Die." But somehow I was safely able to get back home.

The long-haired lady behind the bike

* * *

I heard this story from my brother when he was in high school.

One day, his friend K-san was returning home from club practice with one of the junior members. It was just before 10 p.m. We live in the countryside so there weren't any nearby houses, nothing but the light from the street lamps along the coastline. With his feet on his friend's bike from behind, he helped push him up a large hill with his moped.

Then he noticed 'it.' Something heavy on the back of his bike, like someone was sitting there. He looked in the mirror and saw a girl with long hair sitting right behind him. Her clothes were splattered with blood and her hair was a mess.

It seemed she would look up at any moment, so K-san quickly averted his eyes and focused on what was directly in front of him.

"I can't let her know I know she's there! We mustn't lock eyes!" he thought and continued to look straight ahead.

But he could feel her looking right at him. He kept riding up the hill, refusing to make eye contact with her. Suddenly the weight from his bike lifted, and trembling, K-san checked in the mirror.

She wasn't there. Relieved, he went to call out to his friend in front but when he looked he froze.

She was sitting on his luggage carrier.

He tried to move his feet that were pushing his friend's bike up the hill as far away from the girl as he could and continued riding without looking forward. Somewhere along the way, she turned to look at him, staring at him, but he refused to let her enter his vision.

As they reached the top of the hill, she disappeared.

The next day, K-san decided to tell his friend about what had happened.

He thought he would be scared, but he just nodded and was like, "Well, actually…"

He had noticed her too. On the way up the hill, he thought it strange that K-san was suddenly so quiet and turned around to see why when he saw her sitting there behind him. In a panic, he quickly turned back to the front.

But he was concerned, so he turned back to look several times, and he could see the girl pressed up against his cheek with a dreadful expression on her face.

He got scared after that so he refused to look back and focused just on what was ahead when suddenly his bike felt heavier and he could smell the faint stench of blood. Then he knew she had come for him too.

She was muttering something behind him the whole time, but he couldn't make out what she was saying. After a while the weight lifted, and she disappeared.

As K-san listened to the story, he felt like the girl was haunting him again and got scared. Although he didn't really know what was going on, he made the decision to never return home alone again.

A few years earlier an unidentified woman's body washed up on that coastline, and upon hearing that story I wondered if the girl was still hanging around and it made me kinda sad.

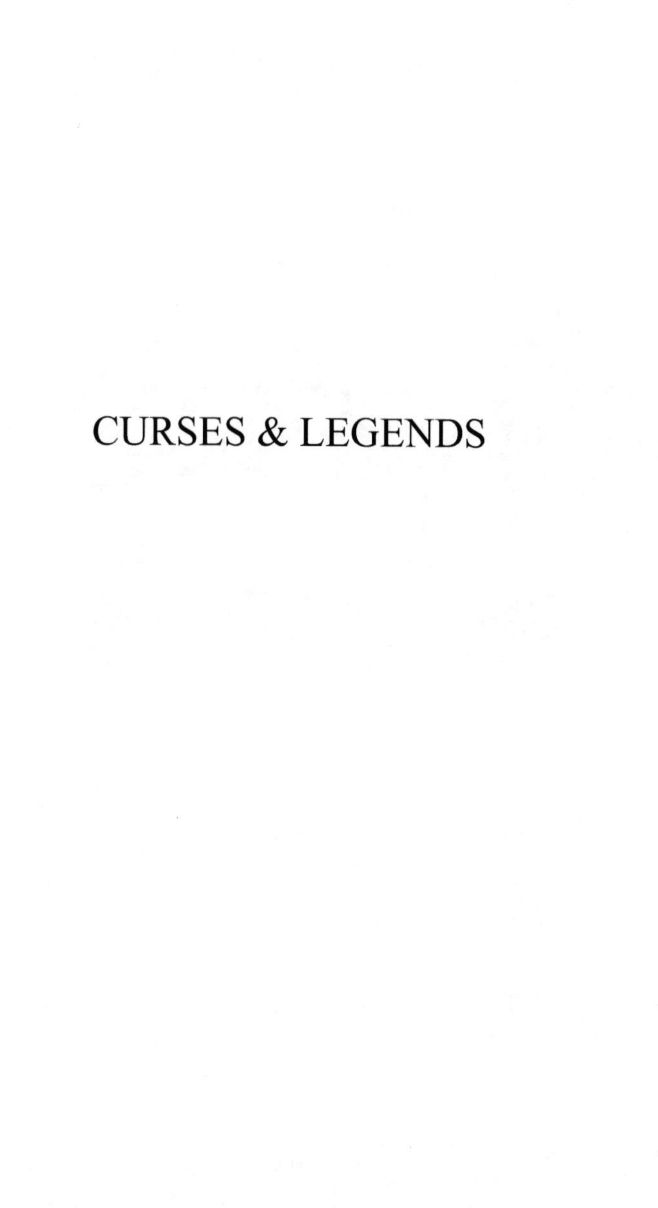

CURSES & LEGENDS

Cursed bread

* * *

Regarding this cursed bread. It's apparently really fragrant and delicious.

But inside you'll find human flesh (for example a finger or earlobe), and when you eat it, you'll become cursed.

The owner of this bread shop was married for a long time to his wife but he accidentally killed her. To hide the body he chopped her up into little pieces, and each day he put a piece into one of the 1000 loaves of bread he made.

The lucky person who got this one loaf of bread would find themselves seeking out more human flesh.

Human flesh is very addictive, you see.

Tour guide's notebook

* * *

Tour guides have the opportunity to visit many places and stay in many different accommodations.

They also often stay in rooms where customers generally refuse to stay, the rooms with interesting circumstances where sometimes things are known to 'appear.' Apparently, there are quite a few tour guides who have had ghostly experiences.

Because of this, word is that the tour guides pass around a notebook where they keep track of the accommodations with ghostly sightings.

They write down which ryokan, which room and what they saw. If customers saw this information, it would harm the lodgings' business, so it's something they keep very close to themselves.

From the front, face the mirror down 45 degrees, then...

* * *

This story is related to mirrors.

I heard this story from my uncle. One day he went to his favourite bar and was drinking sake.

He was talking to the mama (female owner of the bar), who was of Ainu descent. At some point, the conversation turned to mirrors.

Mama: "Facing the mirror, slant over at 45 degrees and look down. Then look over either your left or right shoulder. Once you've done that you should be able to see something within yourself."

Uncle: "Hmmm. (Is that so? Hmm.)"

After my uncle went home and was brushing his teeth, he remembered the mama's story. Thinking it couldn't possibly be real he apparently did exactly as she said in front of the mirror, anyway.

Whatever he saw at that time, he refused to tell me.

But apparently, he saw 'something.'

According to him, the mirror is an object that shows you exactly as you are. For example, even if you're trying to deceive yourself the mirror can see through it.

Supposedly the mama said that "using the mirror is a way to see into the fourth dimension."

Hearing that just made me not want to look into the mirror anymore.

If you're interested why don't you try it?

You might not see anything, but then again you might also see 'something.'

I reached out and touched the notepad by his PC

* * *

When I was in university, I had a friend I'll call A. A had amazing grades, was good looking and had a great personality (he looked a bit like Odagiri Joe). I was just an ugly, gloomy guy, so it was a mystery as to why he wanted to be my friend (not that I'm happy about it, but people say I look like Muga Tsukaji). He was just a really handsome bastard. You would think a guy like him would have a girlfriend and lots of affluent friends but for some reason, he was always with me.

One day I said to him as a joke, "You're a good-looking guy, why don't you go hang out with some people cooler than a loner like me?" His face became troubled and he was like, "I feel safe with you though. Besides, you're not a loner if I'm with you, anyway." I had no idea what he was saying.

A and I met in an occult circle. The group was originally a place we'd go to eat and drink, play some games and so on but it began to change. They started doing group activities less and less so we often ended up at each other's places instead, where we'd spend night after night talking about strange phenomena. Although, having said that, it was really more me just talking about all the things I knew regarding paranormal phenomena and ghost spots and so on. A would sit there and nod his head as he listened like he was having a ball.

This went on for some time before one day I found something shocking at his house. That day A went out to the convenience store to get some cigarettes, and I decided to stay behind. The convenience store was quite a distance away and while waiting for him I began to think I should have gone along too. I looked around his room. There was really nothing there. He didn't have a TV or a sofa, no games or manga either. There was just a desk, the cushions we were sitting on, a laptop, and some difficult looking books in a bookcase.

"Are just these cushions really enough for an unpopular guy? I bet his closet is empty as well. Is he hiding something? Not that I'm gonna look or anything."

While having these thoughts, my hand reached out to the notebook sitting next to his laptop.

I dunno whether he was using it as a notepad but there were shopping lists and electronic model numbers written on it. I had a quick flick through but it didn't look like any other pages had anything on them; they were all blank… but then suddenly, somewhere around the middle of the book, a page covered in letters stood out.

"What's this?" I thought, stopping to read what was there.

"oo die die die die die die hurry up and die die die die die…"

After that, there were a lot of old kanji I couldn't understand or read, maybe some kind of sutra? The page was black with letters. The next page was the same. Why was this happening to A?

He was so gentle. But what shocked me even more was that oo was A's name.

It felt like I'd seen something I shouldn't have so I quickly put the notepad back and pretended to sleep until A returned. There was nothing different about him when he did, and when I got up the notepad had been put away. He just laughed and asked, "Were you sleeping the whole time? You didn't use the computer or anything?"

"You think I wanna look at all your hidden goodies? Nah, there's nothing to do in your place so I just slept the whole time." I replied without mentioning anything about the notepad. Upon hearing that A just laughed and had a smoke.

After that, there wasn't anything particularly different about A. Just like always we'd do our circle activities on our own, drinking and eating and talking about strange things at home. But about half a year later at the start of summer vacation A suddenly died. It didn't seem like a suicide. It was apparently a heart attack.

I was the one who found him. Even though we'd arranged to meet at his place, he wasn't answering the phone or the doorbell. We had keys made for each other's places in the case of an emergency, so I opened the door and went inside. Despite his shoes being at the entrance, there was no response when I called out.

I walked through his empty apartment and he was just sitting there on his cushion, not breathing. He looked like he was just taking a nap. When I realised he was dead, I was dumbfounded. I just cried.

I called his parents, the police, and an ambulance after a bit. It felt like I'd lost everything. I don't really have much memory of what happened afterwards. All I remember is that his family asked me if I knew anything about his private affairs (his diary, his site accounts etc) because they couldn't find anything at all. I said I thought he'd killed himself.

He'd cursed himself, you see. He liked those sort of things, curses, weird religious rites, etc.

A few years after A died I began to realise why A never had any friends outside of me, never made a girlfriend or collected anything at home. I never found out exactly how or why he died though.

I forgot to mention it, but of course, we never found the notebook. I wonder whose handwriting that was in it?

Cursed website

* * *

Apparently, there's a website that appears when you're searching on the internet.

From what I heard, there's a photo of a shrine gate and if you don't go out and find that same shrine gate you'll be cursed with misfortune.

Even when you're not searching for anything in particular, it sometimes appears.

The photo of the shrine gate and rows of cryptic numbers are its main characteristics.

Furthermore, the URL is always changing.

If you don't find the same shrine gate as what's in the photo you'll suffer a terrible fate.

It's a scary website.

Two shrines

* * *

This happened when I was an elementary school student. I think it was a real supernatural phenomenon.

I was a member of the boy scouts as an elementary school student.

Boy scouts are a group that often goes camping and does various other outdoor activities. One day during the summer holidays we went for a 10km hike on the outskirts of our hometown.

We decided on several checkpoints at various places along the hiking route.

We made a small shrine on the corner of the residential area a checkpoint, but when we actually went walking and arrived at that spot were two shrines there.

On either side of the crossroads, there were two shrines that looked the same. They were like mirror images of each other. There was only one shrine gate mark on the map so I thought it was kinda strange.

In any case, we headed for the shrine that matched up with what was marked on the map and took a break. The shrine grounds had a main hall and one smaller building. There was absolutely nothing out of the ordinary about it.

Then our leader, a junior high school student, suggested, “Let’s go check out that other shrine!” We were all intrigued by it so there were no objections.

We noticed something strange as soon as we passed under the shrine gate. It smelt fishy. The smell of rotting fish pierced our nostrils.

Everyone seemed to notice it. They screwed up their faces and were looking around for the source of the smell.

I took a quick look around. It was exactly the same as the other shrine. On closer inspection, however, I noticed the sliding door to the main hall was slightly ajar.

I thought there might be something dangerous inside so I was ready to leave but our leader went straight up the stone path towards it.

"You guys wait here."

As he said that he disappeared inside. We waited several minutes, but he didn't return.

We couldn't wait any longer so we decided to go see where he was.

As we did, he suddenly jumped out from behind the sliding door and screamed, "Uwaaa!!" He laughed at our shock.

"Totally worth it," he said.

"There was nothing there. The smell's probably coming from one of the nearby house's trash or something."

That's the type of person this guy was.

Just like he said, the main hall was exactly the same as the previous shrine, nothing out of the ordinary. We tried to look up why there were two shrines exactly the same but couldn't find anything at the time.

But just as we were about to leave I saw something. From the back of the leader's head down his back was drenched in water. It was way too much to be sweat and there was an awful smell coming from it.

But I only saw it briefly as we passed through the shrine gate. When we reached the road, the water and smell were both gone.

Neither the leader nor the other members seemed to have noticed it. I figured it was just my imagination, so I didn't say anything.

A few days later our leader went swimming at the beach. He got caught in a rip current and disappeared. His drowned body was found several days later.

I didn't have the courage to go see for myself but according to another of the scouts who went to see the place where he washed up the body had been rotting in the summer heat and smelled just like that awful fishy smell from the shrine.

I later found out that it was a shrine for Konpira, the guardian deity of seafaring, and there were hundreds of small shrines around the country dedicated to him.

So, in the end, it really was just a regular shrine. But our leader drowning after visiting a shrine dedicated to the sea couldn't be a coincidence.

I couldn't get it out of my mind so I went one more time to check it out, but when I got there, there was only a single shrine.

Can you tell me how to get to…

* * *

"Can you give me somc directions?"

It was night-time, and I was in an alley when a tall woman asked me this. Her legs were so thin that she could barely keep balanced, swaying to and fro. Her arms were no different, as thin as tree branches, and she was holding a red handbag.

Whether she was sighing or breathing, I couldn't tell. Over and over she kept breathing out, "Haa, haa." Even though she had asked me a question she was looking everywhere but at me.

"Uh… where to…?"

She seemed dangerous.

I figured I'd quickly answer her and leave.

"Kasugayacho 1-19-4-201"

"…"

That was my address.

It was correct right down to my room number.

"I… I don't know."

I answered, really not wanting to get tangled up in anything. With enough force that it seemed like she would break her hip, she bent over and bowed to me, then floated off somewhere down the alley and disappeared.

Gomiko-san

* * *

There's a mountain that exists in central Hokkaido. There was an accident previously where a couple visited the mountain to go climbing. They lost contact and went missing. The police conducted an investigation but they couldn't find any clues. To this day nobody knows what happened to them.

There's a rumour that "Gomiko-san" appears in this mountain. "Gomiko-san" suddenly appears if you're walking around the mountain late at night. She chases after you, screaming, "You threw me away!"

If she catches you she cuts off all your limbs, gouges out your eyes, puts you into a garbage bag and then carries you away. She chases you with inhuman speed, no matter how hard you try to run away you'll always get caught.

If you ever encounter her by yourself, there's no way you can escape her. However, if you're with two or more people, you can split up and try to escape in different directions, leaving one person to become a sacrifice while everyone else has a chance to escape.

Translator's note: "Gomiko" literally translates to "garbage child." The -ko (child) suffix is common in female names, so this urban legend's name is a literal reflection of her story of cutting people up and putting them in garbage bags.

Sugisawa, the cursed village

* * *

In Aoyama prefecture, at the foot of a mountain, there was once a small village called Sugisawa. One day a man who lived there suddenly went crazy and killed everyone with a hatchet before killing himself. In the course of a single day, the entire population of the village was wiped out.

What happened was so horrifying the local government then tried to hide what happened and erase all evidence that the village had ever existed. The village and its name were erased from maps and all official record of it was deleted. For over 50 years the village remained silent, no-one daring to go near it.

However…

No matter how much the government tries to conceal the truth they cannot erase it from the memories of the people. The old folk in the area continue to tell the story of Sugisawa to this day. You could say it's an open secret amongst them.

According to legend, there are three signs that reveal the path to Sugisawa:

1. There is a sign on the road leading to the village that says, "To those who enter there can be no guarantee for your life."
2. There is an old, rotting shrine gate at the entrance of the village, beneath which lies a stone shaped like a human skull.

3. As you head into the village there is an old abandoned building, a former house where if you enter you will find the bloodstains telling of the tragic event that happened there.

One particular story about the village goes as follows:

One day, two young men and a woman went for a drive deep in the mountains when they got lost and stumbled upon an old, beat up shrine gate. Beneath the gate, there were two large stones, one of them shaped like a skull.

The young driver saw it and remembered a rumour he'd heard long ago. The rumour was that a skull found at the bottom of a shrine gate was a sign of the entrance to Sugisawa.

The two men got out of the car, however, the young woman said to them, "I'm scared, let's get out of here." They decided to search the village, however, and all went in together.

About 100 metres after passing under the shrine gate they suddenly found a large open area before them with four old, abandoned buildings. The three of them stepped inside one of the buildings and inside they found a large amount of dried blood on the walls.

The two men felt a shiver run up their spines, and the woman suddenly cried out.

"Hey, there's something strange about this place. I can feel a presence!"

The three of them fled the building in surprise, and as they did, they felt like they were being surrounded by a large number of people.

The three of them ran for the car. However, something was wrong. No matter how much they ran they couldn't seem to reach the car.

From the open space to the car should have only been 100 metres, and it was a straight path so there's no way they could have gotten lost. Even so, as the three of them kept running and running they couldn't escape from Sugisawa.

Unawares the woman suddenly found herself separated from the two men, and as she kept running for what felt like forever she somehow finally found herself back at the car. Thankfully, the keys were still in the ignition. She climbed into the driver's seat to go and get help and turned the key to start the car.

However, no matter how much she turned the key the car refused to start. On the verge of tears, she kept turning the key, over and over, trying to get the car to go.

Then…

Don don don.

A large sound suddenly reverberated from the windscreen. She looked and noticed the windscreen was covered in bloody red handprints.

No, not just the windscreen. Countless bloody red handprints appeared on all the windows as though they were all being beat upon at the same time.

The woman crouched down in fear, and before long she fainted…

The next morning one of the locals, out for a morning walk, stumbled upon the bloody car and the dumbfounded young woman inside. Her hair had turned white from fear overnight.

She was taken to the hospital where she explained her terrifying experience. Afterwards, she disappeared and was never seen again. Her two male friends were also never found.

Akusara

* * *

Have you ever heard of Akusara?

Those who know of Kuchisake-Onna and others should be afraid of her.

Akusara is over two metres tall with long hair, a red coat, and a wide-brimmed red hat. Her left arm is covered in scars. She has no eyes and her mouth has been cut from ear to ear. Nobody knows how she came about. It's said she only appears before men she's taken a liking to.

The most common stories told about her are that she peeks at people from over the top of a fence. If you're unlucky enough to meet her, you're highly likely to face a deadly curse.

Does this story remind you of anyone?

That's right, Hasshaku-sama.

Hasshaku-sama is one of the most well-known and terrifying monsters of the scary story world. At the end of the story, the Jizo statues facing the hero's house are destroyed.

Perhaps… just perhaps… What if Hasshaku-sama broke free of the area she was trapped in and is traveling around Japan looking for men she likes in a slightly different form…

It's possible she'll appear before you too.

I'll say it again. If Hasshaku-sama and Akusara take a liking to you it's almost certain… you'll suffer a deadly curse.

How to open the demon's gate

* * *

The demon's gate faces the northeast, and in *onmyodo*, it's said to be the direction through which demons come and go. For that reason, it's thought you should avoid anything from that direction, and even today this is still a deeply rooted ideology. People are particularly conscious of this when constructing a house, and so if something such as the kitchen, bathroom or entranceway even slightly faces the northeast direction it's said the family will be met with bad luck.

However, whether that's true or not remains to be seen, but they say there's a way to open this demon gate.

How to open the demon gate

If you're truly fed up with life, please give it a try.

1. Take the Hibiya Line from Akihabara Station and get off at Kayabachou. Go to the platform heading towards Hacchoubori and underneath the iron bars there you'll find salt placed on the ground. Scatter that salt with your feet.

2. Change trains to the Touzai Line and get off at Takadanobaba Station. Go to the platform heading towards the Seibushinjuku Line transfer and beneath the iron bars you'll find salt placed on the ground. Scatter that salt with your feet.

3. Once again take the Touzai Line to Kayabachou Station and go through the ticket gate. Take exit 4a and go down the stairs. Scatter ten pieces of rice here.

4. Take the Hibiya Line from Kayabachou to Tsukiji Station and go to the platform heading towards Tsukijihonganji. Beneath the iron bars, you'll find salt placed on the ground. Scatter that salt with your feet.

5. Get back on the Hibiya Line, close your eyes and think about the one thing you want most. Clasp your hands together and continue to ride the train as so.

- - -

The above way of opening the demon gate was written on the occult board of 2chan. About a month after this was posted on July 10th, 2008 somebody posted in the same thread about how they tried this method.

- - -

I was free after work so I figured I'd go and try it out. And like, the salt was actually there, so it freaked me the hell out. What the hell is that salt for? I really wanna know.

- - -

The following day there was a news report.

- - -

On the morning of the 11th in Tokyo, Meguro-ku, a young man was found dead from blood loss in the pool of a company president's home.

The Metropolitan Police Department are investigating whether any foul play was involved in the incident.

At around 6:20 p.m. on the morning of the 11th, a woman living in the residence called the police to report a "young man bleeding from the head" inside the pool in Agariyama, Meguro-ku.

When the police arrived, they found the man lying face down in the empty pool with just a white shirt on. He was pronounced dead shortly thereafter.

The man was not a resident of the household so the police are working to verify his identity while they investigate the possibility that the incident was not an accident.

The scene took place in a peaceful, affluent neighbourhood roughly 500 metres from Nakameguro Station on the Toukyuutouyoko Line.

- - -

To die in some stranger's empty pool is truly a strange way to die. Just what exactly was he doing there? Even more strangely, the man died the very next day after reporting that he'd tried the test, and he was found near Nakameguro Station, which lies to the northeast of the aforementioned Akihabara Station. Perhaps the man followed the information in the thread and really did open the demon's gate…

How to reach a parallel universe via elevator

* * *

There's an urban legend that states that if you follow a certain set of steps, you can go to a parallel universe by elevator. They are as follows.

- - -

What you need: An elevator that reaches 10 floors or higher.

1. First get on the elevator.
(You must make sure you're alone when you do this)
2. While on the elevator go to the fourth floor, second floor, sixth floor, second floor and then the tenth floor.
(If someone gets on while you're doing this the steps will fail)
3. When you reach the tenth floor press the button for the fifth floor without getting off.
4. When you reach the fifth floor a young girl will get on.
(Make sure you don't try to talk to her)
5. When she gets on press the button for the first floor.
6. When you press the button the elevator will go up to the tenth floor rather than down to the first.

(While it's going up if you press the button for another floor the steps will fail. However, this is also your last chance to quit)

7. Once you've passed the ninth floor it's safe to say you've succeeded.

There's only one way to check that you've succeeded. There will be no-one in that world but you and you alone. Nobody knows what happens after that. The one thing we can say, however, is that the person who gets on at the fifth floor is not human…

- - -

[There will be no-one in that world but you and you alone.]

Do these words mean that you alone will be the only living thing in this parallel universe, or perhaps are there things there that aren't human as well? If we think about the fact that the girl who gets on the elevator isn't a human then the possibility of it being the latter seems much higher. It's also been said that she is perhaps just a decoy to lure people to this other world. What happens to people when they go to this other world… it's terrifying to even think about.

There is also a rumour that if you go to the fourth, second, sixth, second, seventh and then fourth floors and then someone gets on, then you can press the button for the first floor and access the other world this way. The original thread on 2chan was full of posts of people who failed, but perhaps this is also proof that if you succeed then you can never again return to this world.

Although there is a way to fail even after the girl gets on the elevator, there's no way to predict what might happen when you mess around with things that aren't human. If you don't want to regret it later, then perhaps you shouldn't mess with things just out of curiosity.

TECHNOLOGY

I worked at a company making graduation albums

* * *

They're bankrupt now, but I used to work for a company that made graduation albums. Photos would come from all over Japan, and there were a few that were kind of like ghost photos.

So such photos wouldn't get published we would trim or photoshop them. One particular photo was from a school excursion. There was a face in a spot where no face should be. Trimming the photo would ruin the balance so I decided to photoshop it.

The work was easy, and I soon finished and sent it to the printer to check, but the face was still there. Maybe I'd printed the old data, or accidentally deleted the editing layer, so once more I opened the file and the face was there again.

I edited it again and this time with the edited file open I sent it to the printer… but again the face was still there!

Of course, the face wasn't there in my open file, so maybe there was a problem with sending the data. I closed and opened the file again, but once more the face was still there.

No matter how much I edited, closed and opened the file, the face would always come back. I called a friend from a photo studio about it but she also replied, "It just won't go away, huh."

My friend tried various things but no matter what the face always returned. In the end, only this class had to have a badly trimmed photo.

In my whole life there's never been another photo like this where no matter what I did, it couldn't be edited.

I watched a ghost ward video

* * *

A few days ago I watched a “ghost ward” video where you could hear real sounds made by ghosts.

The video itself was very atmospheric and the impression the sound left on me was that it was somewhat sad, somewhat angry, but while watching it I never felt it was strange or scary.

When I returned home that night after watching it… the exact same sound rang throughout the house all night.

Day by day it kept increasing.

One day I felt something in the space where the wall meets the roof.

Usually, I make everything dark and go to sleep but there was this spot on the roof that was even darker than usual. I looked away and then back again but it was gone. Instead, I could now feel something directly behind me…

From laying on my side to look at the roof I went to roll over on my back to see what was behind me → sleep paralysis (haha).

The presence was right beside me. But lying on my back there was no way for me to be able to see whatever the black thing was.

I could only move my neck and my eyes were useless. I was terrified, so I forced my eyes shut. Then the next moment…

I could hear something whispering right next to my ear. I had no idea what it was saying.

I was so scared I just tried to go to sleep. Then before I knew it, it was morning (haha).

But the next day, and the day after that, I kept experiencing the same thing… Day by day the voice is getting louder.

There's no end to this story. I don't know how to deal with it either.

Someone help me. Even better, someone please explain that video.

I'm so scared.

So scared.

A single mail changed my life

* * *

Thc following is a true story.

The thing we call life has many ups and downs. We can never truly understand it. The thing that changed my life was a single mail.

Ever since I was young I had a strong sense of justice. Suicide, in particular, I could never forgive.

I don't know whether it was because of a mental illness or not, but in my mind, if you had the strength to commit suicide, then you had the strength to do something and keep on going!

There are less of them around these days but in the past, there were a lot of suicide websites on the internet. I would find those sites and in an effort to stop someone from killing themselves I'd write messages. I'd put down my real email address and write things like, "If you have any troubles at all please feel free to send me a message."

I wonder how many of these suicide websites I wrote on… But for the most part, people either didn't care about what I wrote, the webmasters deleted my messages, or people just ignored them entirely.

Then it happened.

I got a single message.

Together with the site's name, it said, "I've been suffering from a particular mental illness and recently I've been thinking about killing myself. But I saw your message, and it gave me the strength to keep on living."

I was so happy. My message had managed to stop someone from such a stupid way of thinking.

The person who sent me that mail was a girl around the same age as me (who I'll call K-ko), and entirely by chance she even lived in the same city as me.

After that, we often mailed each other and eventually became friends.

Then, around half a year after we first started emailing each other, it happened.

I fell in love with K-ko.

Until that point we had only mailed each other, so I had no idea what K-ko looked like, but at the time it didn't matter to me.

Even if she was some 50-year-old lady, I believed I could still love her.

But I kept wondering if perhaps she wouldn't want to be anything other than email friends, so I could never send her a message asking if she'd like to meet in person.

Then one day I readied myself for the worst and sent her a mail. "Would you like to meet?"

K-ko replied with a quick, "OK."

Finally, the day came where we would meet face to face. Just like she'd said, she was a girl around my age, and she was really cute.

At first, we went out to eat and then to karaoke, and then we started meeting more and more often, and before long we officially started dating.

K-ko invited me to her apartment, and when I got there, I asked her to marry me.

She replied, "I want to stay with you for the rest of my life. Sleep with me."

That night we made love and fell asleep in each other's arms.

The next morning when I woke up, K-ko was nowhere to be seen. When I looked at my phone, there was a message from her.

"I'm sorry. I love you so I wanted you to come to the same world as me."

Whether it was because I'd just woken up or not the message made no sense to me. I quickly tried to call K-ko. I couldn't get through and she didn't reply to any of my messages. I kept mailing her, but in the end, I never got a reply.

A few days passed, and I hadn't been feeling well so I went to the hospital for a check-up. The result? Somehow I'd been infected with AIDS.

My life ended right there.

Luckily, my family is rather well off, so somehow I've managed to live this long, but every day is full of pain. I'm not going to live forever. Soon I will die.

I went to a detective agency to see if they could find out anything about K-ko, but they still haven't uncovered anything.

I couldn't understand people who wanted to commit suicide, but now I painfully understand how they feel. And recently I started to have this strange dream. While I'm making love to K-ko, she's crying, "I'm sorry. I'm sorry. I'm waiting for you on the other side…"

I think the reason I'm having this dream is because I've been pushed to my mental limits. But I feel like K-ko is no longer with us in this world…

The woman in the anime videotape

* * *

"Hey, Atsushi, do you remember?"

My older sister asked me this after returning home for a bit.

"Remember what?"

"It's probably been about 20 years now."

What my sister began talking about was quite different to what I imagined.

After she brought it up, however, I slowly began to remember. Yeah, that really did happen. Both my sister and I experienced something strange at that time.

I was only around five-years-old. We were going to watch a video together. I don't remember what video it was. I think it was an anime or something. My sister put the tape in the deck and when she pressed play there was a dead woman's body on the screen. The woman had collapsed and blood was pouring out of her head.

My sister and I exchanged glances.

"Wha… what's this?"

My voice trembled. Perhaps we had gotten the wrong tape. However, after about ten seconds the anime we were trying to watch started to play. Although we were scared, we tried rewinding the tape. We wanted to check what we'd just seen.

However, there was no sign whatsoever of the woman's dead body we'd just seen. From the beginning of the tape, nothing played but the anime.

I was so scared I burst out into tears. All the colour drained from my sister's face.

... Why did I forget something so shocking?

Perhaps it's not necessarily a lie that when something happens to a person that scares them so badly they forget about it in self-defence. 20 years had passed since we saw that strange video. Then my sister said:

"Do you remember that video?"

"Ah, of course."

"So, do you remember what the woman lying there looked like?"

"Uhhh, I don't really remember that much..."

"Well, I remember it very clearly."

"Okay. And?"

"And these days I've been feeling more afraid."

"Afraid of what?"

"The woman on the ground with blood coming out of her head. I've started to look a lot like her recently... I'm scared because it feels like soon I'm going to die just like that..."

Connection test

* * *

This happened one summer night a few years ago. My colleague and I were in a customer's computer room performing a connection test with a server in another building. The building we were in was one of those so-called "buildings with a shady history." Apparently, in the past, a young woman jumped to her death from it.

According to the computer section head, when he set out for work in the morning… There was a tremendous amount of blood and lines of chalk in the shape of a person on the ground. There were also a lot of police officers and forensics investigating the area.

Ever since then it's said that various strange things have happened in that building.

The connection test wasn't going well for either myself or my colleague so we were getting annoyed. The line was connected and the equipment all new. Our own tests went perfectly. So, was there a problem with the line between the buildings?

"No, that's not it…" my colleague said to me.

"You don't think it's that girl who killed herself just messing around with us, do you?!" I said.

"If so, there's no way I'm gonna let her get away with it. She's just taking advantage of the fact we can't see her and hassling us like this?! She needs to die! Well, she's already dead…"

Just then a sound like that of wooden chopsticks being split or broken rang out throughout the computer room.

Bakibakibaki! Paripari! Bekibeki!

It was like the sound of someone rapping. A few minutes later the connection test that wasn't going well strangely worked. My colleague and I were silent until the test finished. His face turned extremely pale. I felt like I was going to cry.

In the end, we never found out why the connection test didn't work. There's no way that there really was a ghost hindering us and then helping us out… I didn't want to think about it.

As for what happened after that, the company we did the test for went bankrupt and no longer exists. Of course, the company I worked for at the time also went bankrupt.

This is nothing more than my own thoughts on the situation, but perhaps the woman who killed herself was an employee of that company? Did she face some injustice from someone within the company and lose all hope?

Then did she curse everyone connected to the company with bad luck?

That's how I feel, anyway.

By the way, the whereabouts of the computer section head who saw the scene of the accident are currently unknown.

The creepy voice recording

* * *

After I first bought my phone, I got a lot of calls from unknown numbers.

One morning I got yet another call from one of these unknown numbers, only this time they left a message. When I played it back, the voice sounded kind of like that of my mother.

“It’s your mother. It’s your mother. It’s your mother. It’s your mother.”

The entire message was nothing but that. Of course, when I asked my mother about it she said she’d done no such thing.

That same day I got another recording.

“It’s Miyazaki’s mother. The door isn’t open. It’s Miyazaki’s mother. The door isn’t open.”

It went on and on.

When I got home from school that day I saw a note in the basket of my brother’s bicycle in the entranceway.

“I’m here.”

I still don’t know what it meant.

DISAPPEARANCES

He went missing after that email

* * *

There's a forbidden room in our company. It sounds like a lie but it's true, it's really there.

Our company is in a three-story building. At the end of the third floor there's a supplies room, and in that room, there's a door.

I noticed the door when I went to grab some supplies after I first started working there. I asked one of my colleagues about it but he just said, "Don't worry about it."

When I looked from outside, I could see there was a room beyond that door with windows.

The curtains are always closed so you can't see inside. I thought it was a little strange, but I figured it was just a part of the storage room.

About one month ago K, a newcomer, was assigned to our department. His training finished in April and he was now an official, shiny new recruit. As he was the new guy, he was often asked to do odds and ends like I once had.

One day the new recruit K came to ask me a question.

K: "OO-san (my name), um, I went to the supply room just before and…"

I understood immediately.

Me: "Ah, you mean the door?"

K: "Ye… yes, that's right. What exactly is it? Is there another storage room behind it?"

He had the same idea as me. I smiled.

Me: “Well actually I don’t know what it is either. I asked one of my colleagues about it a while ago as well and they just told me not to worry about it.”

K: “Is that so… It seems like it’s locked, so it should open with a key, right?”

Me: “I dunno, I’ve never tried. If it’s a storeroom it should open, I guess.”

K: “Yeah… I’ll give it a try next time…”

He seemed like a curious fellow. I also wanted to know what was back there, so I told him to let me know if he tried.

The next day he came back.

K: “OO-san, it didn’t work. The storage key wouldn’t open it.”

Seemed like he went and tried to open it right away.

Me: “It was no good, huh? Well, there’s probably another key lying around somewhere.”

K: “No, it looks like that door can’t be opened from this side.”

Me: “Huh…?”

K: “The door is locked but there’s no hole to unlock it from this side.”

Me: “Wha…? So like, it’s locked from the inside then…?”

K: “It would seem that way, yes…”

I got chills.

A door locked from the inside. What did that even mean? Whoever locked the door was on the other side? Well, it wasn’t entirely implausible. But something seemed off.

K: "I wonder what it is. Is it someone's private office?"

Me: "Well it's not like anyone's imprisoned in there because they can clearly come and go as they please."

Then I realised something.

K: "That's right, like there are people with autism and social shut-ins, hey~"

Me: "Hang on, something's not right."

K: "What is it?"

Me: "Even if someone can open that door… there's no way to open it from inside the storage room."

I was baffled. You could open that door from the other side, but there was no way to open it from within the storage room.

Aside from the times people went to get supplies from that room, it was always locked. Which meant that whoever was in there was locked in there.

K: "Ah… that's right. Yeah, and then… even at night-time you never see any lights on in there from the outside."

He was right. Even when returning home after working late there were never any lights on in that room. With the gaps in the curtains, you would be able to see.

K: "It's curious, right… Should we look into it a bit more?"

Me: "Well, maybe just a bit."

The next day I left for a business trip. It was three days of apologising to customers and drinking bad sake at corporate dinners.

The first thing I heard upon returning was that K hadn't shown up to work. Then the next day I heard he wasn't even at home in the apartment where he lived by himself.

He hadn't returned home to his parents either. K had gone missing.

Of course, I was concerned about that door in the storeroom. However, having just returned from a business trip I was busy with getting all my things together, and so I was too late in realising.

The day after I left for my business trip K sent me an email. I noticed it three days after I returned.

Although my mail is set up to receive messages from particular senders even on business trips K was new so my server hadn't yet been set up to receive mail from his address. I know, excuses excuses.

The email was one sentence long, as follows.

K: "It opened."

A few weeks have passed since then but K still hasn't been found. I do my best not to go near that room anymore.

I don't know if that door is the reason he went missing but I believe it has something to do with it.

The other day I met the colleague I originally asked about the door. He's working at a branch office now so it was the first time I'd seen him in a few years.

I told him about K. When I did he told me about the door. In summary, it was a little something like this.

* 10 years ago one of the employees who was curious about the door also disappeared (he started around the same time as this colleague.)

* The location of the company is in a bad spot. He heard that it's an easy place for spirits to gather.

* When the company was established a special room was built and 'something' put inside. No-one was allowed to go in.

* Nobody knows what was put in there. Maybe only the president knows? (of course, no-one can ask him)

There were rumours that it was an object of worship, or a strange jar containing a sacrifice. As I listened to his story, however, I asked him something that had been bugging me.

Me: "But why is there a door?"

Colleague: "It's a room. It would be strange if there wasn't a door, right?"

Indeed. Of course a 'room' would need a door. I had one more question.

Me: "So why are there windows? It doesn't need those."

Colleague: "…"

He went quiet for a moment. Then finally he answered.

Colleague: "It needs them to lure people in. Don't look at the windows anymore, okay? If you see something up there just pretend you didn't see anything."

In my mind I pictured K calling me from those windows. Every time I take the road beneath those windows I feel someone looking at me. Someday I feel like I'm going to accidentally look up.

Unable to put up with it anymore I decided to put in for a transfer. Just like my colleague did.

Where is my wife?

* * *

This story happened at the dispatch company I once worked for.

One day one of the dispatch employees asked me, “Is there anything that can cure allergies in a single day?” I have allergies so I told him that even if something said it could cure you in a single day, I didn’t think it would actually work. After that, this person (who I’ll call A-san) fell into a depression, and last month quit the company.

Before he quit, I asked him if he was tired, if he was okay, what would he do if he quit and so on. A-san told me that his wife had disappeared.

Below is A-san’s story.

One day, A-san returned late from work to find his wife wasn’t home. The living room was dark and he couldn’t see anyone. The toilet light was also out, and upon checking no-one was inside either. Wondering if she was tired and already gone to bed, he went to look in the bedroom but no-one was there. She hadn’t told him she’d be going out anywhere either. They lived in a small apartment so there was nowhere she could be hiding.

He turned on the TV and lights in the living room when suddenly he heard the toilet door open. His wife came out. Even though he’d just checked and no-one was there.

“Where did you go?” he asked.

"I didn't go anywhere. I was here," she replied. She said she went to the toilet and when she came out A-san had come home.

From that day on there was something strange about his wife. The wife A-san remembered was allergic to onions. Not just crying when cutting them but her entire face would swell up red. Until now, if she ever wanted to cut up onions she would either wear goggles and a bandana or ask him to do it for her. But there she was, right in front of his eyes, cutting up onions like it was nothing.

He asked her if she was fine cutting them up and she just smiled and went back to her work. He began to feel like something strange was going on, and the more he thought about it the more suspicious it got. But then he started to feel like he was the strange one for being suspicious of her. Thoughts kept spinning through his head and he felt like he was going crazy.

He said his wife disappeared one month before he left the company. It was night, and she was going to take a bath. She went to the bathroom and never returned. The bathroom had no windows, there was only a small vent in the roof. The entrance hall had a window, but it showed no signs of being opened. He called her phone, but it had been left in the living room.

Flustered, A-san called his wife's family, but no one answered. Starting to panic, A-san thought that if he went to sleep, perhaps he would wake up and everything would be back to normal, so he jumped into bed.

Of course, when he woke up, his wife still wasn't there.

When he tried calling his wife's place of work, they replied that no one of that name had ever worked there. He went to visit her family, but despite having gone there several times, another person was now living there. They had been living there for over three years now.

It was as if his wife had never existed.

He visited the police and put out a search, but before he left the company we never heard any word that she had been found.

Disappearing classmate

* * *

I heard this story from Saki-chan, who transferred to our elementary school in the third grade.

When she was still in the first grade, she had a good friend named Yuki-chan. One day, Yuki-chan forgot her homework at school. It was night-time when she realised. She was too scared to go and get it alone, so Saki-chan ended up going with her.

When they reached the school, Yuki-chan went into the classroom to retrieve her homework and Saki-chan waited for her outside. However, minutes passed and Yuki-chan didn't return.

The classroom door was closed and when it opened, it made a sound, so there was no way she could have left without Saki-chan realising it. The classroom didn't have a veranda and all the windows were closed.

Scared, Saki-chan ran home.

The next day when she went to school Yuki-chan's desk was gone. She asked the teacher about Yuki-chan but she just said, "There's no-one by that name here." She asked her classmates and got the same answer.

But Saki-chan refused to believe it, and on her way home, she stopped by Yuki-chan's house. It was an empty lot. Saki-chan's story ended there.

The day after I heard this story, Saki-chan suddenly disappeared. I didn't hear anything about her transferring schools. When I asked the teacher about it she just said, “There’s no-one by that name here.”

“It’s the same as Saki-chan’s story!” I thought, so I asked the other kids who listened to her story about her. One of them remembered her, but the other kids said they didn’t know who she was.

It’s not so scary now, but at the time it really was.

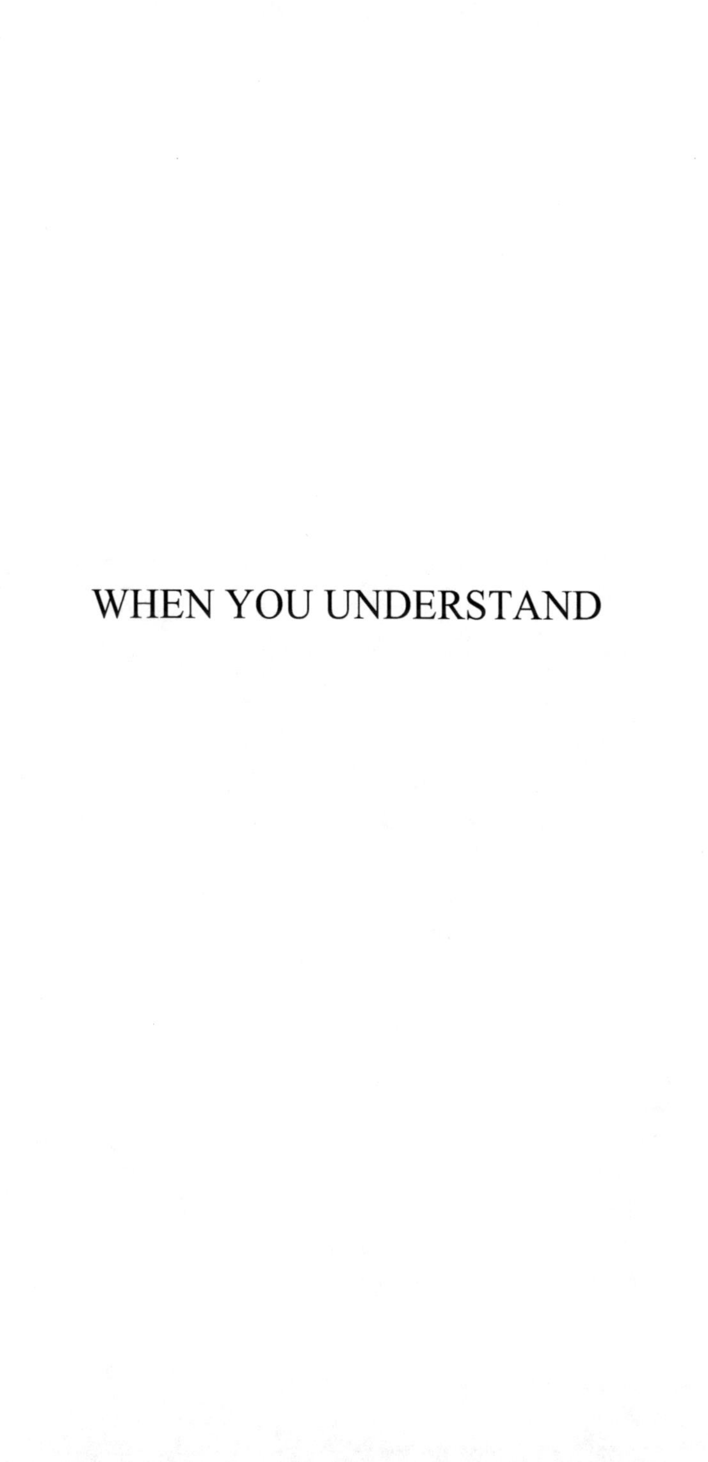

WHEN YOU UNDERSTAND

The names the baby called out

* * *

One day a newborn babe was born to a peaceful family. To everyone's surprise, the just-born baby began to speak.

His first word was "grandfather." The grandfather was so overcome with joy that he couldn't stop the tears from flowing. However, the very next day the grandfather died.

The baby said another word. This time it was "mother." The next day the baby's mother passed away.

The father began to tremble. I'm going to be next, what should I do… he was terribly distressed. For a moment he even considered killing the child, however, there was no way he could go through with it.

Then, finally, the baby said it. "Father." The father became frantic.

The next day his neighbour died.

EXPLANATION

This one speaks for itself. The baby's real father was the neighbour.

Don't open that basement door

* * *

There was once a young girl who always listened to her parents. Her parents often told her, "You must never open the basement door."

However, one day her parents went out and left her alone. Overcome with curiosity, she gave into temptation and opened the basement door.

What stood before her was a bright and colourful world.

EXPLANATION

A bright and colourful world → From the basement to the world above. The girl was trapped in the basement by her parents.

Help me

* * *

She went to work by train. That day, just like every other day, the train was packed. "Just another day," Naomi thought as she got on board.

She soon noticed the girl next to her looked to be in trouble. Her face was red, she was breathing hard, and in a feeble voice she said, "Help me…"

"Oh, no way," Naomi thought, and when she looked, a man's hand was moving near the girl's hips. "I won't let this happen."

Naomi roughly grabbed the man's hand and, pulling hard, she held it up and screamed, "This man is a pervert!" At that moment everyone in the car looked towards them. The train fell silent.

The man's hand was covered in blood. He was holding a knife.

The female high school student collapsed and started convulsing. When the train stopped at the next station, the man exited and ran off.

"I'll never forget what happened," Naomi said, her voice shaking.

EXPLANATION

In forcing the man's hand roughly into the air, Naomi made the knife in his hand cut her even more and made the girl's wound bigger.

When eight of us played hide and seek

* * *

Yesterday eight of us played hide and seek.

I was found in only three minutes.

Three minutes after that another three were found, and then the last four were found five minutes after that.

Usually, it takes about an hour to find everyone, how amazingly fast!

I want to play again tomorrow, too!

EXPLANATION

First three minutes → I was found
Three minutes later → 3 people found
Five minutes later → 4 people found

Although only 8 people were playing, 8 people were found. That's one person too many…

Who became the hide and seek oni?

* * *

This story is about when my friends and I used to play hide and seek at a nearby park a while back. It was a rather large park so hiding wasn't a problem; the problem was when you became the *oni*.

It was already large, so that was a problem, but my four friends were really good at hiding. I really didn't want to become the *oni*. But I won janken and somehow avoided becoming it.

I hid on top of the public toilet with Ken-chan.

"I wonder where everyone is hiding?"

"Dunno~ Everyone's so good at hiding hey~"

"But Ta-kun is so big, I think he'll be found before Shou-kun and the others."

We held our breath and hid there. I don't know how long passed… Then Ken-chan said to me in a small voice, "I need to go to the toilet."

I tried to stop him because he would be found, but he couldn't hold it any longer, so he dropped down below. Then I heard a voice,

"Found you!"

It seemed like the *oni* had found Ken-chan. The next day it was Ken-chan's parents who became the *oni*.

EXPLANATION

What actually found Ken-chan was kidnappers. Ken-chan was abducted.

"The next day it was Ken-chan's parents who became the *oni*."

↓

In order to find their son who had been kidnapped his parents became the hide and seek *oni*.

My clean freak brother

* * *

My older brother is a hard-core clean-freak. He can't sit still unless his room is always sparkling clean. If I had to say one way or the other, I'd say that I'm rather messy. I'm the type of person who doesn't really care even if there's garbage lying around. We share the same room so things are rather uncomfortable.

One day, my brother got so annoyed he finally blew his top.

"That's it! Every day you leave the room a mess! I'm always cleaning up, put yourself in my position! You're doing it on purpose just so you can have a laugh watching me clean up, aren't you? A dirty slob like you is just incomprehensible!"

After saying that he left. He looked really angry.

"What was that about…" I thought and felt a tiny bit of regret. "From now on I'm gonna take care to become someone who keeps things neat and in order!" I decided and went about cleaning up the messy room.

Thirty minutes later, from one corner of the room to the other there was not a single piece of trash to be seen. I let out a sigh of admiration at my own handiwork.

"I can do it if I just try!" I felt my self-confidence grow.

Then my brother returned. It seemed like he went out to buy some garbage bags. All things considered, the bags were rather large.

"Bro, look! I did my best and cleaned everything up! You don't need those anymore, I can do it if I just try!" I told him excitedly.

"Is that so?" my brother said, taking out a single garbage bag.

EXPLANATION

In order to throw out his "messy" younger brother the older brother went out to buy garbage bags. After this, he's most likely going to cut his younger brother into pieces so he can throw him out.

I'll grant your wish

* * *

A robber entered a house and killed the father and mother.

He headed towards the child's room and said to the young boy in there, "I've murdered your parents. Now I'm going to murder you. However, I'll listen to one wish you have. If you say you don't want me to kill you, I'll let you live. I'll grant whatever wish you ask for."

"What does murder mean?" [*Satsugai tte nani*?]

"You'll disappear from this world and never be able to see your friends again."

The boy screamed, "No! I don't like murder!" [*Boku satsugai iya*!]

"That's your wish?"

As soon as the boy nodded his head in agreement, the robber killed him.

EXPLANATION

The explanation here lies in a play on Japanese.

"*Boku satsugai iya*" translates literally to "I murder don't like."

However, if you move the sounds together you get:

"*Bokusatsu ga iiya*" which translates to "beating to death is okay."

Thus, while the boy wanted to say he didn't like the idea of being murdered, the robber took it the other way, “You can beat me to death.”

WANT EVEN MORE?

Also available in *Kowabana: 'True' Japanese scary stories from around the internet*:
Volume One
Volume Two
Volume Three
Origins
Volume Five

Toshiden: Exploring Japanese Urban Legends

Reikan: The most haunted locations in Japan

The Torihada Files:
Kage
Jukai

Read new stories each week at Kowabana.net, or get them delivered straight to your ear-buds with the *Kowabana* podcast!

ABOUT THE AUTHOR

Tara A. Devlin studied Japanese at the University of Queensland before moving to Japan in 2005. She lived in Matsue, the birthplace of Japanese ghost stories, for 10 years, where her love for Japanese horror really grew. And with Izumo, the birthplace of Japanese mythology, just a stone's throw away, she was never too far from the mysterious. You can find her collection of horror and fantasy writings at taraadevlin.com and translations of Japanese horror at kowabana.net.